William McIlvanney

William McIlvanney is one of Scotland's foremost writers

D

North Ayrshire Libraries

This book is to be returned on or before
the last date stamped below.

MOST ITEMS CAN BE RENEWED BY TELEPHONE

For Siobhán McCole Lynch – the best – with love and thanks

Weekend

William McIlvanney

SCEPTRE

Copyright © 2006 by William McIlvanney

First published in Great Britain in 2006 by Hodder and Stoughton
A division of Hodder Headline

This paperback edition published in 2007

The right of William McIlvanney to be identified as the
Author of the Work has been asserted by him in accordance
with the Copyright, Designs and Patents Act 1988.

Extract from *Phoenix Too Frequent* by Christopher Fry © 1946
reproduced by kind permission of Oxford University Press.

A Sceptre paperback

2

A CIP catalogue record for this title
is available from the British Library.

ISBN 978 0 340 65738 6

Typeset in Sabon by Hewer Text UK Ltd, Edinburgh
Printed and bound in Great Britain by Clays Ltd, St Ives plc

Hodder Headline's policy is to use papers that are natural, renewable
and recyclable products and made from wood grown in sustainable
forests. The logging and manufacturing processes are expected to
conform to the environmental regulations of the country of origin.

Hodder and Stoughton
A division of Hodder Headline
338 Euston Road
London NW1 3BH

Ladies and gentlemen, we've been sphinxed
but don't let it spoil your weekend.

One

It was that time when, during an evening's drinking, conversation puts away the telescopic rifle and takes out the scattergun. Jacqui had been the first to reach that point, Alison thought.

'Crap,' Jacqui was saying. 'All men. Crap. Why do we bother?'

Kate was laughing her nervous laugh.

'I could believe you more,' Alison said, 'if you didn't seem hypnotised by the bum-parade at the bar.'

'Choosing a target,' Jacqui said. She went into an American accent. 'I feel like kicking ass.'

Alison managed not to yawn. She didn't like Jacqui in this mood, one which she was putting on more and more, like power dressing. It had been like that ever since Kevin walked out on her. That must have been a traumatic moment, it was true. But it bothered Alison that what had been an understandable reaction was threatening to extend into a lifestyle.

Alison understood how she must have felt but, concerned as she was for Jacqui, she couldn't quite see how she was justified in judging everybody by one dire experience. One creepy man didn't define a species. Why did Jacqui have to come on like an embittered veteran of the sex war when she had only been involved seriously in one skirmish? She sometimes acted like fifty instead of twenty-one. At twenty-six, Alison still felt more open to experience than Jacqui seemed, though not as vulnerable as Kate, she had to admit. But then who was?

Alison watched Kate reacting to any loud laugh or shouted comment that happened in the bar, sensitive as a thoroughbred filly to every shift in the wind. She looked younger than nineteen. She hadn't even realised yet how good-looking she was. The thought endeared her to Alison all over again. Surrounded by people who wore their ordinariness like peacock feathers, Kate's modesty was luminous. In a place where so many voices seemed to be inventing what life owed them, she appeared still to be waiting for life to discover her.

Alison thought of a television programme she had seen some time ago. It was supposed to be an attempt to discover new pop stars. One of the contestants was a weedy boy with an ego so big he should have had an articulated lorry to carry it around. His voice was awful but, when he was voted out, all he felt was contempt for the stupidity of the voters. He explained why, stroking a scrawny moustache that looked as if his father might have given him it for Christmas, like a cowboy suit. But he should never have allowed his son out of the house with it on. 'You see,' the boy said, explaining why he should have won. 'What they don't seem to understand is. You can teach anybody how to sing. But you can't teach good looks.' Nor, it had occurred to Alison, how to recognise them.

The wild egotist would have fitted in perfectly in this bar. Alison was wondering when, instead of waiting for the world to tell us what we need to know about ourselves, people had decided to tell the world what it needed to know about them.

She felt that Jacqui was already hardening into an example of that attitude: take one pinpoint of experience and project it assumptively to infinity. Life is what you say it is, not what it tells you it is.

When Kevin left, Alison and Kate had arrived in Jacqui's flat to help her through the trauma – at least that was what Alison had thought they were doing. They had finished up moving in with her. But instead of helping her to get beyond her bad time, they seemed to have allowed her simply to get comfortable in it. Their sympathy had apparently reinforced her bitterness rather than alleviating it.

As if confirming what Alison was thinking, Jacqui looked round the bar critically, like a judge at an amateur-dramatics competition who wasn't impressed. Kate observed her anxiously.

'I still fancy going,' Kate said.

'For what?' Jacqui said. 'What can you get there you can't get here?' She indicated the busy bar. 'If you want it, that is.'

Alison resented Jacqui's enjoyment of the influence she had over Kate. It was obvious that Kate was keen to go on the study weekend Professor Lawson had organised. It was also obvious that she didn't feel confident enough to go without Jacqui's company. Alison smiled. It was so like Kate to get excited about something as banal as a trip to Cannamore. Peter Pan with tits – to go on a study weekend will be a great adventure. Still, such naïve enthusiasm was refreshing. In deciding to try to help Kate manoeuvre Jacqui into going on the trip, Alison admitted to herself that she had her own reasons for wanting to be in the flat without them this weekend. But maybe altruism was always leavened with self-interest.

'What can you get there that you can't get here?' Alison

said. 'Maybe the chance to explore more than somebody else's crotch.'

'You mean there is more?' Jacqui said.

'Oh, enough with the Cynic-of-the-Year stuff,' Alison said. 'For a start, you'll have a chance to talk to men without any assumptions being made. In places like this, you smile and some of them think you've thrown your knickers at them.'

'Men? You mean like Andrew Lawson?'

'He's nice,' Kate said. 'He's very nice.'

'I didn't say he wasn't.'

'At least he says some interesting things,' Alison said.

'He said I was to phone him tonight if we decided to go,' Kate said. 'He's got two cancellations. He'll be waiting to hear.'

Jacqui turned her mouth down.

'Come on,' Kate said. 'What about it?'

'I went last year,' Alison said. 'It was really good.'

Jacqui took a delaying sip of her Bacardi and Coke.

'Where is it anyway?'

'Willowvale,' Kate said.

'I've never heard of it,' Jacqui said.

'You missed the lecture when Andrew Lawson told us about it. He told us a lot about the place. It sounds really interesting.'

'Willowvale?'

Its foundations had been laid in the imagination of a Victorian mill-owner, Andrew Lawson had told his students. He knew that because the present owner, Gordon Mitchell, had given him a copy of a monograph called *Edward Muldoon: The Other Carnegie*, by P. Vincent J. Witherspoon. Gordon had offered him the pamphlet not just because he was a frequent visitor but because he was obviously as fascinated by the place as its owner was. From the first time he went there with his students, he had sensed the building not just as a place but as a brooding presence. Like a stranger looming large but saying nothing, it challenged him to understand it.

The monograph, Andrew quickly decided, wasn't about to tell the true story of Willowvale. As he read, turning back from time to time to look at the black-and-white cover, it occurred to him that the way the author presented his own name was a clue. P. Vincent J. Witherspoon was as stiff as a starched collar. The date of the printing was 1926 but P. Vincent J., to give him his informal name, would already be old by that time and must have remained a discreet Victorian while the twenties roared around him.

Also, he had been a personal friend of Edward Muldoon, a slightly more youthful, admiring one, and was writing after Muldoon's death. It was an act of homage, a Victorian statue in words, offering a life as a frozen stance rather than a fluid reality. Witherspoon was anxious not only to choose the most flattering posture he could find for his friend but for himself as well. There would be no treacherous deviation into harsh truth from this staunch supporter. That the monograph appeared to have been printed privately with Witherspoon's own money must have allowed his work to avoid any interference from others.

Witherspoon wasn't actively dishonest. Hints of an interpretation of Muldoon's life bleaker than the one on offer here were scattered through his writing like polite coughing, which you were left to interpret as you would. Andrew learned to appreciate trying to work out what the tangential remarks and discreet silences might mean.

'It might be said that his beloved spouse found their splendid new dwelling less congenial than might have been anticipated.' She was probably miserable, Andrew thought. 'Yet even Croesus must have deemed it necessary to curtail the grandiosity of his ambitions.' Muldoon ran out of money?

Andrew even began to enjoy Witherspoon's evasive prose. It somehow suited Willowvale, the monument the monograph had been written essentially to celebrate. Like the building, the words were ornate beyond necessity. They baffled instant understanding of their purpose, as Willowvale did. Through careful rereadings, Andrew found himself engaged in an imaginative inhabiting of a darker life than the one being presented to him.

Witherspoon had a long and florid section near the beginning of his account where he suggested what had been the origins of Muldoon's compulsion to build Willowvale. Many of his expressions reverberated in Andrew's mind: 'He was a visionary among the dark satanic mills', 'a place where truth might disport itself among congenial company', 'wealth metamorphosed into wisdom', 'a sea-girt Eden', 'a dwelling for his dreams'. Bringing the punctiliousness of an academic to such language, trying to sift fact from linguistic fabrication, Andrew worked out his own sense of the life of Edward Muldoon and what Willowvale was supposed to mean. Muldoon had been the son of a Scottish mill-owner whose crass love of money had offended his youthful sensitivities. After a failed attempt to be a painter, he had grudgingly accepted his destiny as a capitalist. Like many converts to a faith, he had become assiduous in the practice of it. Perhaps out of revenge, some thought, he made his father's success look like the work of a dilettante. One mill became many.

But Andrew was convinced that those who thought he was merely extending his father's achievement were mistaken. The intensity of his new religion had an almost mystical dimension to it. Witherspoon had some basis for seeing him as a visionary. The more money he made, the more likely he was to be able to transubstantiate it into his vision, which was Willowvale.

'So where is Willowvale?' Jacqui said.

She saw Kate's face become more animated, presumably because the question suggested serious interest and therefore the prospect of going.

'On Cannamore,' Kate said.

'But that's an island.'

'They have things called ferries,' Alison said.

'I don't like the sea. I get seasick easily.'

'Maybe you should wait till they build an airport,' Alison said.

Alison's superciliousness was beginning to annoy Jacqui again. Because she had worked as personal assistant to a lawyer for a few years before coming to university, she had these moods when she seemed to treat younger people as if they were still in kindergarten. She was like someone who visits London for a weekend and decides she's cosmopolitan and very, very grown-up. She even dressed for the part. For her, casual was formality with a button undone. She was being particularly condescending tonight.

'What's it all in aid of anyway?' Jacqui said, brooding on Alison.

'See it as part of the course,' Kate said. 'We have informal lectures. And discussion afterwards. Andrew Lawson's doing one on *Dr Jekyll and Mr Hyde*. David Cudlipp's talking about *Farewell, Miss Julie Logan*. And Harry Beck's supposed to be tying it all up in some way.'

'I can hardly wait,' Jacqui said. 'I'm surprised there's still free places.'

'I wonder what Harry Beck'll be talking about,' Kate said, as if it were a matter of great fascination.

'He's probably wondering himself,' Alison said.

'What do you mean by that?' Jacqui said.

'I just think he looks like someone with a very dishevelled life,' Alison said. 'Sometimes when he comes into class, he looks as if he's not sure what he's doing there. It can take him ten minutes to focus on the work.'

'You seem to focus on him quickly enough,' Jacqui said.

'What?'

'I've seen you looking at him,' Jacqui said.

'I always do that when I want to see somebody.'

'Staring? With your lips parted?'

'I'm a mouth-breather.'

Jacqui couldn't understand why Alison was being so off-hand about Harry Beck. She had often said he was attractive. The sudden shift of attitude was annoying.

'There's something about him,' Jacqui said. 'I like the darkness in him.'

'He's really got a past him, hasn't he?' Kate said.

'Doesn't everybody?' Alison said.

'Something definitely happened to him,' Kate said. 'And he's having to live with it.'

'You've been reading *Wuthering Heights* again,' Alison said.

'I know what you mean,' Jacqui said to Kate. 'He was married, wasn't he? But he doesn't seem to have any children. Maybe he couldn't have any. Maybe it's that. Or maybe he loved somebody he could never get.'

'There's something troubled about him,' Kate said.

'It's probably a bad back,' Alison said. 'Anyway, now's your chance to find out.'

She looked at Jacqui. Jacqui wondered how she had come to be in the position of having an interest in Harry Beck. It was as if she was being deputised to stand in for Alison.

'They have a free-for-all session on Saturday night,' Alison said. 'The students can do their own thing. Talks. Poetry. Anything goes. The barriers come down. It was great fun last year when I was there.'

'So why aren't you going again?' Jacqui said.

'I've got that history essay to write. It'll take me all weekend.'

'You just want the flat to yourself. With Kate and me away. Peace and quiet.'

'I wish I could go.'

'*You* can,' Kate said to Jacqui.

'I don't know,' Jacqui said. 'I could've pulled Harry Beck here if I wanted to. Without going to the ends of the earth. Anyway, I've heard he's so unreliable, you never know whether he's going to turn up or not. Harry Beck?'

'Harry Beck,' she said, thoughtfully. 'I've been under the covers with you a few times.'

The accent was American.

He recognised an innocent remark wearing garters. He had heard it before and he knew that she meant reading him in bed. He assumed she must mean the column since, as far as he knew, the books were out of print. Dan Galbraith had just introduced them to each other and now he fetched her the gin and tonic she had asked for and left them. As they spoke, he noticed that the man she had come to the party with seemed to have decided to start a drinking competition. He was apparently trying to see if he could drink himself under the table. He looked like succeeding.

He liked how she had met him on a level of immediate flirtation. That way the trivia could at least amplify into a pleasant game.

'I hope I didn't give you a false impression,' he said. 'I'm usually more animated in bed than my photo is.'

'But your photo does look younger,' she said.

'I was a child prodigy,' he said.

He couldn't quite see how that remark related to what she had been saying but he managed to say it as if it were a witty rejoinder. Maybe she wouldn't notice.

'I liked your last one. About the dogs,' she said.

'Thanks.'

'But it wasn't true about that dog you called Snarl, was it?'

'I'm afraid so. Could make you give up on the species, couldn't it? The human one, I mean.'

'And I can't believe what you said about Bruce.'

'You're speaking of the dog I used to love. I wouldn't lie about Bruce. He would have skated any canine *Mastermind*.'

'Do you like cats?'

'Of course. We used to have hordes of them, too, when I was a kid. Not all at once, of course. But I've always been fond of cats. A bit like having somebody from MI5 billeted in the house. You never know what they're up to. But I like that about them.'

'We have a cat.' The 'we' was ominous. Was she married to the peripatetic vat? 'Maisie. She has the run of the house. Sometimes sleeps on my bed.'

'My' bed. Green shoots of hope showing again.

'Oh, we'll have to see about that,' he said.

She looked at him, slightly startled.

'What do you mean?'

'Well, it could be dangerous. Maybe pass something on to you. All that proximity of fur.'

'Oh, that.'

'Also. Could maybe do some physical damage when you least expect it. Bite your bare bum or that.'

'And why would your bum be bare?'

'I honestly can't think of a reason offhand. But I'm sure there must be one somewhere.'

They were smiling at each other when a man, walking as if he had a brass band behind him, came up and shook hands without preliminary, introduced himself and said, 'I'm a lawyer.' Harry just managed to stifle an impulse to say, 'Ssh. If you don't announce it, maybe nobody'll guess.' Instead, he introduced the lawyer to her, allowing her to supply her name, which he couldn't immediately remember. Mary Sue. He was trying to resign himself with grace to a three-way conversation when he realised this was to be a monologue. The lawyer was here to put him right about something he had written in his column. The man was obviously one of those people who mistake fluency for

13

articulacy. As long as he kept talking, he assumed he was saying something of significance. He thought conversation was a one-way street. As Harry had dreaded, it was a street where she wasn't going to loiter. She turned down her mouth at him and drifted away.

Time passes, like a three-legged tortoise sometimes.

'What you don't seem to appreciate,' the man was saying, 'is that those lawyers were simply fulfilling a public service by being there.'

He was trying to remember which column the man was going on about. It must be the one where he had attacked that legal firm which was picketing its local casualty units, distributing leaflets on how to claim for compensation if anything went wrong with your treatment.

'I admit it's possible that some few may be a trifle over-zealous,' the man said.

'Hm.' (Excuse me while I go and throw myself off a cliff.) 'But —'

He had lost track of her. That had been pleasant for a moment there, relaxed nonsense behind which their eyes had been reading each other like a sub-text. He had enjoyed her presence. He figured her about mid-thirties, maybe slightly over that. She had an attractiveness that made him not just wonder where she had been but wish a little he could have been there with her. Her body had reached the point of being opulently fleshed without yet being heavy. The soft blonde hair imbued her maturity with a warm glow. Given the almost anorexic fashionability of most of the younger women in the room, she had been like coming upon a Renoir in a gallery of Lowrys. Not that he didn't like Lowry but he knew whose figures he would rather get physically involved with.

'I don't see why lawyers should be criticised for finding enterprising ways to ply their trade.'

His eyes were wandering round the room when he saw her. She was standing among a group of men. Well, she would be, wouldn't she? But she was looking at him. The glance congealed into a stare. He didn't know how long it took her eyes to turn away towards one of the men. Five seconds? Fifteen? But it had been as if they were looking at each other down a private, silent corridor. If that was just a glance, it was one your imagination could feed off for a month. It was a glance that felt like an assignation.

'I say, good on them,' the lawyer was saying.

Had he imagined it? She was talking with the men again. They weren't a bad-looking group either. Especially two of the three. And they were young.

He hadn't imagined it. To think that would just be giving himself an excuse for not trying to connect. She hadn't come in with those men. The man she had come in with was looking as if the stomach pump might have to be summoned at any moment. He knew him as a friend of Dan Galbraith. Alec Something he was called. Maybe his connection with Mary Sue was casual.

He had to do something. He suspected that if he tiptoed away from the talking man, the absence might not be noticed. The man was so busy listening to himself, he didn't need anybody else.

Maybe he had shut down his reception system automatically as a mode of self-protection, but he could no longer follow the lawyer's monologue in detail. It had degenerated in his ears into a babble of soundbites in contemporary non-speak – stopping bucks and care in the community and final analyses and, bizarrely zooming in from outer space, the trial of Oscar Wilde.

'Excuse me,' he said. 'I'm just going over to the table here.' (It's either that or suicide.) 'Maybe we'll connect with each other later.' (Say, if you've got a lasso.)

'Hold on a minute,' the man said, putting his hand on his arm. 'I don't think you've got my point at all.'

'No,' he said. 'I don't think you got mine. The main thing I was saying in the piece was that a democracy functions on consensus. Mutual goodwill. Take that away and it caves in on itself. If you've got one of our crucial institutions skulking round the premises of another for profit, and one that happens to be the most important one in our lives, you've got consensus disintegrating. Every dingo dog for himself. I admire the NHS. Apart from women's emancipation, I think it's the single most important piece of legislation we had in the twentieth century. You haven't confronted any of that.'

'No, no, no. Listen.'

'I've listened. Two things. Take your hand off my arm. And – as Oscar Wilde probably didn't say – piss off.'

He went over to the table which had been set up as an improvised bar. He was angry at himself for getting angry. This was Dan's party. Once at the table, he loitered, waiting to calm down. He was also waiting for an amazing plan to arrive. All he could think of was that she drank gin and tonic. That was what Dan had given her. He made one carefully, turned and walked towards her group.

She noticed him as he came towards her. She smiled at him and was about to say something. Anything. Maybe 'Hello again.' But he took the almost empty glass she was nursing and replaced it with a full one. He looked at her and turned and walked away. The men around her had gone silent. She took a tentative sip from the glass. It was gin and tonic. She was impressed that he had remembered. The voices started up around her again.

'What was that all about?'

'Is he the part-time barman?'

'Who is he anyway?'

'Harry Beck,' she said.

They obviously had never heard of him. She was remembering the sudden darkness of his eyes. They were intense. She liked that.

'Anyway,' the one called John said. 'Then we started on the champagne. And it was Moët. That was a party.'

She watched him cross to the table and mix himself a drink. Whisky and water he took. Dan Galbraith called to him and he went over and sat on the floor beside Dan's chair, leaning his back against the wall. She enjoyed the way he moved. She wondered what they were talking about.

'I need a bit of company tonight,' Dan was saying. 'I don't want to go into my fifties alone.'

'You've got plenty of that, then.'

'I don't know about Sylvia's insistence on the long dresses, though. A bit formal, isn't it?'

'I like it. I like seeing women like that. I don't know. It makes me imagine a more romantic time. *Fin de siècle* or something. End of the nineteenth century.'

'In a way it's quite a good wake, I suppose,' Dan said.

'Burying your forties. That was a nice funeral oration you gave.'

'It was meant to be about the future as well as the past.'

'I know, I know. It's all right for you. You've still got most of your forties to come,' Dan said.

'Uh-huh. But what am I doing with them?'

It was a remark thrown out casually that came back to attack him. He was mugged by his own question. While Dan reminisced gently, he found himself trapped among thoughts the question had released in him. His part in the conversation became mainly nods and vague sounds of assent.

What *was* he doing with his forties? He sometimes felt his nature was a beast he hadn't learned to domesticate. It did what it wanted rather than what he tried to train it to do.

'Remember the party we had when your first novel came out,' Dan said. 'That was an event.'

'It was.'

And thanks for giving me a memory I don't need at the moment. How many years ago was that? Fifteen? Sixteen? It was in a wine bar which had since disappeared. Passing the place where it used to be, he sometimes wondered if he had dreamed it. It was a Pizzaland now. He certainly seemed to have dreamed the possibilities with which he had sensed the place shimmering that evening.

Lodgings in Eden had been out for three weeks then. He had decided to wait before having the party in case the book sank without trace and people wouldn't know what they were supposed to be celebrating. But all the reviews that were in had been good. The book had reached number nine in a bestseller list. Since he had never again appeared on any such list, he had, of course, realised that they were things of no

18

serious significance. But then that entry at nine had seemed an omen of a bright future.

So many other things that evening had supported the feeling. He was standing among a lot of people who were happy for him and wishing him well. He was twenty-eight. He had already written a book that he was entitled to call, however briefly, a bestseller. Maggi was still with him and they had plans to choose somewhere to live where she could take a job teaching and he could write his next book. The publishers were happy and waiting for it. He had ideas for evermore. If this was what he could achieve at the first attempt, what might he be able to do over the next few years?

Not a lot, as it transpired. He still couldn't understand it. How had something as solid as that moment turned into a mirage? Perhaps the first thing he had done wrong was to work so hard on the second novel. Perhaps success, like some women, is turned off by being courted too abjectly. It took six years for him to deliver *Winter in August*. When it was finally published, it felt like his second first novel, so long had it come after *Lodgings in Eden*. It emerged to a thunderous silence. Something in him died with the book.

His confidence was broken. It was as if another Columbus had set out to discover new worlds and landed on Rockall. The bleakness of where he found himself spread like a blight into the lives around him. He didn't blame Maggi for leaving him. If he could have found the way to do it, he would have parted with himself. He made a half-hearted attempt at it by leaving Skye and coming back to Glasgow. But he brought his dead ambition with him, like a corpse in a suitcase. He unpacked it with his clothes and had sat staring at it for years, willing it to breathe again.

But the book of short stories he had published five years

later merely reaffirmed where he thought he was – trapped in a fantasy of his own making. They could have sold more copies of *In Places at the Time* if he had gone round the houses with them. He almost did.

He knew his reaction to his own failure was exaggerated but he couldn't control it. Since his teens he had invested almost all his hopes in being a writer, and the high of his brief initial success had been so intense that he couldn't adjust to the experience of coming down. He seemed to have spent the time since the failure of *Winter in August* in a kind of unsuccessful psychological rehab. Even sitting here with Dan Galbraith, he still couldn't believe that what he had thought was an infinity of promise had contracted by now to waiting for a letter, which still hadn't come. His future, he was thinking, had reduced itself to the contents of an envelope.

'Sometimes,' Dan was saying, 'I wish I had achieved half of what you have.'

'Do yourself a favour,' he said. 'Don't.'

'You've written something,' Dan said. 'Me? I've reached the dizzy heights of being a sub-editor. Your books'll be there when you've gone.'

Where would they be? Recycled into toilet-tissue? If they survived, they would be like some of the more egregious tombstones you sometimes saw in cemeteries – proclaiming not the importance of the people who lay under them, just their misguided sense of that importance. And very seldom read.

The truth, he realised again, was that other people's assumptions about his success were, in a strange way, what hurt him most of all. They were such a contradiction of what he felt was the truth about himself that they made a performance of much of his life. He sometimes felt he was going around pretending to be somebody else.

Even his invitation to come here tonight had been partly related to the mistaken sense of him that people had when they knew of the books. He had been friendly with Dan for years and he would have been glad to come anyway. But he was also aware that Dan had been especially keen for him to be there because he was the nearest thing Dan could get to a half-baked local celebrity. Hence the speech. It was the equivalent of getting somebody who was known slightly for being known slightly to cut the ribbon at the opening of the supermarket.

'And what have I achieved?' Dan was saying.

He looked round the tastefully furnished room, saw the attractiveness of Dan's wife and two daughters.

'Look around you,' he said.

'I know, I know,' Dan said. 'I'm grateful for what I've got. I'm very proud of my family. But all I've managed to be is a sub-editor on a paper. I still envy you the legacy of words you're leaving.'

Some bequest to the nation, he was thinking. Still, maybe they could use it as a warning to others on the folly of misguided ambition. He heard fake laughter somewhere, not so much a laugh as a shout with bells on.

He traced it to the man who had come in with her. He was sitting in a chair, gesticulating wildly at someone or something. It was hard to tell which, since his focus didn't seem too precise.

'All the same,' Dan said. 'You could have written a lot more. If you hadn't been such a madman.'

'Comes with the territory, I suppose. A sane writer's probably an oxymoron. Anyway, journalism's writing. Although

I'm not even a real journalist. I just write a column. But I'm not knocking it. I need it. I've got into the habit of eating.'

'What about the poetry? You never try to publish any of that?'

'I don't write poetry. Who are we kidding? I write daft verses. Light verse, my man.' He said it with a BBC accent, or what had once been a BBC accent. 'So light, if you breathe on it too heavily you could blow it away. The only place I might get it published would be on a greetings card.'

She had crossed the room to the windmill in the chair. She seemed to be trying to reason with him, which couldn't be an easy trick. They were obviously going to be leaving soon. He had missed his chance to connect seriously with her. When he had done the thing with the gin and tonic, it had felt dramatic and peremptory. Now it felt stupid. What was that supposed to achieve? I'm the drink-delivery man. Boldness was what was needed.

She had partly succeeded in calming the man down. He had gone into muttering mode. Now she was talking to Sylvia, who had been hovering – hostess in a state of mild alarm. Sylvia brought her a piece of paper and a pen, and began to use her mobile. It was taxi time.

She was writing something. He had hoped it would be a love letter to him but it was too short for that. Dan rose and went to talk to Sylvia. Putting the pen down, she started to walk. He was taken aback by how exciting it was to know that he was the one she was coming towards. She came and stood beside him, her back to the wall, and so close that her dress overlapped on his outstretched trouser leg. She sighed. 'I'm going to have to leave soon,' she said. 'He's just a friend. He asked me to partner him tonight. But I'll have to see he gets back safely to his place.'

'I'm sorry to hear that,' he said and put his hand under her dress.

He thought: What the hell am I doing? Get the handcuffs ready.

She thought: Ooh. No. That can't be what I thought it was. It is. It is.

In the time it took her to believe the incredible, what she thought would have been her response was displaced by pure sensation. His hand was resting at the top of her calf. The hand didn't feel aggressive. It felt as gentle as a bird nestling there. It was less threat than plea. By not rejecting him immediately, she became part of a conspiracy of two against the rest. She found that she was enjoying the conspiracy. She had wanted him to make some kind of move all night. Well, he had certainly done that. They were standing in a busy room sharing a secret intimacy.

Not having been arrested, he began to stroke her calf gently. She wanted to talk casually, about anything, she decided. She felt it was a way of adding to the clandestine sensation.

'I still think you made up that stuff about Snarl,' she said.

'Only the name. Sadly enough,' he said.

'And Bruce?'

'Bruce was real. Probably realer than most of us. Although this feels quite real.'

'I know what you mean.'

'The weather's been pretty mixed, eh?'

'I see they've had rain in California.'

'This is a lovely way to spend an evening.'

'I feel as if I could sing that.'

'Feel free.'

Sylvia was signalling over.

'Why do taxis always come at the wrong time?' she said. 'I

23

have to go. No, don't get up. I want to remember you this way. But I do think you should leave now.'

His hand gently squeezed the back of her calf and then was gone.

'Here,' she said, giving him the piece of paper she had written on. 'I was wondering whether to give you this. Now I'm sure. I'm going to check that article sometime for lies.'

He watched her get her coat and usher the man out with the help of Dan. He looked at the paper she had given him. It contained her phone number and her name: Mary Sue. Mary Sue.

His hand closed round the scrap of paper as if it were a nugget of gold. He leaned his head against the wall. He folded the paper and put it carefully in his hip pocket. He hoped he would still want to phone her when he was sober. Then he saw her come back in, taking off her coat. She said something to Sylvia. He watched her mix two drinks at the table. One seemed to be whisky and water. She turned and walked towards him until she was standing beside him, exactly where she had stood before.

'He's all right,' she said. 'The taxi-driver was nice. Said he'll look after him.'

She handed him the drink that looked like whisky and water.

Sometimes the gods smile upon the lunatic, he thought.

'Cannamore?' Alison said. 'Ends of the earth? It's about an hour on the ferry.'

'Her sense of geography is prehistoric,' Kate said.

'At least my sense of men isn't. Like you, Kate. Dark pasts and romantic figures wrapped in mystery. Like a bloody opera-cloak. What're you waiting for? To meet Byron in Tesco's? He's dead. Long time dead. Look at them.'

She indicated the young men at the bar. Kate followed her nodding head. She saw, first of all, the living representation of a thought she had often had: the physical variety of people is amazing. Wasn't it incredible that, with all the people there were in the world, you couldn't find two exactly the same? Even identical twins weren't really identical. The term didn't describe the reality, just the carelessness with which people observed the reality. And beyond a category like that, all was blatant and mind-blowing difference.

What life managed to do with limited materials was astounding. After all, how many different shapes could you give to something as basic as a nose? A bone, a lump of skin and two breathing holes. It wasn't exactly, you would have thought, the stuff of infinite variation. How many eye-colours could you get? Not a lot, and you weren't allowed to have different colours within any one iris. You couldn't, for example, have striped eyes. That might have helped to vary things a bit. And mouths. Two soft folds of flesh around a set of teeth or the lack of them, as the case may be. It really was amazing.

Look at those men at the bar. Everything was slightly different about each of them. Height, weight, hair, features – everything. Looking at them, she realised what exactly she had against Dolly the sheep. Well, not against Dolly person-ally but against the whole idea of cloning. (Come to think of it, could you have anything against a clone *personally*, since it was not itself in the first place but merely an imitation of somebody else? It would be like, say, standing in a cave with someone. And they insult you. And the insult has an echo. It would be like starting an argument with the echo. Instead of with the person who insulted you. Something like that.)

But that was what was wrong with cloning. People were always discussing the ethics of it. It didn't seem to her it was so much a matter of ethics as a matter of the nature of experience. The whole nature of life, it seemed to her, moved towards difference, unique individuality. At least, among people that was true. In a sense, life never repeated itself. Cloning was a precise, deliberate repetition. Cloning was anti-life.

Yet, watching the men at the bar, she was forced to wonder if cloning had been invented before Dolly had come along. For all their immediately obvious physical differences, these men seemed determined to pretend they were all one another. It wasn't just their clothes. The behaviour of each was like an echo of everybody else in the group. They had the same self-assurance, the same way of glancing arrogantly round the pub. They laughed like a convention of mimics. They were trying, she decided, to clone themselves *psychologically*.

It was sad. It was sad because it couldn't be true. There had to be some who felt a little insecurity. Maybe one didn't feel tough at all. Maybe one was afraid of spiders. Maybe one was even still a virgin. But you couldn't have guessed it.

It wasn't that she would have expected them to declare such things publicly. She didn't expect them to walk about with placards round their necks. Fragile – Handle with Care. Arachnaphobics Anonymous. Vagina might as well be a state in America for all I know about it. (That would have to be a sandwich-board, she supposed.) But she would have hoped the truth of themselves might be honestly, if obliquely, expressed in the way they acted towards others. Otherwise the most interesting aspects of themselves, the places where they really lived, were being denied all the time. So how could you hope ever really to meet them or, perhaps more importantly, allow them to meet you?

With these men, she didn't even want to try. They were all acting in close harmony, like a repertory company that had been together a long time. You were allowed to watch but they were the only ones who knew the plot. It was as if only they were natives here. Everybody else was just a tourist. She certainly felt like one.

'You see what I'm saying?' Jacqui was saying. 'Just look at them. Romance? They think that's a long run for their team in the Cup. Don't waste your time looking for more than sex with them. They can only relate to you from the waist down. They look round the women in this pub, all they see is a lot of convenient spaces. Somewhere they can park their amazing equipment. Till the urge passes. And they can get on with what really matters again. Mainly beer with the boys and football matches. The rest is patter. Just the money in the meter that lets you stay there till you get your business done.'

Jacqui took a bitter gulp of Bacardi and Coke.

'Well,' she said. 'If that's the game, more than one can play it.'

Kate winced. Some suspicion in her was worried that Jacqui was right. She didn't want her to be right but almost envied her for her certainty. At least it made her connect directly with the world around her, even if she did it rather abrasively. At least she was dynamic.

She seemed strong. Kate saw her as a kind of Boudicca figure. She *drove* through situations and her chariot-wheels had blades on them, very sharp blades. So what if some people were hurt? It was mainly men she did the damage to and, post Kevin, she saw them as her enemies. At least she got where she was going. Didn't she?

Kate always felt that she wasn't going anywhere. She was hanging about in the anteroom to her own life. If Jacqui was Boudicca, she was the Lady of Shalott. Weaving fancies inside herself and hardly daring to venture out into where things actually happened. Catching echoes of what it might be like.

And Jacqui was honest – often brutally honest, but honest. She wasn't. But to be honest you had to know what you thought about things. She didn't. Maybe that was why she accepted so many situations without reacting to them in the way she really wanted to. She hesitated too much. At school she had been the type of pupil who knows the answers but is afraid to put up her hand in case she is wrong and makes a fool of herself. She would have liked to be able to run home, check it out in the *World of Knowledge* book her father had bought and run back into the classroom with her hand up. She was the type, except with Alison and Jacqui, who was likely to listen to nonsense or swallow a mild insult and postpone a reaction until she had gone back to her room and reprocessed the entire occasion in her head. She always thought exactly what she should have said when there was no one there to say it to.

It was a kind of lying, not having the nerve to own up to the truth of where you were. It was a condition that had become more serious recently. It no longer applied only in incidental moments. It had taken up permanent residence in one particular area of her life. She could still hardly believe that she had lied to Jacqui and Alison about not being a virgin.

28

That was one of the problems with lying. You spent so much effort sustaining the lie and elaborating on it that you almost began to believe it. There were times, remembering real situations like the one where she had had her pants off, when she could almost convince herself that what had happened was really a kind of sexual intercourse. She had to remind herself that it wasn't. She was the only supposedly sexually experienced woman she knew with her hymen still intact. At least, she assumed it was. If it wasn't, and her father insisted the culprit made an honest woman of her, she could probably look forward to marrying a bicycle.

But now she was trapped in the pretence. She knew that in any future conversations with Jacqui and Alison she might have to wheel in another imaginary lover. She had even thought of a couple of names. It was getting ridiculous. There was only one way to stop it: do it for real.

That wasn't the only reason she wanted shot of her virginity. It was a total embarrassment, like a pimple that never burst. It was so unmodern. She felt she might as well be going about in a bustle and having the vapours. She had to do something. She didn't know what but she had the vague idea that if she kept putting herself in promising situations it might happen to her before she could stop it. That was one reason she wanted to go to Willowvale. At least it would offer possibilities. A lot of men and a lot of bedrooms. Like her father's lotto card. Permutations there. But she needed Jacqui to go with her. It might give her the nerve to put herself about a bit more. It would open up the possibilities.

'And there's David Cudlipp, of course,' she said.

She noticed Jacqui and Alison exchange a glance she didn't understand. Jacqui seemed to become more thoughtful. Kate took it as a hopeful sign. Perhaps she was considering David Cudlipp . . .

. . . who was standing in his flat looking through the window down into the street, where one teenager was pushing another along in a supermarket trolley. Both seemed to be shouting some incomprehensible challenge to the street's residents. David drew back from the window a little in case he became the focus of their marauding arrogance. He remembered a thrown stone coming through the window about a year ago, for no other reason he could see than that the room was lit, with the curtains undrawn, and must have looked like a warm and pleasant place.

We've lost the streets, he thought, as he watched the two careen out of sight, bellowing like berserkers. The propriety of home no longer extends outside to walk the pavements sedately. The roughness of the roads invades the house, estranging us from each other within our own walls. Was that really his wife sitting on a chair and using a magazine she wasn't interested in like a stage prop?

'So you're definitely not coming?' he said.

'There's so much to do tomorrow.'

'We did promise Andrew Lawson.'

'But what difference does it make? The room will still be taken. It's just that it'll become a single instead of a double. At least, I hope so.'

She was smiling at him. He ignored the implication.

'What do you have to do that's so important?'

'My own work has fallen behind in the library. I have to go

in. Anyway, it's not as if I have any significant contribution to make. I'd just be a spectator.'

'All right,' he said. 'Suit yourself.'

He didn't want to pursue it in case she changed her mind. He thought of Veronica Hill . . .

. . . a thought that seemed to be troubling Jacqui.

'Veronica Hill?' I thought you said there wasn't much competition.'

'There isn't,' Alison said.

'Veronica Hill? She looks like a L'Oréal advert.'

'But she disqualifies herself. She'll hardly look at anybody. Let alone talk to them. She doesn't just come to uni. She makes royal visits.'

'That's true.'

'It's more people like Marion Gibson and Vikki Kane.'

'Listen,' Jacqui said. 'Vikki Kane could really look something special. She's got a lovely figure. Good bones. It's just the clothes she wears.'

The idea of Vikki Kane gave Kate comfort. There was somebody else who didn't seem to belong in a modern context, so demure and reserved. She was so uncertain of herself it was hard to believe she was in her thirties. Maybe she wasn't the only Lady of Shalott, Kate thought, as she held in her mind the image of Vikki Kane . . .

. . . who was studying herself in the wardrobe mirror.

The white Lycra top and the black jeans looked good on her. The shop assistant had approved in the passing, saying the jeans made her look like one of those photographs where they've painted an outfit on somebody. 'Know what Ah mean. Robbie Williams did it. All he wore was his underpants. And somebody had painted blue jeans on 'im.'

The Lycra moulded itself to her breasts. They had hardly sagged at all. Maybe that was one advantage of having had only one child. Her bum looked firm in the jeans. Maybe her half-hearted visits to the gym, before she abandoned them two or three months ago, had done some good after all. Maybe it was the supportiveness of the cloth. It wasn't just that clothes could accentuate your good points and minimise the bad ones. Used carefully, they could amount to a kind of temporary cosmetic surgery. These jeans not only made her look more attractively tensile from the back, they also made it hard to imagine the cellulite underneath. Still, if this weekend fulfilled the promise she saw in it, she might have to take them off in company. Love me, love my cellulite. But perhaps by then the shadowy, faceless man would be too preoccupied to notice.

The thought returned her to the glass of white wine on the dressing-table. She took another sip, fully aware of what she was doing. She was keeping her recently acquired sense of abandon topped up. She was grateful now that she had hardly ever drunk. It meant that it didn't take too much to shift her mood from brooding to carefree. There must be a lot of bottles of self-confidence she could take before any physical damage caught up with her. Whatever she died of, it was unlikely to be cirrhosis of the liver, she thought bitterly.

The idea released her from any self-criticism she might have felt in sitting here, watching herself in the dressing-table mirror as she took the wine. She toasted herself in the glass. If she was going to free herself from dead behaviour, she would have to uncork a few more bottles in the process.

She was missing Jason already. But her worry about him was diminished by the realisation that he seemed perfectly happy to be away from her. When she had phoned for the second time tonight, under the pretence of reminding him that he had forgotten his football boots (although she had known already that he wasn't going to the training tomorrow), he had seemed impatient with her interruption of his evening. It was almost as if he knew she was just fussing and felt she was an embarrassment to him in his different context, spending the weekend with Alan and his new wife.

There was a strange emotional law in broken marriages, she thought: the one who spends less time with the child or children is the one who is valued more. Wasn't that a swine of a law? The more time you spent ironing clothes and making packed lunches and helping with homework and nursing colds and delivering them to mud-caked playing-fields on winter mornings, when the wind chafed your cheeks to soreness, the more you merged with the furniture. You became an incidental fixture in their lives, about as sensitively treated as the doormat they usually failed to wipe their feet on. But vanish for weeks at a time and you were much thought of. The rarity of your appearances turned them into greatly appreciated events.

There had been stretches of many months in the three years since they had divorced during which the occasional phone-call from Alan was his only presence in Jason's life. He had maintained his alimony payments, it was true. But direct contact had been subject to his personal whim. He turned up only when he chose, like a wayward uncle who had so many other things to do. He always arrived with the air of someone doing them a favour. The incredible thing was that Jason seemed to agree with him. He made excuses for his father, no matter how many times he had promised to come and didn't turn up.

Now Jason seemed to think Christmas had come early when his father suggested they all spend some time together, Alan and Maureen and Jason, to get to know one another. The enthusiasm with which Jason welcomed the idea had hurt her and she was surprised at the jealousy she felt for Maureen. But she had bartered her misgivings in exchange for the time the arrangement gave her to come to terms with the new sense of herself she wanted to find before it was too late. It also gave her next week free for what she had to do.

She leaned close to the mirror and stared into her own eyes, as if waiting to see slowly surface there the confident woman whose clothes she was wearing. She knew she still looked good but she had looked better than this for years and nothing had happened. Could it happen now? It had to. Alan's remarriage had been one sign. It had been like the final switching-off of what she had come to realise belatedly was a baleful influence on her life, always had been.

She looked across at the dress lying on the bed, its grey cloth so familiar. She put down her glass of wine. She stood up and took off her jeans, laid them lengthwise on the bed, wriggled out of the Lycra top, straightened it out and put it beside the jeans. She turned and looked at herself in the mirror.

The Janet Reger underwear had been her one serious indulgence for this weekend, a bigger one than she could afford. She was glad she had overcome her misgivings about the price. The silk bra and pants made her feel sensuous. Perhaps they would make somebody else feel the same.

34

Sensing tears almost come to her eyes as she contemplated her still attractive breasts so long starved of touch, she fortified herself with wine.

She picked up the grey dress from the bed and slid it over her head, smoothing it down past her hips. She took the broad black belt from the bed and buckled it round her waist. The alterations to the dress had taken the waist in, made it sleeveless and brought the hemline up. With the roll-neck, she thought it made her look like a nun who had broken out of the convent and made a few adjustments to her habit. She smiled to herself. That seemed appropriate. It was the last thing that Alan had bought for her and, in its original box-like style, sleeved and coming below her knees, it had made her look like a nun. 'Where's the wimple?' she had asked him. She ran her hands down the contours that the dress emphasised. The libido strikes back.

She took off the dress and laid it carefully on the bed. She brought the phone across and put it on the dressing-table. She topped up her wine-glass and dialled Marion's number. Marion answered after a long time, as usual. Vikki sometimes wondered if she was waiting to find out if the caller would give up.

'Marion. It's Vikki. You all set?'

'For what?'

'The trip. Tomorrow.'

'Oh, yes. That.'

Even when you were sitting beside her, Marion often gave the impression of not quite being in the same room with you. But tonight she sounded as if she was in another country.

'You did remember?' Vikki said.

'Of course. I'm packed. I wasn't absolutely sure about going at first.'

'Marion!'

Vikki immediately set about persuading her. She had phoned to give her own stalled sense of purpose a psychological tow from Marion's imagined enthusiasm. Now she was dreading catching her inertia. By the time they had finished talking, Marion was saying she would definitely go. But when Vikki put the phone down, the conviction she had managed to impart to Marion seemed to have cost her her own. Aware of how much she might shock Marion, she stared at herself in the mirror, thinking she saw there a belated reveller who was turning up when the party was over. That was when she really cried. Turning the wine into water, she told herself. She let the tears work themselves out. When she looked back into the mirror, the mascara she had applied to have the full effect of her new appearance had spiked itself round her eyes.

Maybe she should be a Goth for the weekend, she thought. That would really shock Marion . . .

. . . who was sitting very still, as if imitating the nickname she knew some of the other students had for her: the Mouse. Why had she agreed to go on this trip? It intimidated her. Nearly everything did.

She sat with her cup of coffee going cold in front of her, resting on a copy of *Hello!* so that it wouldn't leave a ring on the glass of the table. She wasn't enjoying the coffee. She had never been sure if she went on buying this brand for the taste or because it had been advertised a while ago on television as part of a romantic serial. Did she imagine it was an elixir? Drink the brand, find the romance. Perhaps romance by proxy was becoming a way of life for her. She glanced at the famous face staring at her past the rim of her cup.

The romance didn't necessarily have to involve a relationship. That would have been a pleasant bonus but she had ceased to take that possibility seriously some time ago. If she was a mouse, she was a well-fed one. It wasn't that she thought the not-unpleasant roundness of her figure disqualified her from attracting a man. It was just that, in her experience, it had so far disqualified her from attracting the kind of man to whom she would have been attracted. Being perilously close to forty, she found it difficult to imagine that she would attract him now.

'The only talent you've got,' her father had told her more than once (as he told her most things more than once), 'is your stubbornness. And that won't do you any favours.'

Perhaps it hadn't. She remembered him lying in his coffin, his face having achieved that expression of unchangeable conviction about the nature of things it seemed to have been rehearsing all his life. Told you I was right, it seemed to say to her as she stood in his dim bedroom with the curtains drawn, and especially about you.

Maybe he had been.

'People who only want to wear glass slippers always end up barefoot,' he had told her, more than once.

She reflected what a cruelly sententious man he had been but she stifled the thought, not out of respect for his memory but out of respect for the memories of her own she still hoped to make. She had decided soon after his death that to spend too much time reacting against the powerful effect someone or something had had on you was to recharge that power. You defined yourself against its terms rather than finding your own. It became a continuing necessary part of you instead of something beyond the negative influence of which you could finally go.

Looking at the holiday brochures showing through the glass of the coffee-table, she wondered again if she shouldn't have spent all the money she once had on travel. Those two months travelling in Europe after her mother's death could have been extended into her final freedom, she was thinking. She had enjoyed being in strange places so much. Even visiting the bullfight had been an unexpected thrill. Instead, she had been sensible and taken a mortgage on this flat.

Now she had to admit that her money wouldn't last for ever, unless she saw for ever as a couple of years or so. She had decided already that, if she completed her degree, she wouldn't be going into teaching. And the idea of being at university as a mature student no longer seemed as attractive as it had done, except for the creative writing class.

Perhaps she could just sell the flat and travel until the money ran out in some foreign place and she quietly brought out the bottle of Valium she had kept as her secret travelling companion. She thought of herself expiring romantically alone, having experienced many places, in a quaint hotel room in Paris or Vienna or Venice. Or Padova. She liked Padova. Especially the little square beside the Basilica of St Anthony. There was a small hotel where, when you closed the shutters, the darkness in the room was total. The staff had been kind to her.

But she couldn't quite see herself as a romantic heroine. She worried about ring-marks on the table. Her escape from her stifling dissatisfaction with herself would have to be something more practical. She had always known that she would never have eloped without a road-map. She knew, sitting lumpily beside the coffee-table, that she would never be flying to freedom. But maybe she could painstakingly tunnel her way out.

She thought yet again of the box-room. She thought of it as the entrance to her tunnel, had been conscious of it for a long time now as the only place from which she could seriously start. She had lovingly equipped it with the tools she needed. All that was lacking now was the will to begin to use them, the purpose for applying them. Maybe this weekend would help her find it. She rose, took the cup and went to the kitchen to rinse it out.

She went back and sat down on the couch beside the coffee-table. She hoped she had given some reassurance to Vikki, who was so vulnerable just now. But then the operation next week was not something any woman could face with equanimity, especially for someone who, as an only child with her parents dead, had no immediate family.

Vikki was being very brave about it. This weekend was to be her last outing before surgery. As far as Marion was aware, she was the only one Vikki had told about it.

It was interesting how much she knew about the people who were going to Willowvale. Perhaps seeing her as the Mouse (they had never called her that to her face but she was good at eavesdropping), people felt free to say almost anything in front of her. Perhaps they liked to feel they were shocking her. They weren't. Nothing about people shocked her. Every horror she read about in the newspaper or saw on television she liked to confront calmly because it was telling her the way things were. She had always sent her imagination into situations and experiences she had never known herself, so that she could feel what others felt.

She knew the story of Jacqui Forsyth's break-up with the apparently appalling Kevin. She suspected from certain remarks Alison Miller had made that she had been involved with David Cudlipp at last year's weekend. She knew that Andrew Lawson's life outside university was devoted to his wife, who was housebound with illness. Devoted to her and the bottle, she suspected.

She thought of them a lot. She thought most of Harry Beck. That was inevitable, given that the key to his writing class was mutual honesty, and he led by example. She knew that he had had problems with the book he was working on.

'I think I've discovered a new neurosis. The Penelope Syndrome. You heard of her? She was the wife of Odysseus. While she was waiting for him to get back from Troy . . . Twenty years it took in all. How do you explain that one to your wife? "That was some traffic jam on the M1." She was pestered by men who wanted to marry her. Eventually she had to give them a time-limit. She said she would choose a new husband when she finished the tapestry she was working on. Every day they could see her weaving it. Every night she unravelled in secret what she had done during the day. The never-ending tapestry. That's me. Every night my head un-ravels my belief in what I've written during the day. Just call me Penelope. But not in public, please.'

He had finished it now and had submitted it to a publisher. She had read all his published work, finding his books on Amazon with great difficulty, and that told you a lot about a person, she felt. She had seen him once in a bar called the Ubiquitous Chip. He hadn't noticed her, of course. But the company he was in had dismayed her. One man in particular looked like a caricature of an aging gigolo. But there was more to Harry Beck than that. Most of the notes on the table in front of her were transcriptions of things he had said.

'Does it matter? A day or a lifetime. Or one crowded hour

of glorious life. I suppose every book creates its own wilful timescale. Certainly, you can't tell a story without it inhabiting time. Once upon a time, as they used to say. I suppose every story really begins: It was that time when . . .' There was a pause. 'Of course, you could get twenty different people writing about the same event and using that beginning. And still have twenty different stories.'

She leafed through some of her other notes, transcriptions she had extracted from his tutorials, which he had allowed her to tape. She had taken them mainly from the free-ranging chats they always had at the end of a class. She liked those times best. Usually then, with assignments decided, Harry Beck was just responding to their general questions about writing.

'I don't think you teach anyone to write, really. You might give them something useful to react against, right enough. That's healthy. But what we do here is still valuable, I believe. You can let people see their mania is shared. They're not alone in the padded cell. And, at the very least, it's going to make you a more appreciative reader.'

'I can only speak for myself. Writing a book feels for me like trying to ride a bucking bronco. And trying to go somewhere at the same time.'

'How can you know there's actually a book there when you start out? I don't see how you can. I can't anyway. It's like a mirage. Sometimes you think you can see it. Sometimes you suspect there's nothing there. You're deluding yourself. But you have to keep going. And even once you've arrived. I suppose only other people sharing your belief that you've arrived somewhere real can confirm it for you. And then, these days, often the people publicly confirming your book's reality aren't very real themselves. I think you have to leave it to the individual lay reader. The dread of mirage remains.'

'Posterity? Who says you can trust posterity? Think about it. This is posterity for all the writers who are dead. And look how undervalued some great writers are today. And how overvalued some chancers are. Nah. You're on your own. No guarantees. Place your bet.'

She would be taking her notes with her and hoped she would be adding to them and finding out about more people.

'Mickey Deans is going,' Kate said.

'I'll leave him to you,' Jacqui said. 'I don't rob cradles.'

Kate thought she might not mind. At least he might be more accessible than the men at the bar.

'Does that mean Donnie Davidson's going too?' Alison said.

Jacqui touched both nostrils and sniffed, as if her nose were running.

'With a truckload of pharmaceuticals.'

Kate realised that Jacqui had just spoken as if she would be going. It was necessary to encourage her with something more.

'And it's supposed to be haunted.'

'Sorry?'

'Willowvale. It's supposed to be haunted.'

'Ooh,' Jacqui said. 'There's an idea. Maybe I could lay the ghost. That would be a first.'

Andrew enjoyed telling his students about the ghost of Willowvale. A recuperating soldier was first to claim he had seen it in 1919. Having turned a corner in the house at dusk, he saw a woman in a floor-length black dress at the end of a long corridor. She had a fierce white face and she appeared to be gliding towards him threateningly – perhaps, Andrew thought, because her dress concealed her feet. The soldier apparently didn't wait for her to introduce herself.

Having been brought to the public's attention through an article in a local newspaper and become a tourist attraction after Willowvale was a hotel, the black woman decided to make many more visits. For a time she was something of a fashion. Perhaps people felt they weren't getting their money's worth if she didn't appear for them, rather as if they had gone on a safari holiday and not seen an elephant.

Andrew told his students that she might well be Elspeth Muldoon, the disgruntled wife, come back to express her unexorcised distaste for Muldoon's folly and to make sure that no jumped-up tourist would be entirely at ease in the place she seems to have hated. Or perhaps she was looking for her dead son, Edward. It wasn't that Andrew believed in her. His credulity had certainly not been encouraged by the discovery that the soldier who had first seen her had ended up in an asylum. It was just that he thought a ghost might be another inducement to going away for a weekend to talk about books. It wasn't exactly an indoor swimming-pool but it might help. Considering the diminishing numbers on these trips, he needed all the help he could get.

Also, there was for him a certain appropriateness in the idea of a ghost. He felt Willowvale was, in a way, haunted, though not by a woman in a black dress. It was haunted by something less easy to escape.

Willowvale might be a monument to Edward Muldoon's failure but it was a big monument. The grand exterior might now be undermined within by small, often gimcrack rooms full of one-night lodgers and squabbling families waiting for good weather, but the grandness of their surroundings made the smallness of their presence all the more questionable.

The real inheritance left by Muldoon's vision, Andrew came to think, was not the building but the warren of dreams it housed, the inevitably shifting terms our lives have to inhabit but seek constantly to make over into dubious certainty, whether complex or simple, important or trivial. What haunted Willowvale, Andrew believed, was the revenant of human aspirations. What people met in its corridors was perhaps the ghost of something in themselves, the unfulfilled stature of their dreams, looking for flesh.

Ghosts didn't bother her, Jacqui was thinking. People did. Faced with the living dangers people presented, ghosts were an indulgence. Come to think of it, how many ghosts had she heard of haunting working-class houses? They always seemed to be found wandering through castles and mansions. Maybe there wasn't room for them in a high-rise flat. Poor people's lives were too crowded with harsh reality to leave space for a ghost as lodger. They had to give their full attention to the real dangers.

She was doing that now. Standing alone, along from where

Kate and Alison were using Alison's mobile phone, she could hear the sounds of a street-fight coming from somewhere that sounded closer than she wanted it to be. She couldn't see it yet but it had come nearer in the last minute or so. The swearwords going off like fireworks were louder. The frightening noises (flesh hitting stone?) and the shouted names and instructions were threatening to invade her space.

She shouted along to them, 'Hurry up.' Alison nodded but Kate continued talking, presumably to Andrew Lawson. How long did it take to tell him they were going to bloody Willowvale? She was still considering the possibility of backing out when the two of them joined her, laughing and saying it was all fixed.

'We'd better get home and packed,' Kate said.

'It's no big deal,' Jacqui said. 'We're going for a weekend, not a fortnight.'

'What's that?' Alison said.

'Something you don't want to know about,' Jacqui said, as she led them in the opposite direction from the sounds of violence to look for a taxi.

'Don't expect too much to happen till Saturday night,' Alison said. 'That's when the Willowvale effect takes over. It takes that length of time for things to happen.'

Jacqui looked at her.

'I can hardly wait.'

'Andrew Lawson,' Kate said. 'He sounded as if he wasn't sure who he was, never mind who I was.'

'He would be pissed,' Jacqui said.

'Unlike us,' Alison said.

'I think he was. Or maybe he'd been sleeping. He sounded like that.'

They were laughing.

'In fact,' Kate said, 'I think he'd gone back to sleep before I put the phone down.'

When he woke up, he was still sitting in his chair. Daylight was remaking the furniture. The stiffness in his neck told him reproachfully that he had slept here all night. He waited for his brain-cells to regroup. How long was it since he had checked on Catriona? Hopefully she was still asleep. Oh, hopefully. The fervour of his wish made him feel guilty. This guilt replaced the guilt that she might not be sleeping.

He waited. Sometimes it seemed to him that he was always waiting. For what? For death? But whose death? His or someone else's? He shied away from a thought that confronted him with guilt yet again. He wondered how he had come to be trapped in such a warren of guilt. He hated guilt, how destructively addictive it could become. It paralysed you. There was an ironic thought. Could you develop paralysis by association, by proximity to the paralysed? The self-pity of the idea was enough to make you feel guilty, he thought, smiling bitterly to himself. He noticed the residue of whisky in the glass beside him.

He knew he was drinking too much. Every glass he took brought questions with it. What if a crisis arose and he was drunk? What if he fell asleep and Catriona needed him? It was as if every impulse had to submit itself to a committee before it could be fulfilled. Even this trip – two nights away with a couple of colleagues and a group of students – spoke quietly to him of selfishness.

At least he was going. This was the one time away he was

sure of every year. Perhaps the number of trips he had already taken made it easier to do it again. Perhaps the repetition of an action numbed the guilt of it.

Certainly, most times when he had a desire to do something solely for himself, the intention became so enmeshed in complications of doubt that he usually finished up doing nothing. It was easier that way. Perhaps that's why his work had become, outside Catriona, so all-consuming in his life. There could be no guilt in that. It was something he had to do for both of them. It was how he could provide a carer for her. It was how he had been able to afford the alterations to the house that took her increasingly limited mobility into account as the disease progressed. It was how he had been able to promise her that she would remain in her own place to the very end.

Beyond Catriona and the university, his life had been, for a long time now, something that took place mainly inside his head. His life, too, *had* been paralysed in a mild way. He lived among endless circular thoughts that seemed incapable of finding their way through into action. What action? Catriona was there and she needed him more than any other demands on him that he could think of, even those that were born inside himself.

The thought did what such thoughts always did. It overcame his self-pity with the reality of Catriona's vastly greater suffering. She was the only one of them who had any right to complain about life and she hadn't done much of that, even when she'd had the means to. Perhaps she couldn't afford to or she would have gone under more quickly. These days, he was largely guessing about what she felt.

He was wondering now. He put down his glass and went out into the hall. The railings there and the stair-lift attached to the wall struck him as poignant. They had been fitted at different stages of her deterioration. Now even they were useless except as milestones along a dark road she had gone alone.

At the door of the room he paused and listened. There wasn't even the sound of breathing. He pushed the door open gently. Light filtering through the curtains reached as far as the bed she lay in. He crossed quietly and stood looking down at her.

For a moment he panicked. Then an expression – indicating what, he didn't know – brushed her face as gently as a cobweb, stirred her features infinitesimally and left them. She was alive.

He watched her. In this flattering light and given the position of her head, the weight loss was somehow minimised. He saw her almost as she had been once. He remembered them making love and was glad he hadn't been with anyone else since her illness had made them celibate. He knew the gladness had a doubtful basis, was another of those expressions in his life whose meaning he wasn't sure of. Was it the result of noble self-denial or a lack of sexual drive? He felt the gladness anyway. Perhaps even the gift she was unaware of was still a gift, futile yet an expression of love, like flowers laid at the grave of one of the dead.

Watching her, he felt anew the injustice of what had happened to her. The innocence of her face was no illusion. He had once told her that it took her about three weeks to work out that somebody was being nasty to her, so alien to her was such treatment of others. What had she done to deserve this? Well, at least he knew it couldn't be too long now.

On that casual day in the kitchen she had begun a life sentence for which there was to be no remission but death. He should complain? He had been no more than a conscientious visitor to her prison.

Nothing he had done entitled him even to believe that he could effectively imagine the refined complexities of her suffering: learning to live within ever narrowing physical limits, so that each agonising adjustment of the spirit was merely a rehearsal for an even more brutal one, and then another; having your sight progressively blurred and your speech progressively muffled little by little; knowing yourself receding gradually behind thicker and thicker walls of silence and stillness and darkness.

He would have kissed her, except that he knew she could have no greater happiness in her life now than sleep, so he gave her the gift of not touching her. He crossed the room, pulled the door to and came downstairs.

The sense of what she had endured and how she had endured it chastened him. He would have his weekend, which she wouldn't have grudged him, and come back to look after her in the evenings. It had been arranged that Mhairi would stay with her till Sunday. She would soon be here. He would have a quick shower and be ready for the changing of the guard. But first he should give Harry Beck the wake-up call he had asked for. He stood in the hall.

He regretted again that he could never remember phone numbers. He went through to the sitting-room and found the list of people going on the trip. He lifted the phone and dialled. He listened to the relentlessness of the tone drilling into the strangeness of another life.

Someone or something was burrowing towards him. He seemed to be buried alive. He didn't want to be reached. But his hand had already taken hold on another world before he was fully awake.

'Yes?'

Who said that? He was lying among ashen light where vague shapes drifted. A mirror floated somewhere, containing a fragment of the ceiling and cornice of a room, a jigsaw piece that didn't fit anywhere. A voice buzzed in his ear like a trapped midge. It was bothering him.

'Who?'

'Harry. It's Andrew. Andrew Lawson.'

'Andrew?'

He shook his head, whether to clear it or to deny the name, he didn't know. He saw some single-masted boats floating on dappled water. That was Argenteuil. But where was he?

'It's your wake-up call. It's eight o'clock.'

'Hm.'

'Okay?'

'Yes. Yes.'

'See you at nine?'

'Fine. Thanks. Cheers. Andrew.'

His hand put the receiver down clumsily.

What plans? He had plans? The only plan he had at the moment was to work out where he was. Who had a Monet painting in their bedroom? What he had in his bedroom was a Russell Flint watercolour of nude women bathing in a sheltered waterway in what he had always assumed was Venice. He missed the women's unselfconscious company. Yet that painting of boats moored at Argenteuil was familiar. He had it in his sitting-room. It was then he remembered that he had switched the prints a couple of days ago. He was in his own bedroom. He was relieved.

The relief was short-lived. He didn't need painted nudes in his bedroom this morning. He had a real one in his bed. He sat up very carefully and leaned on his elbow to contemplate her as if she were some piece of extra-terrestrial matter that had fallen from the sky. Except that she was very much of this earth, thank God. Any planet she was on couldn't be such a bad place.

He closed his eyes tightly for several seconds, then opened them wide. She was real. It was the reality of himself he wasn't sure about. She lay there, effulgent as a lighthouse leading someone lost at sea back to land. He took his bearings from her. Her blonde hair was marvellously dishevelled on the pillow, evoking a raunchy night. Had he been part of it? Her breasts were carelessly displayed above the duvet. A thrown arm leaned against the headboard.

The image of her lying there slowly filtered other images into his mind in fragments, like disjointed scenes from a grainy film that hadn't been edited yet. He remembered her coming up to him at the party to say she knew his writing. This wasn't a bad result of literary appreciation: the word made flesh. There was a man who was drunk being persuaded to leave. There were streetlights observed from the darkness of a taxi. He was seeing them through a screen of fair hair. There were coilings in the dark, luminous bodies turning there.

He had been able to make love to her satisfactorily, drunk as he had been. At least, it had seemed satisfactory to him. But, then, he probably hadn't been the most stringent of judges at the time. He was trying to remember her name. The need to remember developed urgency as her breathing told him that she wasn't sleeping. Her eyes, opening lazily on him, bright blue, became an accusation.

'I have to go,' he said.

'I didn't know that,' she said softly. 'I didn't know that writers were on call as well. Like doctors.'

The accent was American. Had she had it last night? She smiled. He caught her mood.

'People don't know the half of it,' he said. 'My life's not my own. Us linguistic paramedics have it hard. The language would grind to a halt if it wasn't for us.'

She shifted slightly. The heavy movement of her breasts made radar contact with his loins.

'So what is it?' she said. 'Emergency parsing?'

He stroked her arm.

'What it is,' he said, wishing he could think of something to sustain the levity. 'I've got to deliver a mixed metaphor. Seems to be a tricky one. Sounds like a breech birth. The writer's in agony. Coffee?'

'That would be nice.'

She lay watching him as he got out of bed and put on his boxers. He was self-conscious before her eyes, hoping that what had been posing as a battering ram during the night hadn't turned into a toothpick. He paused on his way out of the bedroom.

'Oh,' he said. 'How do you take it? The coffee, I mean.'

'Black, no sugar.'

'Interesting social inversion, isn't it? I know how you take sex but not how you take coffee.'

'Well,' she said, smiling at him. 'Some of the ways.'

'There's more?'

'Hm.'

'May I study long at the encyclopedia of your body.'

'You certainly passed first grade,' she said.

He saw his kitchen with a stranger's eyes. It was a shambles. He found it hard to believe that such a small place could contain so much untidiness. Had she been in here last night? He wondered what could possibly have been the point of stacking these empty milk cartons neatly on the draining-board. He understood when he raised the lid of the bin and found it full to overflowing. He crumpled up the cartons and stuffed them ineffectually into the bin. The lid wouldn't shut properly.

He turned around vaguely in the kitchen, wondering where to start, and saw that there was no way he could finish until he had a spare day to work with. To hell with it. Presumably she had found him out already. Caliban in his cave, living among the debris of his loneliness.

Boiling the water for the coffee, he remembered her name. She was called Mary Sue. She came from New York. He was troubled about something. Staring out of the window, he located it among the leaves of a sycamore tree outside, as surely as if it had been sitting there like a bird, watching him. That was it. He felt too much at ease with her too quickly. Hers was an effortlessly comfortable presence to be in. It was like having known each other already and they had just been waiting for circumstances to get round to introducing them, exchanging names.

The feeling was so strong that he was tempted not to go to Cannamore. That was ridiculous, surely. Decisiveness gelled with the coffee-grounds in the water. He was going, all right. Last night was fine. It was a sweet short story. Why try to turn it into a novel?

When he brought the coffee through, she was sitting in her bra and pants, freshening her makeup. He regretted that. He liked the way she had wakened, with her eye-shadow lewdly wrecked. Courtesan was turning into housewife.

'Is this all you want?' he said.

She eyed him questioningly over her compact.

'More is possible?'

'Well,' he said, 'I could scrape the mould off some bread and toast it. Or there's a chocolate biscuit through there we could break with an axe.'

'I'll forego the breakfast menu,' she said, taking the coffee. 'Thanks.'

'You've obviously seen my kitchen.'

'Only from the outside. I didn't want to go in, in case something bit me. But this is lovely.'

'Okay, smartass,' he said, getting as close to Humphrey Bogart as he could. 'You gonna push your luck too far.'

'Hm. He speaks my language. Almost.'

'You know I've got to go to this weekend thing?'

'You told me last night.'

'I did?'

'Oh, yes. And many other things.'

He waited, wondering what the other things were. She didn't say. He decided to dress potential embarrassment in more levity.

'I hope I didn't mention the three murders I committed?'

'Three? You only mentioned two. But you can tell me about the other one next time. If there is a next time?'

'Yes, please.'

He left it at that. By the time he was shaved and dressed and had packed his travelling-bag, she was sitting demurely on the bed, which she had made, finishing her coffee. He checked that his notes were in the bag, then remembered the short story Mickey Deans had given him. He packed the two copies

54

of it with a certain trepidation. He still didn't know what he was going to say about it. He put his jacket on.

'Can I drop you?' he said.

Her eyes widened as she looked at him.

'Somewhere,' he said, spreading his hands. 'In a taxi.'

She smiled. That smile could become addictive, he thought.

'You afraid I'll ransack the house if you leave me here alone?'

'Anything you take will be doing me a favour. It's mostly stuff I can't be bothered to throw out. I'm just trying to be polite.'

'After last night, why bother?'

He laughed.

'Okay. I've ordered a taxi. I have to go now. I'll be happy to drop you at your place if you want. If not, stay here the weekend. My dumpster is your dumpster.'

'I'll leave with you,' she said.

'You want my number?'

'I have it.'

'You're some machine.'

The taxi sounded its horn and he gestured that he would follow her. At the bottom of the stairs she picked up the mail and passed it to him.

'Three letters,' she said. 'Impressive.'

'A thin day, my dear,' he said pompously.

He noted that one was from a publisher. It had a red square on the front advertising a new novel. Surely they wouldn't have the insensitivity to do that if they were rejecting *his* novel. He knew the thought was nonsense but he indulged it the way he had indulged himself long ago in avoiding stepping on the cracks in the pavement before an exam. He didn't know who the other two letters were from. One had a typed address. The other was handwritten in impeccable script. He put all three in his inside pocket. *Poste restante*. To be left until called for. He decided to try not to open any of them till the weekend was over. If he could fulfil that promise to himself, he decided, the news would be good.

Two

One of the problems nowadays with Stevenson's *Dr Jekyll and Mr Hyde* – Andrew Lawson was saying in his not unattractively portentous voice – is that it is familiar to us before we have read it. Mr Hyde has become a cliché of anti-social behaviour. Everybody knows one. Like Don Quixote or Hamlet, he has entered popular culture by a kind of osmosis. We feel we know him before we ever meet him. It is hard to come at him fresh. We may lessen the impact of the book because of the flabby assumptions we bring to it. But try to imagine the shock of his sudden appearance in Victorian society.

Open-mouthed, Marion pushed the pause button on her tape-recorder, as if enacting the shock Andrew Lawson was talking about. Someone was trying the door of her room. She was sure she had seen the handle turn. She thought she might also have heard the infinitesimal, flat click of a lock refusing to yield.

She was sitting cross-legged on the bed in her pyjamas with

the lights out. The moonlight that infiltrated the thin curtains made a daguerreotype of the room. The impression had been pleasing to her, as if she were sitting inside a nineteenth-century photograph, had re-entered the time in which this building was conceived. She had been imagining the ghosts of old inhabitants wandering the corridors, while the deep voice on the tape seemed to be talking of an era when they would have done so in the flesh. It had been an eerie feeling.

Suddenly, imagined eeriness had become real, and with it her fear. She had been gazing abstractedly at the door, listening to the hypnotic sound, when the handle had turned. Her finger had pressed automatically on the machine, erasing the voice as if it had been a medium calling up dead spirits.

Holding her breath, she continued to stare at the handle. It turned again. She managed not to call out. She forced herself to go on staring at the door-handle. Very slowly, nothing happened.

She looked at her watch. 2.15. Well into Sunday. She wondered who could be trying her door at this time. If it had been Vikki, she would surely have knocked. There was no one she could think of. There was no reason she could think of. She laid the tape-recorder on the bed and very quietly crossed towards the door, wincing at the creaking moan a floorboard made under the carpet, like the sound of the past buried in modernity but not yet dead. Crouched at the door, she listened. The only thing to disturb her was her breathing.

Very carefully she tried to release the lock, her tongue sticking out as if the elaborate expression of a dread might forestall its consequences. The lock clicked softly, reverberating like a rifle shot in her head. She clenched the handle, leaning instantly against the door to withstand any sudden pressure from the other side. She turned the handle slowly.

She pulled the door open. There was nothing in front of her but blank wall.

It was a nondescript off-white, she noticed. The thought was like common sense returning. She put her head out, looked left and right: carpeted corridor and dim, dead light. She was about to shut the door again when she sensed that something wasn't as it should be. She put her head back out and looked left. Two rooms along, on the opposite wall of the corridor, the door was open – an oblong of darkness where polished wood should be. Beside the open door, sitting on the carpet against the wall, there was what looked like a toilet bag. Was that the room from which she had heard shouting earlier and had been too frightened to come out? The noise had been so violent, she wondered what could have happened.

She stepped out into the corridor and listened. No sound came from the darkened room. She tiptoed towards it on her bare feet. She stopped and craned round the door jamb.

She thought at first she really was seeing a ghost. The motionless figure of a woman sat with its back towards her. She was facing a window with open curtains, against which the moonlight sharpened her outline. Beyond her the sea was turgid.

'Excuse me,' Marion said.

The woman remained motionless.

'Excuse me!'

The woman's head turned slightly to the left but it was her only movement. She said nothing. Her head turned back towards the sea.

Marion walked into the room, feeling embarrassed to be in her pyjamas but unable simply to walk away. When she stood beside the woman, Marion paused, transfixed by her utter self-absorption.

She sat like a woman in the waiting-room of a railway station where no trains came any more. She seemed dressed to travel but unable to move. Her cashmere coat was buttoned. A small travelling-bag lay on the floor beside her. There were some objects on the table in front of her. The only one Marion identified clearly was a small coolbag. The woman was staring through the windows at the moonlight on the sea. She was as bleak an image as Marion could remember seeing. Marion followed the woman's eyes out into the darkness. Diseased and deadening pallor on the waters and the land. It was as if, Marion thought, the night was painting her mood. The world had leprosy.

'Are you all right?'

The woman turned almost towards Marion without confronting her directly. Her face was cadaverous in the moonlight. 'I'm not sure,' she said.

'Can I help you?'

'I wouldn't think so.'

'Can I do something for you?'

The woman shook her head.

'You see, you left your door open.'

The woman had an expression vague enough to suggest that she didn't know doors could be closed, and turned again towards the window.

'Shall I close it for you?'

'If you like.'

Marion felt reluctant to leave but the woman was watching the sea again.

'Who are you?' Marion said. Once she had expressed it, the question seemed slightly impertinent. It had surfaced automatically because she couldn't identify the woman as a member of the study group. The woman thought about it for a moment.

'Sandra,' she said. Something like a smile that died in embryo happened in her face. 'I think.'

Marion smiled too but the woman didn't notice.

'I'll close the door then, shall I?'

Marion went out and closed the door. Back in her own room, she turned the lock again. If Vikki decided to come back now, that was her problem. She went and sat on the bed among her notes. She wondered what the woman was doing there. She didn't know whose room it was or if it had been occupied until tonight. She lifted her tape-recorder.

She was glad Andrew Lawson had given her permission to tape all the lectures. She wasn't going to be able to sleep tonight and the tape gave her something to distract her from herself. She would make notes of the parts that had interested her. It would take her mind off the embarrassment. How could she have done what she did this evening? Perhaps that was why someone had tried her door. Maybe they imagined she was available. The thought would have been laughable last night. No doubt it was still laughable but she didn't find it as easy to be amused now.

She looked at the tape-recorder. She was almost at the part about the names, the part she had found most interesting. She pressed the button.

Perhaps one of the most striking things about the novel is the scarcity of event. What does Hyde actually do on all those occasions when he escapes from the body of Jekyll? It's very vague. Of course, Victorian convention would forbid too many details. Perhaps that's why a Hollywood version of the novel introduced Ingrid Bergman to proceedings. But Stevenson turned this limitation to his advantage. There is a story of Michelangelo confronting the marble from which he would carve the statue of David. Someone had started to work on it before him and had lost his nerve. But not before he had cut a large piece from it. The story is that Michelangelo contrived to conjure the damaged marble into the posture of David's body. He made a virtue of necessity. Stevenson does something similar. Obliged to work with an enforced reticence, he induces us to inform the silence with our own imagination. We fill the void with ourselves. And isn't that what we try to do with our own lives?

And Vikki, Marion was thinking. What about Dr Jekyll and Mrs Hyde? Marion had woken up this morning alone in a room beside a bed that hadn't been slept in. Vikki hadn't explained herself when she came to change before breakfast, rather bizarrely dressed. There had only been raised eyebrows and knowing smiles between them. But the knowledge wasn't Marion's. What had happened?

Just before midnight on Friday evening Vikki had sat in the room she was sharing with Marion. Marion was already asleep. She hadn't taken any alcohol tonight, saying she was saving herself for a Saturday night blow-out. That probably translated into gin and tonic twice.

Vikki had opened one of the four bottles of wine she had brought. She filled herself a glass. She sat down on the single bed in the Janet Reger underwear she had put on after Marion fell asleep. She told herself she was toasting the weekend ahead but the toast stuck in her throat. The wine might as well have turned back into grapes. She had already lost faith in her ability to make the weekend more than a passionate encounter with words, an affair with dead men called R.L.S. and J. M. Barrie. No first names here, please.

After arriving at the hotel she hadn't changed out of the jeans and top she had travelled in. She didn't have the nerve. Maybe it was just as well. Most of the students had dressed so casually that the clothes she had brought would have made her look like a fading actress who had lost her way to the première. Yet the young women students had still managed to be sexily attractive. Perhaps that was what being young did for you. Nubile bodies could look enticing in baggy combat trousers and a tank top. Youth was the ultimate cosmetic, one you couldn't buy in any shop she knew of.

She glanced across at Marion, lying demurely immobile in her own single bed. She slept like a dead one and Vikki saw in her the corpse of her own future. Nights of rest untrammelled by the searching hands of men. She remembered the weight of Alan's arm across her body, heavy in sleep, and suddenly missed it with agonising intensity, as if it were a limb of her own identity she had lost. It wasn't him she missed, she knew. It was who she had been and could never be again. She was mourning herself.

She saw her clothes hanging in the open wardrobe. Their empty stillness accused her – the disembodied alternative selves she might have been, if she'd had the courage. Maybe she should have had the nun's dress lengthened and bought the wimple to go with it. A wimple for a wimp. She brought the dress determinedly into focus. It palpitated in her vision like a neon sign in Soho. It mocked her. You don't dare come in, do you?

Why didn't she? She remembered a boy in the woods near her home when she was fourteen. She was taking a shortcut through the trees to get to her house when she became aware of him, maybe thirty yards away. She could see him still. He had black hair that hung over his forehead almost to his eyebrows. His head was framed among leaves, turned fixedly towards her, watching. He was unlike any of the boys she saw in the classroom or the playground or on the street, swathed in attitudes that were too big for them, like adult clothes they were dressing up in. He seemed as startled as she was, raw with surprise. He was utterly who he was, an anonymous being caught in a shaft of sunlight, staring at a presence he had never seen before. He stood, as natural as an animal.

She stopped, transfixed by the intensity of his stare. He was transfixed by hers. A bird sang somewhere. Leaves tinkled in the breeze, like muted wind-chimes. She felt as if they couldn't move. They were trapped in each other. Something had to happen to release them. It did. Suddenly he shouted across the green distance between them. At first, in her state of trance, it was sheer sound, as basic as the bellow of a beast. It troubled her. But as the noise resolved itself into words, she reverted to being a girl who had to get home. And quickly. 'D'you want a ride?'

She swerved and ran. There was no sound of pursuit, no breaking branches, no battered leaves. Against her own wishes, she stopped and turned. She was gasping but it was not an unpleasant sensation. He stood exactly where he had been, still visible down a tunnel of leaves, still watching her. He looked forlorn, as if he had been trying to pay her a compliment in a language that was foreign to her.

It wasn't foreign now, she thought. As she raised the glass to her lips, she heard herself laughingly whisper 'Yes!' into it. She smiled and reflected ruefully that he was too far away to hear her.

Did such times accumulate till they defined you, trapped you in the refusal of yourself? There had been other times when rules that came from nowhere she could precisely locate (her mother, her father, what teachers said, conclaves of girls comparing notes?) had pre-empted what she felt, so that she prejudged the possibilities before they could happen and sentenced them to death, and thought it good.

The man at the café table in Madrid came back to her. Alan was visiting the stadium of Real Madrid. She couldn't remember its name. She didn't want to. They had spent a morning of loneliness in the Prado like vandals, their mutual displeasure spoiling everything they looked at. Their mood had desecrated Velázquez, defaced Goya. Only one painting hung in her memory from that visit. It was very small, easily missed. It showed the frontal image of a man's face gazing pleadingly upwards, framed in flames. It was called *Un Alma en Pena*, which she later found out meant a soul in pain. The melodrama of her mood at the time had sympathised with the man in the picture.

They had been arguing about something she couldn't recall. That memory lapse wasn't uncommon. Any relationship, she imagined, must be familiar with those lost quarrels that had seemed so vividly important at the time, graveyards of unremembered angst. Perhaps, though they didn't retain their substance, they came back to haunt togetherness remorselessly till it proved uninhabitable.

Whatever discontent had been alive that day, it had breathed its contagion on the city. She had wanted to be anywhere but here. When Alan suggested visiting the stadium, it was no more than she bitterly expected. He knew she hated football. As he walked angrily away from her, she stood still and decided, not for the first time, that their marriage was over.

She began to walk nowhere briskly, as if she were distancing him from her life. She sat down suddenly at a café table. It was not an action but the absence of an action. She did it because there was nothing she wanted to do. She ordered a brandy, which was something she never drank. But as she sipped it, the very strangeness of what she was doing made her feel different from herself. She felt she might be interested in meeting her. She felt the thrill of being beyond a routine sense of herself.

She was aware of people all around her, walking, going to places she would never reach, and she wanted to have her own strange places to go. This city excited her.

She knew that a man at the next table was watching her. She looked at him. He smiled. He had a thoughtful face, dark eyes, a mouth like cruelty waiting to happen. It was an interesting mouth. She looked away.

An old man and woman were walking down the street towards her. The slowness of their progress was awesome. Each step seemed a task they might never finish. People were passing them as if they were stationary. It looked as if the sun would fell them before they made another yard. Before she could avoid the arrogance of the thought, she found herself wondering what point life could possibly have for them any more.

Involuntarily, she glanced again towards the man at the next table. She had the disconcerting feeling that he had read her mind. He raised his eyebrows, still watching her. He nodded towards the old couple. He pointed to her, he pointed towards himself. 'Soon now,' he mouthed in English. (He must have heard her ordering.)

She smiled dismissively but she did not take her eyes away from him. He nodded sombrely. He pointed to her again, he pointed again to himself.

He made a gesture with both hands towards the street. She knew that he meant they should go off together. He mouthed again in English: 'I have a place.'

She turned her head away. She knew she wouldn't dare to look back at him. She lifted the slip of paper that was her bill. She cursed the almost indecipherable faint blue numbers on the paper, afraid that he would come across and interpret them for her. She left what she decided was the price of the brandy and a tip. She stood up and walked away in the direction opposite to which the man had gestured.

She had been walking away ever since, she felt. Would she ever find the nerve to stop and turn back towards the risk? All she had done with the weekend so far was listen to Andrew Lawson's lecture and phone three times to try to find out how Jason was getting on. But nobody had answered the phone at Alan's place. Nobody needed her there. Nobody needed her anywhere.

Now here she was, sipping wine alone, unless you counted Marion lying like a figure carved in stone. She could have been doing this as easily at home. She stood up with the glass in her hand and gazed at herself in the full-length mirror fixed to the wall. She thought she was looking good. She struck what she felt was a seductive pose and stared at herself provocatively, as if daring the woman in the mirror to step out of it and merge with her.

Perhaps the woman needed more encouragement from her. If she hadn't had the nerve to put on anything daring in public, why shouldn't she at least do it in private? Maybe she just needed practice. She was already wearing beautiful underwear and suspender belt and stockings. She had even put on her highest heels, as if she were drinking in a brothel, waiting for her next client, with Marion the unwitting sleeping partner. Why not complete the ensemble?

She drained her glass and put it on the desk against the window. She took the dress from the wardrobe and wriggled into it. She put on the black leather belt. The dress showed a lot of leg.

She contemplated herself in the mirror. She had an urge to walk up and down but was afraid her heels on the thin carpet might waken Marion. She wasn't satisfied. The dressing-room wasn't where you performed. She smiled to herself. You needed a stage for that, even if the theatre was empty. She smiled at herself again. In her case, especially if the theatre was empty. Why not? They must all be in their beds by now. She giggled. If anybody saw her, maybe she could pretend she was sleep-walking. If she couldn't brass it out under these conditions, when would she ever?

She refilled the glass and drank the wine in one gulp, trying to make sure that the fuel for her boldness didn't run out. She put the glass down and looked at Marion as she tiptoed across the room. Opening the door, she waved theatrically to the sleeping figure. She stepped out into the corridor and closed the door softly.

She listened. There was no sound. She walked regally along empty, carpeted corridors until she came to the main staircase. She paused there. The ridiculousness of what she was up to put a wobble in her self-confidence, like a broken heel. Surely she wasn't really going to do this. Yes she was, some desperate dread of returning sheepishly to that room was insisting. If she went back now, the door she closed would close on her for good. She could always say she had thought the bar was still open. Swingers were like that.

The way she came down the staircase, Rhett Butler might have been waiting for her at the bottom. Through the glass door in the hall below, she could see most of the reception area. No one was there. In the silence of early morning the building seemed to hum, like a generator. She walked towards the large residents' lounge which adjoined the small bar. As she came nearer, she noticed that the lounge wasn't completely dark. A dim light seeped out to stain the carpet for a short distance in front of the door. She stopped beyond the reach of the light. Listening, she heard an intimacy of murmured voices. She thought she should turn away but she couldn't resist approaching. She peered carefully through the doorway.

A lamp in the far corner made a small bell of light within which two people sat. Their faces were leaning towards each other. He was dark and she was fair. They had the attractiveness of the utterly preoccupied, the innocence of those completely absorbed in being with one another. Their postures were not passionate but totally intense.

From this angle she couldn't make out who the girl was. The boy was Mickey Deans. He had a reputation for aggression but she had always thought he had the kind of dangerous good looks that could make a woman wish she were young again. She was glad she couldn't hear what they were saying. It would have felt like a profanation of their closeness.

She turned quietly away and walked towards the door of

the bar. The place was shadowed, only a little light from the corridor mitigating its gloom. She went and walked among the tables, imagining herself unfazed by many people sitting there.

She stood at the end of the bar, ignoring the metal shutter. She turned towards the door and said, 'Oh!' before she could stop the sound.

A dark shape, not unlike a bear, stood just inside the doorway. She wasn't sure what it was, let alone who it was.

'Vikki,' a dark voice said. There was a pause. 'You look amazing.'

She was startled first that the shadow knew her name and, second, that she knew the name of the shadow.

Names are interesting. Jekyll. Hyde. Utterson. We should, of course, be careful of deducing galaxies of significance from atoms of meaning. But the primitive belief in the sympathetic magic of names has maybe a particular resonance in this story of a man who renamed himself. Naming as incantation. A summoning forth. As you call it, so it will be.

Sandra, Marion was thinking, as she looked round the room, wondering about Vikki's absence for the second successive night. It was such a pleasantly ordinary name for such a bleak, dark woman. Presumably the incantation her parents had been performing in naming her hadn't worked too well.

Maybe they should have called her Deirdre. Sorrow seemed to suit her. But perhaps all christenings are unintentionally ironic, adult wish-fulfilment imposed on a contradictory reality.

Marion imagined her still sitting there, merging with the emptiness outside her windows. She seemed to Marion at the moment the core of Willowvale, as definitive of the place as the female gargoyle she had noticed on one of the outer walls had become for her. It was as if, in Marion's mind, the labyrinth of corridors and rooms could lead only to the woman.

The Dr Jekyll who becomes Mr Hyde seems almost to illustrate Christopher Fry's observation on the nature of names:

> Our names. They make us broody; we sit and sit
> To hatch them into reputation and dignity.
> And then they set upon us and become despair,
> Guilt and remorse.

We can begin to wonder what our names represent.

'David?' she said.

She was on the only chair, reapplying her makeup. He found her concentration impressive. It was as if this was all there was, as if the small circular mirror in her hand showed her the whole world. Presumably he had fallen off the edge of it for the moment. Maybe that was one way to handle the situation. For what the hell was there to talk about? He hoped she would go on making love to her face for the next few hours. Then they could both escape. But that seemed unlikely, even for her. He could always pretend to be asleep, except that his head was going like a factory, trying to process the chaos of the future into some kind of usable commodity. He wouldn't be able to keep his eyes shut. They were too busy staring into the sudden unknown.

He had opened the curtains and he was standing at the window. She wondered what that was about. There was nothing to see, unless he was getting messages from the moon. She hoped he didn't start howling or growing hair on the back of his hands. He had enough there already. She would have to stop putting on her face soon. People had been known to take less time painting the Forth Rail Bridge. But she had to take her time. She had to think. This took careful playing. There were possibilities here. Especially now. And they weren't just academic. He hadn't been bad. Not at all bad. Her eyes were looking good. They stared back at her vividly as if they were trying to tell her something.

She glanced across at him.

That was ominous. He mustn't look back. Only disconnect. The longer he managed to maintain silence, the less time they had to talk. The less time he had to say all the things he didn't mean. But if they did start talking, he would have to say them. He was vulnerable to her now. Telling her the truth was not an option. He had to get through the next few hours without angering her. The truth would certainly do that. He needed to get clear of this situation, defuse it. Then he would have the time to work things out. She could interpret the silence any way she wanted. Silence was proof of nothing. They had to stay quiet till time and distance disempowered her. This room was a hand-grenade sitting in his life. Talk might pull the pin. She was gazing in her mirror again. Good. Enjoy the view.

But she was no longer applying makeup. She was communing briefly with her face in the glass. At least you have me to work with, it told her. Not a bad start. If you can't make effective use of this, you're hopeless. He was still staring out of the window. He hadn't returned her look. This could go on all night. But it wouldn't do to tell him to snap out of it. He was sensitive Byronic man, gazing appreciatively into his own sadness. Enter his female counterpart – understanding woman, handmaiden to his sorrow. She practised a compassionate face.

The compact snapped shut.

Since she was sitting to his left, he turned slightly to the right, grimacing into the moonlight. This was it. Curtain up. This was a play he didn't want to be in. The script was going to be crap. But he'd better try to be convincing.

'I'm sorry that had to happen,' she said.

'So am I.'

'I'm really sorry it happened.'

'I know.'

'Really sorry.'

Jesus. Put a hammer through the CD.

'Don't let it worry you,' he said. (Not that I imagine it will. It's not like smudging your makeup, is it? That would really be a tragedy.)

'I feel so guilty,' she said.

'It happened.' (You probably don't go to bed without putting your face on. In case you get burgled.)

She put her compact in her handbag, put her handbag on

75

the floor. She noticed the bottle of wine they had gone to fetch, still lying on the bed where he had thrown it when they came in. She fancied a glass but thought that perhaps the timing wasn't right. It might come in handy later.

'We were having such a good time, too,' she said.

'Yes, we were.'

At least he was moving from the window.

'I blame myself,' she said.

'Hey. Don't, love.' (Don't flatter yourself.)

He sat down on the bed, leaned his elbows on his knees, clasped his hands and stared at the floor as if he could see through to the flames of hell. It was amazing how men could put on a conscience with their trousers.

'I'm just wondering, though,' she said. 'Where do we go from here?'

She said it softly but the remark went off in his head like a klaxon. His reply was on tiptoe.

'Who knows?' (As far as possible in opposite directions?)

'I wish we'd had more time to get to know each other properly. Before this.'

It won't stop us being together again, was what he mustn't say.

'I suppose that's the way it goes,' he said.

Oh, do you? I know too much about you to pretend that one discovered infidelity is blighting your life. You had Alison Miller last year. And who knows how many others before and since? Now it's my turn. I can take that. I know that's the game you play. But at least I'll have some say in when the game is over. This time I decide when the dumping's done. And it's not yet.

'Uh-huh,' she said.

He put his right hand over his eyes. Then he took his thumb

76

and forefinger and worked his eyelids vigorously. What was he trying to do? Make her disappear?

'David,' she said. 'What is it you want?'

Total silence. How about that? A moratorium on your voice. Peace. Perfect fucking peace.

'Just tell me,' she said.

He kept his fingers on his eyes.

'Jacqui,' he said. 'Have some sensitivity. Please. Think of how I must be feeling. Could you leave me alone with my thoughts for a minute?' (Or alternatively shut the fuck up.)

Pardon me. Now that your cock's gone AWOL, your head has reattached itself to your body. That's nice. Sensitive, is it? You were very sensitive when you were riding me like a roller-coaster and wailing like a banshee. You were so sensitive I was afraid the management was going to turn up and chuck us out.

'Of course, David,' she said. 'I understand.' (I understand that the performance of your phoney pain is going to take longer than I thought.)

This might be a good time for the wine. She crossed and took the bottle from the bed, being careful not to touch him. With a man as sensitive as he was, it might leave a bruise. She went to where she had left the corkscrew she had brought and lifted it from the desk. It was then she noticed that the wine bottle was a screwtop. She managed to lay the corkscrew gently back on the desk instead of throwing it. The noise might shatter his concentration. Screwtop wine. Maybe that was why he was in despair. With taste like his, he should be. No worries here about whether the wine was *chambré*. She unscrewed the metal top, missing the evocative popping of a cork that always came to her like an invitation to a party. She thought about rinsing the two glasses they had used earlier, which were sitting on the desk. To her, they looked poignant there, small memorials to pleasure past. She made a sentimental decision not to wash them. Anyway, he wouldn't notice. Despair did that to people, made small niceties irrelevant. She filled the two glasses with the new wine, which promised to be a less uplifting vintage than the previous one, and not just because of the screwtop, which she replaced on the bottle. She lifted the glasses and moved to where he was. He was still covering his eyes. She put the cold edge of the glass against his forehead. His hand came away quickly and his eyes opened. They were beautiful eyes.

'Here.'

He smiled ruefully.

'Thanks.'

He took the glass and held it, facing the wall.

She crossed back to where the chair was and sat down. She noticed that his right foot was resting on her discarded thong but perhaps it wasn't the best time to mention it. The image looked like a corny metaphor for something. Virtue trampled underfoot? Except that any virtue which was trampled hadn't been wearing the thong. Of course, neither had she been at the time. She felt sorry for his wife. She had looked like a permanently sad soul. But the real fault was in the pathetic naïvety that could put its trust in a man who would have chatted up a barber's floor because it had curly hair on it. She wasn't about to give too much sympathy to someone hiding behind marriage like a mask. Welcome to the real world. She had had to learn to live there herself. How long was he going to sit here? Harry Beck wouldn't have done this. But he wouldn't have done the other stuff as well, it seemed. Nor Mickey Deans. With him, you would have to put your lust on hold till he grew up. That could take a long time. About as long as this was taking.

She had finished her wine. She stood up and moved back to the desk. She screwed the top off and refilled her glass, wondering why hotels always provided you with thimbles. Still holding the bottle, she turned and gestured with it towards David.

His stare didn't waver. The wall was more interesting than she was. She screwed the top back on and put the bottle down. She lifted her glass and walked back to her chair and sat down and took a sip of wine. This was long enough.

'Let's at least talk about it,' she said.

'We have to talk,' she said.

Only the walls, it seemed, had ears.

'For Christ's sake. I'm here as well, you know. I'm involved in this. There are two of us involved here,' she said.

She watched his eyes bounce off the wall to stare at her. It was meant to be intimidating so she tried, with some difficulty, not to smile. Contact.

'Three,' he said savagely.

'Three?' she said innocently.

'My wife,' he said, 'is marginally a part of this mess, too. In case you hadn't noticed. I have to think about my wife as well.'

Afterthoughts were nice. Better than nothing at least. Not quite in the same class as forethoughts, but never mind. So that's where he was.

'You think I don't know that?' she said. 'I'm very sorry about your wife. But I wasn't even sure you had one.' (Until last year.) 'At least you don't have any children.'

He seemed to be renewing his friendship with the wall.

'Do you?'

He said nothing.

'Well, do you?'

'No, we don't as it happens.'

That was one possible problem out of the way. Any real guilt he might have was localised. You wouldn't have to go all around the houses to confront it.

'I don't know her name,' she said.

She waited.

'What's her name, David?'

'Don't even go there.'

Did she think because she'd dropped her knickers once she owned his private life? If you could call those knickers.

His foot flicked the thong aside. She watched him calmly.

'It's a simple question, David.'

No, it's not. I know what you're up to. You lure me into talking about my life and suddenly you're inside my head. You're part of the furniture in there. And whatever removals I make in my life, you're liable to be going along with them. No way. You think I'm still in nappies? I've got possibilities. I'm not sure what they are yet. But I think I might know one. There's somebody who might be delighted to know I'm on my own. I think so. If I'm jumping ship, it won't be into another leaky boat. You were just a fuck by the wayside, darling. Watch me go.

'All I'm asking—' she said.

He was back fixating on the wall and his right palm was commandingly towards her. No through way.

'All I'm asking—' she said pleasantly.

'We don't talk about Sandra.'

He grimaced, and then his face relaxed in incredulity. He couldn't believe what he had said.

She could. He was open now. He might take difficult

handling but voiced anger was a lot better than silence. It took you places you hadn't meant to go. And who knew what might happen there?

'Hm,' she said. 'That's it?'

He didn't look at her.

'Sandra,' she said.

He stared at her warningly.

'Sandra,' she said. 'Nice name.'

She watched his fists clench. He made as if to rise but didn't. She knew now that passion of some kind was coming, let it fall where it would. It was better than discreet silence or disappearing without warning into the distance. At least there would be fireworks. All she had to do was provide the match.

'Sandra,' she said. 'Sandra, Sandra, Sandra.'

She looked at the surface of the desk that stood between her and the window. The objects on it had an eerie definition in the moonlight, a weird still life. The French term for it would have fitted her mood more exactly: *nature morte*. Her nature certainly felt dead. All she thought remained to her at the moment was an autopsy on her past.

Before her were the means she had given herself to perform it. It seemed a random and incongruous collection, the purpose of which would have baffled anyone else, like the tools of an esoteric trade. Perhaps one no longer commonly practised. Say, fletcher or lorimer. But the despair she was about to open up and explore was peculiarly her own. She thought she knew what they were for.

She moved them around absently on the desk. Maybe she

was simultaneously reminding herself of their purpose and arranging them in some mystically advantageous way, as if they might form a pentagram within which to summon up the meaning of the past.

The thought was laughable when she considered what the objects were. She had bought the packet of sandwiches on the ferry. They were egg-and-cress. The irrelevant exactness of that fact overwhelmed her. Egg-and-cress? The meaningless multiplicity of things was endless. The stiff triangular plastic container appeared strange to her. Who had made it? She thought she might need an instruction booklet to open it. Maybe it wouldn't come to that. She hadn't eaten anything since this morning. Why should she start now?

The coolbag contained two bottles of champagne. She had brought them as a way of celebrating.

The irony of it twisted her mouth into the death mask of a smile, one which extended to the bottle of sleeping pills, sitting squat and practical. She had persuaded her doctor to prescribe them more than six months ago, when she wondered if she would ever sleep again for a full night. She hadn't taken one. She had brought the bottle with her this weekend because she had thought she might be too excited to sleep without them. They might still have their uses.

The glass had been rinsed and dried with the hand-towel in the bathroom. It sat shining and empty on the desk. Its innocent emptiness offered interesting possibilities. It could deaden the pain or end it, depending on how she decided to employ it. She would see. The Polaroid photo lay face down beside the pills. The black back of it was all she could bear to look at just now.

She arranged her five objects into a pattern that pleased her. Then she simply waited. She felt empty. Perhaps, she thought, friendship and love and trust are the clearest mirrors in which we see a reflection of ourselves. Break them and we are left wondering if we exist. She felt hardly present in this room, barely physical. But mind remained – self-generating, the mad amoeba. Its endlessness frightened her.

In order to block out the image her mind was endlessly presenting to her, she had already crossed the room and locked the door that the strange woman in pyjamas had closed for her. She had taken off her coat and put it on the bed. She had lifted one of the glasses and replaced it in the bathroom, as if that were erasing the evidence of her folly.

But she knew none of this activity would work. The glass seemed more immediately present in the bathroom than it had been on the desk. In her head the door was always swinging open, ushering in the moment that had atomised her understanding of her own experience. It was a door she couldn't effectively lock. Through it were still coming David and a woman she didn't know, like an incessantly repeating scene in a bad film from which she couldn't take her eyes.

Hyde seems obvious enough: the hidden asocial nature of a man who is socially thought to be known and much admired. But the name has other echoes, which trouble the clarity of this first impression. Hyde is also the name of a famous park in what was the most famous metropolis in the world. And a park can be seen as an obeisance to the country made by the town. A shrine to the natural in the heart of the man-made. That normalises him somewhat perhaps. Is he so alien to society after all? Is he so different from us? Another possible meaning reverberates beyond this one. Hyde can also be a pun for the skin of an animal. So who is hiding? Him or us? What are we naming when we name him? We take names as defining a coherent identity. But his name melts into a confusion of meanings. May not our own?

The words gave Marion a brief shiver as she imagined the people she had vaguely assumed she knew, inhabiting all the dark and silent rooms around her. What were they doing? Perhaps just sleeping.

Harry Beck sat on the bed in black boxer shorts and a white T-shirt. He looked at the virginal white of the two pillows behind him. Only one would be rumpled in the dawn light. Maybe his next haircut should be a tonsure. Welcome to the monastery.

He caught a glimpse of someone and wondered for a second if he had come into the wrong room. But it was only the wardrobe mirror showing him a stranger. He was strange, all right. He recognised the hair – thick and not yet going grey. It was the same hair that had dripped playing football in the park and had gone to the disco with him and accommodated the long and the short of changing styles. But who was that underneath it? When had life switched faces on him?

Maybe the strange man in the mirror was telling him who

84

he was now, forbidding him to go on with the charade of pretending to be someone else. Maybe his sense of himself had stripped to its underwear as well. It wasn't a pretty sight.

When Jacqui had come and sat down beside him in the lounge tonight, an old conditioned reflex had pre-empted any genuine reaction. He found himself smiling automatically and remembering the signals she had been giving him earlier. But, as she started to talk, he suddenly knew the role he was expected to play and felt that it wasn't him. Without warning, even to himself, he was changing the script.

'I really enjoyed your talk, Harry,' she said. 'I enjoyed yours the most.'

It was the first time she had used his Christian name to him.

'Thanks.'

'It was so true.'

'I don't know about that. It was only some thoughts.'

'It was, though. Especially that stuff about us all being just animals. No matter how much we try to hide it.'

'I don't think that's quite what I said, Jacqui. It's certainly not what I meant to say. In fact, I think what I was trying to get at is that we can't just be animals any more. And that we can't quite effectively be anything else. We're kind of deformed hybrids, I suppose. There's a cheery thought. Let's drink to it. Can I buy you one?'

'No, thanks. This animal is going upstairs. To sleep alone.'

She smiled. He smiled.

'My room-mate has deserted me.'

'I'm sure it's not a matter of personal hygiene.'

He had meant to deflect the offer with suave levity. Once he had said it, he felt it had all the suavity of a kick in the crotch.

Were there good turn-off lines as well as good turn-on ones?
She didn't seem bothered.

'I could easily prove to you it's not.'

He looked at his glass.

'What's your room number?'

He glanced up at her. She was watching him steadily. He
didn't know what to say.

'I never give it out, Jacqui,' he said.

It was news to him.

'Come on,' she said.

'What?'

'You can't be that old.'

'Maybe not. But I'm trying to be.'

Into the awkward silence, as if somebody had turned up the
volume, came an awareness of laughter and loud voices. He
felt bad for her, as if he might have made her feel the laughter
was directed at her.

'Jacqui,' he said.

'See you,' she said and rose and moved away.

He had noticed that she didn't go upstairs. A few minutes
later he had seen her talking to Mickey Deans and then to
David Cudlipp.

He lay back on the bed. His behaviour towards Jacqui
couldn't have come out of nowhere. He was trying to work
out what had brought about his reconversion to being fully
human, instead of a sexual urge with identikit man attached.

He had spent the time since he came here doubling back in
his mind. Willowvale had become where Mary Sue was, inside
his head whether he wanted it or not.

He had been trying, he suspected, to rediscover in himself
enough stature to accommodate the feeling he had for Mary
Sue. He had been trying to make himself worthy of her. It was

86

embarrassing but it was true. Shades of courtly love. Perhaps that also explained the torture he had put himself through to try to make good his bad treatment of Mickey Deans.

He swung his feet on to the floor and sat up. He looked at the man in the wardrobe mirror and thought it was time to try to get to know him better. How could Jacqui Forsyth have imagined he was open to her proposition? He had never considered being with a student in his life. Maybe he had become so estranged from himself that people thought he was someone else.

He was ready to make acquaintance with himself again. He thought affectionately of Mary Sue turning at the bottom of the stairs to give him the letters. He decided it was time to read the letter from the publisher.

The layers of implication in the name Hyde contain inherent natural contradictions. The first meaning, with its under-tones of hypocrisy and presenting a sham image of who you are, carries pejorative weight. Read from this viewpoint, the text can be taken as a critique of individual social duplicity. But the second meaning, punning with the name of a park, compromises the first one. For the second meaning acknowl-edges by implication the acceptance of the natural, the comparatively wild, as an inevitable part of the socially constructed, the man-made. In a somewhat domesticated form, it is true. But it does to some extent normalise both Mr Hyde and Dr Jekyll. The first meaning would have distanced us from them, as criticism of another tends to do. The second meaning puts a bridge between them and us. Hyde becomes not merely a part of Dr Jekyll but a part of ourselves. Read from this viewpoint, the text becomes a less comfortable examination of our own inner lives set against our attempts to conform to the supposed norms of social behaviour – the instinctive self that is housed in the social person, the park within the city. The third meaning casts us further adrift from any fixed or predetermined point of view and challenges further the initial implication of one-sided criticism. The hide of an animal is its most blatant characteristic, the means by which it shows itself most fully. So Hyde is paradoxically not hiding. Dr Jekyll is. The text can be seen as being not merely a condemnation of the evil of Mr Hyde but of the evil of the society that would deny the truth of him utterly while exploiting it, exemplified by Dr Jekyll.

The need to use the toilet woke him, as it always did these nights. Two trips a night as a zombie was his average. Noticing his travelling alarm glowing beside him to his left in the dark, he found that he was lying on the wrong side of the bed. He wondered vaguely how that had happened. Then he remembered why he was on this side of the bed.

As he groped his way upright, trying not to disturb her, he was glad he had insisted on an en-suite room for all lecturers. Female students would have one, too. Only male students would have to go on safari to the nearest toilet on their floor if they felt the need during the night. It was a way to keep the cost of the trips within budget. No one had ever complained about gender discrimination – no doubt, he suspected, because they would simply use the wash-basin that was in every room which wasn't en-suite.

When he switched on the bathroom light, he was startled to see that he was naked. He slept in pyjamas. It was like being embarrassed by what he didn't want to see. The grey and heavy looseness of his body confronted him with a familiar dismay.

He held his penis over the bowl and waited for the urine to arrive. When it did eventually come, it fell sheer into the water of the lavatory pan in heavy droplets. It occurred to him again that those contests of projectile peeing he had witnessed as a boy (who can pee the highest?) hadn't been as pointlessly silly as he had thought they were at the time. They had been an instinctive expression of growing virility. Young men can pee like stallions. Old men can't. He wiped his penis with a small piece of toilet paper to avoid the dreaded residue, and flushed. It was then that he was aware of the heaviness of his penis, as if it were trying to tell him something (I'm not just here for this, you know).

He crossed to the wash-basin and turned the hot water on quietly. He painstakingly tried to coax some lather out of an oblong of soap so small he found it difficult to locate it in his large cupped hands. He was taking his time, less out of commitment to hygiene than as a way to let him adjust to the strangeness of where he was. He dried his hands and peered into the bedroom, into which the open bathroom door threw a shaft of light that diffused gently through the rest of the room.

She was still asleep, he was glad to see. He needed to be alone to work out what he felt. Looking at her, he couldn't believe that someone so attractive was lying in his bed. He tiptoed through and put on his underpants, trying to draw in his stomach as he pulled them up. She seemed fathoms down in sleep. Maybe the wine had helped with that. He looked for the bottle and saw that it was still half full. Not half empty. Was her presence teaching him optimism? He found his drained glass and refilled it. He sat down on the cushioned chair, took a sip of warm white wine and stared at her.

He still couldn't understand the sequence of events that had led to her being here. It was like spinning random numbers on a safe to which you had lost the combination long ago and suddenly it sprang open, and you couldn't believe the forgotten wealth that was inside. He contemplated her as if she had been conjured out of some half-forgotten poem, say 'The Eve of St Agnes'.

If a careless mistake could yield such riches, maybe he should have cultivated more carelessness in his life. The half-bottle of whisky he had brought with him had been an ill-advised attempt to ration his consumption. When he had gone to his room on Friday night he had decided to celebrate completing his main responsibility, having delivered the only lecture he had. The celebration had got slightly out of hand. Shortly after midnight, the half-bottle was empty. He excused himself by remembering that he had taken a couple of drinks from it before dinner.

He had thought of going to bed but decided he really needed one last nightcap. Perhaps the bar was still open. When he stepped out of his room into the corridor, the omens weren't good. Nobody was celebrating Mardi Gras tonight. He walked through a silent hotel, meeting no one. Before he reached the bar downstairs, he noticed a dim light in the lounge. Glancing in, he saw Mickey Deans and Kate Foster sitting under a single light, talking with quiet intensity. The tableau they made went through him with such a pang of the unattainable, they might as well have been in the Garden of Eden. He turned away without making a sound.

The dark silence of the bar had already told him it was closed but he went in anyway. He was wondering if they had shuttered it. Some of these country hotels didn't. It was no good. Fort Knox with a gantry. He went to the end of the bar to see if he could get in that way. Everything was locked up. He wandered back across the bar and stood against the wall just inside the doorway, reluctant to accept the hopelessness of things. He had a vague idea that, if he could just reach one of the optics, he could fill a glass and pay in the morning. He was being silly, he knew, but his silliness was suddenly rewarded in an unforeseeable way.

A woman he had never seen before was walking into the bar, as if it were open and full of people. He thought perhaps he was hallucinating. She was certainly dressed for an occasion which wasn't now. Was she the ghost of the hotel? If she was, he was pleased to meet her. But surely no ghost ever had flesh that was so sweetly solid against the light. In the completely unimagined suddenness of the moment, he felt something he had trained himself for years not to feel. He felt desire for a woman. It happened in him before he had time to reason with it. By the time the woman went to the end of the bar and turned, and he realised that he had seen her before, it was too late. It was no longer his sense of himself that was meeting her. It was a part of him that sense had for so long denied. Something in him, so patiently domesticated, had snapped its chain. When he spoke, his words sounded, even to himself, more growl than speech.

'Vikki,' he said. 'You look amazing.'

It wasn't the kind of thing he said. The strangeness of the words was like an alternative self speaking. But that self was out now and in control.

'Dr Lawson,' she said.

'Andrew,' he said, as if naming himself for the first time. There was a pause.

'Andrew,' she said, almost submissively.

'I was looking for a drink,' he said, and was pleased to hear he had made no attempt to conceal what he was doing. 'Whisky.'

'I don't have that,' she said. 'Wine, though. I have some wine.'

'You do? Where?'

'In the room.'

'I can adapt,' he said.

She hesitated.

'Lead on, Vikki.'

She turned and began to walk out of the bar. He followed her. As they came out and turned towards the foyer and the staircase, he noticed that the light in the lounge was out. Mickey Deans and Kate Foster must have gone to bed. Together or separately? he wondered. But he felt no envy at the moment.

As they went up the staircase, he put his hand on her arm. He hoped it looked as if he was helping her in a gentlemanly way but he knew it was an act of possession and he enjoyed that it was. She didn't object. Outside her room she stopped. She seemed to be having doubts.

'Marion's asleep,' she said. 'Marion Gibson. I'm sharing with her.'

'You want *me* to get the wine?'

He hoped she wouldn't say yes.

'No, no. You don't even know where it is.'

But she seemed uncertain. She looked at him. He made a drinking gesture with his cupped hand.

'I'll try to pass it out to you quietly,' she whispered, as if her voice was practising the stealth her body would need.

'Pass it out? Vikki. The idea's to have a dorm feast. I've got some biscuits. You wouldn't ask a man to drink a bottle of wine alone? You'll be back before she wakes up, all right.'

Vikki giggled and tentatively opened the door, grimacing. As he waited for her, he relished how a dead night had turned into a small adventure. She passed a bottle of wine out to him and disappeared. He was dismayed until he noted that the door was still open. Presumably she was coming back. He glanced at the label. It was an anonymous Chardonnay but the company might improve the vintage. She emerged with two more bottles of wine and her handbag. He took another bottle from her to prevent the clinking of glass. She closed the door.

'I don't have a corkscrew,' he said conspiratorially.

She held up her handbag and widened her eyes.

It had been as simple as that. Watching her lying asleep in his bed, he couldn't believe how easily it had happened. They had slept together two nights now. But who had been sleeping with her? It wasn't anybody he recognised. Was he the same man who had sat in his house yesterday, thinking of his wife?

The name Jekyll itself further disperses the reader's ability to locate any fixed moral centre in the text. If these narrow, cackling syllables connote anything, it must be jackal. And the jackal is not only an animal but a scavenger. Something that haunts the edges of the kill. Feeding off the savagery of other creatures. Long before the advent of Hyde, Henry Jekyll ('He was wild when he was young') has come to acknowledge the animal impulses in himself, to accept that 'man is not truly one, but truly two'.

Andrew Lawson's voice made Marion think of herself. What she had done at the Free-for-all tonight had been like another person suddenly emerging from some hidden place in her to declare that this, as well, was Marion Gibson.

Enter Edward Hyde. Like part of some unnatural compact between the jackal and the lion, personal purveyor of ferocities off which Henry Jekyll may feed. For Hyde is the animal almost, if not quite, pure. The truth is, just as Henry Jekyll is part social man, part bundle of asocial impulses, so Edward Hyde is hybrid too. The aftermath of the early incident of the trampling of the child shows that he can act with great social circumspection when necessary. The animality of his nature is diluted by social pressures. The loose entity that is Jekyll–Hyde is neither quite one thing nor the other – neither sheerly social man nor sheerly animal.

It was a dead calm in the middle of a storm of words. He sensed her sitting behind him, watching. He told himself he must not get angry again.

'I'm sorry about that,' he said, as he unscrewed the bottle-top.

She said nothing. He filled his glass. He turned and walked towards her with what he hoped was that expression of boyish shamefacedness women had innocently taught him they liked. He filled her glass. She watched him go back to the desk and put the top back on the bottle. He took his glass and went and sat on the bed again. He took a sip of wine. She studied him. He looked nice sitting there. She had enjoyed his anger, too. The flaring eyes. Those eyes.

'You know,' she said, 'I think maybe I could get used to being with you.' (For a few months anyway.)

He smiled at the floor.

'Same here,' he said. 'With you.' (But a fakir gets used to a bed of nails.)

He sighed.

'The thing about it is,' he said. 'She didn't want to come, you know.'

'Sorry?'

'Sandra. She didn't want to come here. A place was arranged for her and everything. She was supposed to be coming. Then she reneged at the last minute.'

His voice faded away but she recognised the bait it had left trailing behind it. She decided not to take it. Suddenly he wanted to talk about Sandra. That was dangerous. It was all right to demystify her sacred name but to make her a significant presence in the room with them would leave no space for herself. Digression time.

'I can't say I blame her.'

'What?'

'No, no. I can see how anybody would want to be with you. I just mean this place. Willowvale. It's a crap place. A pile of

95

old rubble passing as a building. Why not bulldoze it and build a modern hotel?'

'That's a bit extreme.'

'I don't think so.'

He was suddenly animated and looking at her directly. It was interesting how a neutral issue had reconnected them. With the image of Sandra out of the way, they could see each other clearly.

'I heard so much about it,' she said. Kate's few references were hardly a history of the place but how was he to know? She decided to go for it. The more she talked, the quieter Sandra might be in his head. 'It was supposed to be an amazing place. I wasn't at the lecture when Andrew Lawson told them about it. But now that I see the place, I'm glad. Kate Foster was full of it. Ghosts and crap. It's just a place where the past keeps getting in the way. The plumbing sounds medieval. You know the male students don't even have an en-suite? I don't know why they put up with it. It's a cranky place made by a crank. And gargoyles, for God's sake. Have you seen them? What are they supposed to be? References from past guests? Photos from old summer holidays? This is us at Willowvale. You can see how much we enjoyed ourselves.'

He was smiling.

'The lectures have been all right. Especially yours. I enjoyed yours the most.'

He seemed to understand her feeling.

'But what a place. And I haven't even seen the ghost.'

He was nodding.

'Well,' he said, 'I've always liked coming here.' He noticed her raised eyebrows. 'Come on. Behave yourself. I mean because of the place.' Banter already. 'Oddly enough,

96

basically for the same reasons that you hate it. I know what Andrew's on about. But he's a terrible old romantic. I see what you mean. But.' He was going into lecture mode. She could sense him almost reaching out for a lectern to hold on to. 'It's the absurdity of this place that makes it worth visiting. It's a lesson in living. Muldoon, the man who built it, is a parable. The parable . . . of the foolish non-virgin.' He seemed to like that. 'This is such a pretentious crock of shit that it tells us to go forth and do otherwise. It's Victorian egotism cast in stone. Every time I come I'm confirmed in the way I live my own life. Nothing cast in stone. Everything's relative.' Like fidelity, perhaps. 'Don't look out for certainties. Look out for yourself.'

She would.

'God, yes,' she said. 'I can see what you mean.' (And so much for Sandra.)

But it wasn't quite.

'But Sandra likes this place. I don't know why she didn't come. I tried to persuade her. I wanted her to come.' (You see how close we are?) 'And then she appears tonight. I don't understand it. Why?'

Maybe it was cheaper than hiring a private detective.

'You see where I am, Jacqui?' (If you do, I'm doing something wrong.) 'I mean, she was weird on Thursday night. Nothing I said could persuade her. She's never been like that before.'

He stopped, staring intensely ahead. He looked so genuinely stunned that she didn't want to break in on him. She didn't know how to play it, so she waited. He *was* genuinely stunned. His performance had stumbled into a truth. Sandra had never been like that before. The reason the truth of this hadn't struck him until now was that he had been so pleased

97

she wasn't coming. He hadn't bothered to wonder about her motives too much. She said she had work to do, and that was fine. He couldn't believe his luck, so he didn't question it in case it changed. At that time Veronica was supposed to be coming. And what had happened to her? He began to wonder if there was anyone he could trust. Sandra had been really weird on Thursday night. She was too casual about not coming. She put him off too glibly. 'You go and enjoy yourself.' She had been hiding something. He couldn't believe she would do that to him. But what had she been hiding? One thing he knew: it wasn't another man. How could it be? And why come on Saturday? Could she really have been setting him up? Well, if that was the game she wanted to play, she had her result. He hoped she enjoyed it. She should have left well enough alone. He thought he knew what the problem must be with Veronica. Of course. She had thought Sandra was coming. He hadn't phoned to tell her she would have him to herself. She probably couldn't bear to be around to watch him and Sandra playing at happy families. He should have been more considerate. But he could sort that out. He would.

'Anybody in?' she said.

He looked at her as if he was surprised to find her still there.

The surprise was real. He saw her as isolated as a painting: *Woman Sitting in a Chair*. It was some painting. It was her apparent unawareness of the effect she was having that made her compelling. She was wearing the short black satin dress he had noticed earlier this evening. He imagined everybody must have noticed it. When she walked, it had made a series of lewd suggestions, hinted at the delicious curve of her arse, the sweet weight of her breasts. The dress had not been lying, as he had found when she pulled it off in one sweeping revelation.

Welcome to the pleasure garden. Now she sat with her right leg carelessly extended, her left arm over the back of her chair, her wine-glass in her right hand. The thick black hair was a careless tangle, evidence that she hadn't bothered to erase of what they had been doing earlier. (No wonder Sandra's rage had been instantaneous.) She hadn't put her bra back on. The neckline of the dress was distorted by her posture so that one firm breast was visible almost to the nipple. Her face, bold with makeup, looked arrogantly lovely. Her left leg, bent naturally in sitting, had pulled the ruffled material of the dress up her stretched right thigh. The tautness of the cloth made a darkness between her legs. He knew she was naked up there where the dark hair was, the only burning bush he believed in.

'Anyway,' he said, trying to distract himself. 'You can see why I'm preoccupied. There's things here I have to work out.' (Like, why the hell did Sandra come anyway?)

'Oops,' the woman had said.

The word kept surfacing in her mind, as if her memory were burping. Oops. It suggested nothing more than a trivial accident, like the breaking of a cup rather than the disruption of a life, and maybe that's what the whole thing was – a series of small mishaps.

She had been so late in deciding to come that she was sure she would miss the ferry, but she felt compelled to try to make it. Fortunately – as she had thought then – the ferry was delayed. The delay turned into hours. The rumours that circulated among the prospective passengers hinted nervously at some kind of technical failure, which they were trying to rectify. Some people went away, perhaps thinking the delay was a bad omen. Others remained vociferously present, expressing their need to travel that night and apparently believing that the louder they talked the more seaworthy the ferry was likely to become. Crisis made for comradeship among them and, by the time they sailed into the darkness, a man with his car on the ferry had offered to drive her to Willowvale.

When she arrived there, everything was quiet. Gordon Mitchell, the owner of the hotel, was looking for something behind the desk in the foyer. They recognised each other from the visit she had made two years ago with the students, when they had talked together quite a lot. She liked him and she was surprised that he seemed less than effusive towards her. She had assumed that it was because he was preoccupied in looking for something. Now she wondered if he couldn't meet her directly because he had been hiding something. When he told her the number of David's room, he made a point of adding that a group had gone out for a late stroll along the shore, and it was possible that David was with them. He wasn't sure but it was possible. If David's room was locked, he could give her another key.

She remembered coming up the staircase. She had still felt good. She had a secret to tell. After wandering several corridors and hearing occasional strange voices in rooms she passed, she found twelve and tried the door. It was unlocked. She opened the door into a moonlit room placid with anonymous furniture. She put on the light and closed the door.

The bed was perfectly made (obviously not by David) except for the indentation of someone who had sat there. She imagined him working on his lecture, doing that thing he did of going over his notes again and again. The key to the room was on the bedside table. He was such a careless man outside his work. He must have gone out without thinking to lock the room. There was a bottle of red wine sitting beside the key. It was untouched. Maybe he was saving it for when he came back in. He wouldn't need a corkscrew. It had a screw-off top. That was so unlike him; he liked to pride himself on the wine he bought. French only, that was what he liked to say. He must have had a problem getting what he wanted and settled for anything liquid. She smiled. At least he would be having something better now. Krug. It was his preferred champagne.

She set down her bag and laid on the desk the coolbag and the packet of sandwiches she had bought on the ferry. She took off her coat and threw it on the bed. She went through to the bathroom and checked that there were two glasses. She washed and dried them. She brought the glasses through and set them beside each other on the desk. She collected the shirt, underpants and socks he had dropped on the floor. She found his travelling-bag inside the wardrobe and put the used clothes in it. She paused, wondering if she should go down and wait for him. But she wanted that there should be just the two of them when she told him and she wanted no intervening small-talk to postpone what she had to say.

She sat down. As she gazed out to sea, rehearsing her news, she heard voices outside. The late ramblers had returned. She took out the photograph and set it face down on the desk. She waited, smiling to herself. Voices infiltrated the corridor and gradually receded. Nobody came. She waited. She rose and stood in the middle of the room, wondering if she had better go down to look for him.

It was then the door clicked suddenly and swung open.

'Behave yourself, woman,' he was saying. 'I'll get the wine.'

He was turned away from Sandra, his right hand round the edge of the door. His head was bent towards a dark woman with wild hair. Her face was raised to kiss him. When she had kissed him, her face turned towards the room. Her shock was silent. It formed her mouth into a perfect circle. Perhaps it was the sight of that which made his head turn quickly to see what the woman was seeing.

'It's you?' he said, looking upwards pointlessly, perhaps just noticing that the light was on.

Time stopped, became a tableau that she seemed to be able to study at leisure. His hair was dishevelled. His pupils dilated into a confession. The woman's face looked naked of makeup. Her lips were bloated with kissing. As her mouth closed, her eyes became hard and assessing, as if measuring an opponent. The proof was incontrovertible. These were people who had been making love. She knew it instantaneously and undeniably.

'This is my wife,' he said, to the room it seemed.

For seconds there didn't appear to be any more he could think of to say. It sounded as if he wasn't sure who it was he was talking to, whether to the woman or himself. Perhaps he had just remembered he *had* a wife. His statement loitered awkwardly in the air, like someone in evening dress who has turned up at a funeral. Someone who doesn't know what to say. But the woman did.

'Oops,' she said.

It was that sound which released the surging anger in Sandra. She had no idea where it came from. It possessed her in a primal way, a power in her she hadn't known existed, something molten shifting underground. She was screaming.

Now she couldn't remember much that she had said. It

seemed to her to have been hysteria in a foreign language, most of it swearwords she couldn't remember using before. Something in her must have stored them and now the repression of years gave them a terrible force. They geysered from her mouth.

She could remember screaming, 'Ex-wife, you bastard!' and the rest was malignant gibberish to her now. He started to say something but she drowned him out. While she ranted, she took his travelling-bag from the wardrobe and flung it at him, a shirt spilling out as the bag hit him in the chest. While he scrabbled to collect the shirt and stuff it back in, she became angrier. Was his only reaction to what he had done to make sure he retrieved all his shirts? 'Oops, you fucking whore,' she screeched at the woman. 'I'll give you oops.'

Her rage had blow-torched them into the corridor. He made a feeble gesture with his left hand, indicating that she should tamp down the noise. 'Here,' she shouted. 'Take this with you, you fuck!' She ran and collected the bottle of wine from the bedside table and made a missile of it. (Why had she done that, she wondered. To remove every trace of him from the place?) He fumbled it in mid-air but didn't drop it. At least some things were important to him.

'I'll speak to you when you've calmed down,' he said feebly.

'Phone me in ten fucking years then,' she bellowed. 'Get out, get out, get out, get out! And never come back. Bastard!'

They moved swiftly out of her vision. She put on her coat and buttoned it. She lifted her bag and put it back down. She went through to the bathroom, put his toiletries in the toilet-bag and left it against the wall outside the door. She put out the lights, as if preparing to leave, and her sense of what she might do went out with them. She became very still. She sat down at the desk and was suddenly aware of the wreckage of her life.

The image of him and the woman standing in the doorway subverted every memory she had of their marriage. Past moments that had confirmed the reassuring routine of their time together were now shadowed with strange possibilities. She could only imagine what might be hiding in the shadows.

His preference for working late at his office in the university rather than at home (because, he said, it was where the books he might need to refer to were) seemed sinister now. Casual remarks he had made at dinner parties with friends began to sound ambiguous. Phone-calls he had taken separated from the name he had put on them and whispered around her like conspirators. Her past was a code of lies she must try to decipher.

Dear Mr Beck

It is with some reluctance that I write this letter. Before taking a decision on Alms for Oblivion, *I managed to catch up with some of your earlier work, so that my reading of your latest book would have some kind of context. I feel your earlier work showed promise but it is my opinion that that promise is merely repeated in* Alms for Oblivion *with a dying fall rather than fulfilled. Since — it is my understanding — your previous publications proved not to be successfully marketable, I can find neither personal enthusiasm nor commercial viability as a motivation for*

publishing. Therefore, with regret, we cannot make an
offer for Alms for Oblivion.
   I wish you the best of luck with another publisher.
   Yours faithfully,
   Harold Walters

He woke up with the impact of his rejection hanging over him
in a darkness nacreous with moonlight, as if inscribed there in
letters of fire. The writing on the wall. He was sorry he hadn't
gone on sleeping.

He wished briefly that he hadn't opened the letter tonight.
(At least he had managed to put it off for two days.) Then he
felt this was a pathetic wish. Whether you wore a blindfold or
not, the firing squad still got you.

He applied thought like a painful tourniquet to a bleeding
wound: anyway, this was just another failure. He had had
plenty. This was their time to visit. All you had to do was wait
and out of the blackness would float the shapes of failure.
They were never far away, the night whisperers. They kept
their distance until they could get you on your own, conspirators who plotted endlessly to persuade you that you were
not who you might have been.

He hated to waken at this time in the morning, when every
foothill of a problem seemed insurmountable and there
gathered round you in the gloom the orphans of ambition
and the casualties of error. Their familiarity was no comfort.
He thought again of Maggi and wished her well, hoping his
wishes didn't bring a blight with them. The arrogance of his
ambitions to be a writer had been a lodger she couldn't live

with either. How long could promise last before it turned into a contradiction of itself? He thought of his mother dying. He thought of a woman he had betrayed at twenty-two. Old, apparently imperishable accusations by himself against himself filed past like mourners looking for a funeral.

But a stranger jostled in among them. He waited to recognise the newcomer. The new self-dismay didn't lie in rejection by a publisher. (Critics, he had long ago decided, are people who begin by telling you you never had it and end by telling you you've lost it.) It lay in the effect rejection had had on him. He felt as if the letter was a punishment for the way he had spoken to Mickey Deans about his story. Embarrassment flooded him. The scene still sat in his mind, landscape of the moment when malice came out of his mouth like venom on the tongue of a snake.

The sun had been a disc of mildewed pewter in the sky. The breeze was soft. They were sitting on adjoining rocks above a mildly restless sea that shifted lazily like cooling lead that never cools. It could have been a low-rent idyll – a pleasant shoreline scene in mild weather, the veteran and the novitiate. He was holding Mickey Deans's very short story in his hand, three sheets of careful typing double-spaced. The paper riffled in the small wind.

Mickey Deans was waiting. His face seemed to be trying on reactions, changing expressions in readiness to meet what he was going to say. He hadn't known himself. He had read the story several times, but as if through his fingers. The truth was he couldn't see it clearly because it was blocked by his own feelings. Maybe he had more than writer's block. Maybe he had reader's block.

Every time he read it, he was reading that he hadn't written a word he could believe in for months. He saw the absence of himself. It was not a pleasant sight. He resented the piece of paper he was holding in his hand, the effortless self-confidence it expressed. It negated him.

Mickey Deans was waiting. He looked so young. The whites of his eyes seemed as if no lines of red could ever come there. The irises were as blue as Mary Sue's. The black hair was ridiculously abundant. Nobody had the right to look as young as that.

He couldn't remember exactly what he said, perhaps because he wasn't really talking about the story, just busking his own disillusionment with the story as the instrument. But he said a lot of technically negative things. His attack on the story was an oblique way of defending himself.

Even as the words came out of his mouth, he was disgusted by them. He was stunned into inarticulacy by his own aimless malice, which was unretractable between them. He watched the face of Mickey Deans helplessly as it absorbed his words. The eyes widened in surprise, seemed to lose perspective, hardened slowly into focus on his own eyes.

He was reminded ridiculously of a moment in an old Danny Kaye film. It must have been Boris Karloff, he thought, who was portraying a madman explaining to Danny Kaye how to commit the perfect murder. An icicle inserted in the brain, Boris was saying in his best thespian manner, will melt before rigor mortis sets in, thus leaving no trace of a weapon. No trace here, Boris, he thought, but a small kind of death surely.

He was looking for words to try to modify what he had said. It wasn't easy. As he opened his mouth, hoping some sort of magic ointment might come out, Mickey Deans leaned across and said something and took the paper gently from his hand and stood up and walked away. As he watched the receding figure, he felt as dead as the stone he sat on. It was only then he made sense of the words Mickey Deans had said and was still left wondering what meaning they were hiding.

'I suppose that covers it. Thanks for taking the time to read it, though.'

('What I actually meant,' Mickey Deans said to Kate Foster, 'was: you fucking wanker! When did you last have the guts to write anything? Except fucking newspaper columns. Still, he came back from the dead a bit, didn't he? I suppose it took balls to do what he did.')

What he did afterwards was at least a penance, he thought, as he lay in his bed. It was a feeble one. Mickey had come to his lecture in the afternoon but only, he suspected, to ask the most awkward question he could think of. He left as soon as Harry had tried to answer it. Kate Foster left with him. Mickey hadn't looked satisfied. He wasn't there for the evening meal. He wasn't even there for the traditional Saturday evening Free-for-all session, when students could make any contribution they wanted to the jollity of the evening, with Andrew Lawson acting as MC. While Calum Smith, the boy who had read everything, offered an appreciation of Bob Dylan, with musical illustrations, and Naim Choudhry gave what was meant to be a humorous talk called 'How to Pass English Without Reading a Book', Harry still couldn't find Mickey Deans.

He made a decision. It was a dubious one, which he hadn't the right to make. He slipped out of the lounge and went upstairs to his room. He was glad he had asked Jean in the office to photocopy Mickey's story in case he lost it. He had some trouble locating it. He had put it at the bottom of his bag, perhaps to avoid noticing it when he didn't want to, which was liable to be anytime.

He smoothed out the three sheets. He checked that the story was all there and went downstairs. When he came back into the lounge, Apollonia, the beautiful Greek student, was reading some of her poetry to a hushed audience. He found it strangely ethereal stuff, involving things like an imaginative flight over the roofs of a city and an emotional epiphany in a greasy-spoon café. He could see why the audience was hushed, though. She was perched on the table at the front, bare-footed, wearing very tight jeans and a short top, which the protuberance of her breasts made even shorter. Her brown, flat midriff wasn't difficult to look at. Her delivery was very animated. She moved a lot and her right hand kept flicking away some fronds from a forest of blue-black hair. Take away the words, she would still have been a riveting mime. She was the real poem. When she finished, he suspected that many of them were applauding the wonders of nature.

He walked to the front and told Andrew he wanted to read something. Andrew's introduction made the natural mistake of assuming it was something he had written himself. The students greeted Harry generously. It might have been just how he was feeling at the time but he thought he could detect some gentle jeers among the cheers.

'I'm going to read a story,' he said.

The applause broke out again. He waited.

'It's not my story. It's a student's story. I didn't give him a very good review when I was talking to him about it. I think I was wrong.'

He had them then. Officialdom divesting in public to reveal the frailty of itself is not without its interest. Casual attention had become concentration on a hoped-for emotional strip-tease.

'I'm reading it without his permission. I hope he'll forgive me. The student's name is Mickey Deans. The story is called "Brass". You can let him know what *you* think.'

He read it. He found he was reading it very well. His audience – Mickey's audience – was held. Not a dismissive expression stirring. He was surprised how well he knew the story, how accurate his shifting intonations were. A benign part of him, a survivor from the generosity he used to have, must have been reading the story a lot more appreciatively than the failed writer in him was able to. Maybe he was curing himself of reader's block.

When he reached the sentence relating to the husband's feelings about the potted plant, some mouths were open. It was about then that he almost lost his rhythm. He suddenly noticed Mickey Deans standing at the back of the lounge. The blue eyes were on him like lasers. He managed not to atomise.

The ending caused a long pause in the audience. Their faces sat in parenthesis for several seconds. Then they got it. They liked what they got. The applause was real. Word passed among them that Mickey was there. Several people rose and went to congratulate him, until he was standing among a small crowd.

He came from behind the table and walked towards Mickey. He waited patiently. He noticed that Mickey had a black eye. When the others were dispersing, he gave the pages to Mickey.

'Here,' he said. 'This belongs to you. It's worth keeping. Maybe I should be the one with the black eye. I think I misjudged it. I couldn't have written anything as good as this at your age. It's a pretty melancholy accolade, but it's meant as one.'

'Thanks.'

'Is it okay to have read it?'

Mickey nodded towards the people around him.

'Well, it is now,' he said.

Before any more could be said – something for which Harry felt perhaps he was glad – a strange thing happened. Marion Gibson, known not unaffectionately among some students as the Mouse, had taken the microphone from its stand and was giving an unaccompanied rendition of 'Hey, Big Spender'. The lounge was amazed into silence, staring at her with an intensity born of the need to verify that what was happening was really what was happening. It was like watching a demure spinster suddenly doing a can-can on a coffee-table. It holds you.

Remembering Marion Gibson's performance, Harry discovered he was smiling inanely into the darkness. The action of the smile ambushed his solemnity, became the cause of a mood rather than the result of one. Wasn't life incorrigibly various? Just when your pomposity was in danger of turning you into your own statue, life dropped birdshit on your head. Thank you, Marion.

He swung his legs out of bed. All that had happened was that another publisher had rejected his novel. There were plenty more where they came from. It wasn't cancer. It occurred to him that he had been so paralysed by the news of his rejection he hadn't even opened his other two letters. They might be good news. He could use one of those messages life sometimes sent, telling you things were all right.

They were stopped at the lights. Through the rear window of the car in front a hugely fat man was staring at them, with a Baby on Board sticker beside his head. There was no sign of a baby.

'I wouldn't fancy changing *his* nappy,' David said.

Sandra laughed and her laughter seemed to crystallise the mood she was in. The sound was a spontaneous confirmation of the happiness they were sharing in the car, a conspiracy of two from which the pointless balefulness of the fat man was excluded. They were going to have Sunday lunch at Peter and Myra's in Langbank. It was bright and hot, the kind of day that always reminded her of childhood, a segment of sunny innocence kept in storage for her from the past. They would have cold wine in the garden and eat there and talk pleasantly about their lives. Last night they had made love at what she had worked out was the best time in her cycle. If things went well, she might have a baby on board herself soon enough, though she thought she could live without the sticker. What were people without children supposed to have on their cars? No Baby on Board – Ram Me If You Like?

Fidgety with pleasure, she aimlessly pressed the button of the glove compartment. As the door came down, something small and bright that flashed in the sunlight rolled slowly out. As it dropped over the edge of the door, she caught it in her hand. It was metallic. She opened her hand, letting the object nestle in her palm.

'What have we here?' she said jocularly.

'What's that?'

He glanced across, released the handbrake and put the car into gear.

'It's a lipstick,' she said, just realising it herself.

'Surprise, surprise. Must be yours.'

She didn't recognise it. She unscrewed the cap and looked at the stub.

'This isn't mine,' she said.

'Who else's would it be?'

'This isn't mine.'

'How can you tell?'

'I would never use this colour.'

'Well, neither would I.'

'David. Who does this belong to?'

'Listen. If it's not yours, who the hell's is it? You use the car as well. Maybe you should tell me.'

'Whose is it?'

'Hold on a minute,' he said. 'This fat bastard's getting on my mammaries. He hasn't stopped staring at us. I'm beginning to think he's a cardboard cut-out.'

He pulled out slightly, checking if he could overtake. He let one car pass in the other direction and swung into the middle of the road. There was a car coming towards them but he put his foot down. The sudden panic she felt in the next few seconds left her wondering if she would be found dead with the lipstick in her hand. She thought irrelevantly that they might think it was hers, and the colour was awful. As he drove back on to their side of the road, the car he had just missed that was coming towards them and the car he had cut in front of blared their horns.

'Piss off,' he screamed. And then in a quiet, if shaky

voice, 'Might make the fat bastard sweat off a few pounds anyway.'

He maintained his speed, leaving the car behind far in his wake. While she waited for her flock of startled nerves to settle again into quiet indignation, he spoke.

'Oh, wait a minute,' he said. 'I know whose that is. Jean Hadley's. It must be hers.'

She was a secretary in the English department. Sandra had met her once briefly at a departmental get-together. She hadn't seemed the type who would favour post-box red.

'So how does it come to be here?'

'Look. I gave her a lift. She was going into the town and she asked if I could drop her.'

'Where? I wouldn't have thought this was Jean Hadley's style.'

'I wouldn't know. But she was going for a night out with her girlfriends. When I stopped to drop her off, she decided to freshen the warpaint. It was only after she was away I noticed that lying on the floor.'

'So how did it come to be in the glove compartment?'

'Jesus, Sandra. What d'you think? I slung it in there to give to her later. Must've forgotten all about it.'

'But you said you thought it was mine.'

'Because I forgot about the whole thing, I'm telling you. It's a bloody lipstick. You think I made a note of it in my diary?'

'I don't know.'

'Jesus, what is this? I can't believe you.'

He drove in silence for a time while she turned the lipstick over in her fingers. Suddenly, he swerved into a lay-by, stopped, wrenched on the handbrake and sat staring through the windscreen.

'All right,' he said. 'You think if I was going to play away from home, I'd pick Jean Hadley? No offence to Jean. But I would think the only cock she's ever seen was in a farmyard. Think about it.'

'It's funny you didn't think of this right away. That it was Jean Hadley's.'

'I'm not exactly Aristotle. But I hope I've got more to think about than a bloody lipstick. Okay. Imagine I'm having a mad affair with Jean. You better imagine it for the both of us. There are places my limited imagination just can't reach. But there we are. Having it off all over the place. Given that scenario. You think I'm going to put her lipstick carefully in the glove compartment? Think about it.'

'But you're the only one that's saying it's Jean Hadley's.'

A car tooted at them as it passed and she recognised it as the one they had overtaken.

'Drive carefully,' he shouted. 'Into a fucking brick wall.'

He sighed.

'I see,' he said. 'The plot thickens. Now it's somebody else I'm screwing. Or maybe many somebody elses. Who knows? You don't believe me, do you?'

He sighed again.

'Okay, Sandra. Tell you what. You keep that lipstick. And tomorrow you phone Jean Hadley at the office. You explain to her where you found it. Ask her to verify that it's hers. Question her about the night I gave her the lift. Once she passes the test, you can give it back to me and I'll return it. God, it's going to be one embarrassing situation. But if it puts your mind at rest, let's do it.'

He leaned across and kissed her.

'Okay?'

She made a rueful face at him. He kissed her again.

'If that's what it takes for us to trust each other,' he said, 'let's do it.'

She put the lipstick back into the glove compartment and closed the door.

'When you give it back to her,' she said, 'don't mention what bad taste she's got.'

They both smiled.

It had been a good day at Peter and Myra's, she remembered, but what stayed with her most vividly about that day was the small shiny object she had unearthed from her thoughts. She contemplated it again, wondering what it was telling her about her past. She never saw it after that day. He said he had given it back to Jean Hadley. She had never checked the truth of his statement. She had met Jean Hadley again much later but it had seemed ridiculous to revert to her suspicions after all that time and, besides, things were particularly good with David and her then.

Now she wondered. Had he suddenly decided to overtake the car to give himself time to think up a story? Had he embarrassed her into burying her misgivings? How many other times had he diverted her from the truth about their marriage with which she was now confronted? There must be others.

To find the man who seems completely socialised we have to turn to Mr Utterson. And a dismal prospect he offers us. The name forewarns us of what we will find there. He is an utter son – someone conditioned from birth, it seems, to obey all the rules he has been taught. He is hardly more than a collection of negative conventions. He can only live so successfully within society by the continuing total negation of his natural self. He has a 'rugged countenance, that was never lighted by a smile'. Presumably because a smile would be too dangerously spontaneous, an ambush of relaxation, the consequences of which cannot be foreseen or controlled. 'He was austere with himself; drank gin when he was alone, to mortify the taste for vintages; and though he enjoyed the theatre, had not crossed the doors of one for twenty years.' This man lives by negatives. He drinks gin not because he likes it but because it controls the pleasure he takes in wine. Because he likes the theatre, he makes a rule of never going there. He lives in a cage which he has made for himself and which requires the maintenance of his constant vigilance. This cage locks from the inside.

He was weeping. It was a strange feeling. It was something he thought he had forgotten how to do. The tears came without warning, welling from some mysterious source, like a spring in dead soil. All he could do was let them happen and wonder where they came from. He didn't understand his tears. He simply felt the wisdom of his eyes in weeping.

His mind couldn't leave it at that. Like a fussy undertaker at a funeral, it was trying to give his grief a practical form. His betrayal of Catriona was appalling. What did a lifetime of being faithful to her mean if he could subvert it in a moment? Perhaps that he had never really had the opportunity before. In one weekend he had made a nonsense of his life. It hadn't meant what he thought it meant. That was surely cause enough for crying.

But it was more than that, he knew, which had made him an overweight, aging man sitting in his underpants crying in a hotel room. It wasn't just Catriona he was crying for. Catriona would never know. He would always know. Perhaps he was crying for himself.

The guilt he had always felt about Catriona had multiplied into contradictory feelings like opposing armies. They seemed to be fighting one another to the death in him, and he could see no victory.

Just as he was guilty of betraying Catriona, he was guilty of betraying the potential of his own life over so many years. He looked at Vikki sleeping. This was what he had denied for so long after the time it could have made any difference to Catriona. His celibacy hadn't been serving her. It had been serving a dead sense of himself. You didn't help someone who was on breaking ground by joining them there. You needed to stay on the firm ground of yourself to hold them up. He had gone down with Catriona. He felt as hopelessly shut off from possibilities as she was.

He had destroyed what he had thought was the meaning of his life with Catriona but he could see no other meaning. He had pretended to Vikki to offer more than he had to offer. He was old, older than his years said he was, and the feelings that would make a meaningful relationship for a woman he did not believe he could find in himself any more. And, even if he could find them, he did not believe he could sustain them. The weekend had implied a promise he couldn't keep.

In his falsity to both he had lost his sense of himself. He could see no habitable life now. He felt he had been sleep-walking in a play, taking cues from other people, and had wakened in the last act to find he didn't know the words any more and didn't believe in the part he had been playing. But there was no other.

He remembered a phrase Witherspoon had used when he was writing about the death of Edward Muldoon: 'the peacocks mourning on the lawn'. There were no peacocks now but he imagined he could hear them. In his mind they were mourning more than Muldoon.

He rose quietly and moved to the window. He gently pushed aside one of the curtains. Had Muldoon stood here in some dark times? Had he stood at a window and looked out at what he had achieved? If he had seen it in this half-light, it must have looked more like a cemetery than a garden. The other Carnegie. Had he been as disillusioned at the end as Carnegie had been? He sought solace for himself in thinking of Muldoon.

Witherspoon's device for circumventing what looked like the sad details of a private life and giving it an aura of public significance was obviously that comparison with Carnegie. Incorporating the name of Carnegie into the title must have been meant as a way of generating interest and implying importance by association. But there was some validity in seeing Muldoon's career as providing a local imitation of Carnegie's global one.

The parallels Witherspoon suggested between the two held for much of the way. Each man had built an impressive Scottish mansion by the sea. Each wanted to turn his money into social progress. Each ended with a sense of failure that was catastrophically defined by the First World War. Each created a private place that would end as a resort for the paying public. The attempt of each to go beyond the making of money became after death merely another way of making money.

He pushed the curtain further aside softly, as if a fuller view of the grounds would give him a better sense of the scope of Muldoon's failure.

The difference was only one of degree, not of kind.

Carnegie's Skibo at Dornoch was much grander than Muldoon's Willowvale here on Cannamore. Carnegie's impact on the world was huge, Muldoon's more or less nonexistent. Carnegie's reaction to the First World War was that of someone with massive international influence. Imagine being a man who could, with some justification, feel personally insulted by the outbreak of a world war. Muldoon's reaction was a small, personal bitterness. His son, Edward, had been killed in the first year of the war at the age of nineteen. It was many years after Carnegie's death that Skibo became an expensive bolt-hole for the enormously wealthy. It wasn't long after Muldoon died in 1916 that Willowvale became a rest home for soldiers and then a sanatorium and finally a hotel, which went rapidly downmarket.

A shape suddenly appeared from the trees at the other side of the lawn and hobgoblined through the darkness in the direction of the hotel.

Welcome, he thought. I hope you enjoyed your night. He wondered who it was.

But didn't Muldoon's failure have more human resonance than Carnegie's success? What Carnegie had achieved had not finally matched the scope of his ambitions but it was still tangibly there, in countless libraries and scholarships and the Peace Palace at The Hague. Against the awesome extent to which his aims had been fulfilled, it was difficult to sustain any compassion for Carnegie's sense of disappointment. His vision survived his death. It had become a complex of institutions that impinged daily on the lives of many people.

The well-known story of his life told us nothing about ourselves except that we would never be like him. His impact on the world was too diffuse, too vast to be related to personally. It shut us out.

Muldoon's only lasting achievement was Willowvale and it survived in part as a negation of what he had meant it to be. It was a failure so human that anybody could take a holiday in it. The largely unknown story of his life had ended in something that accommodated the ordinariness of our own lives. In spite of its intended grandeur, it had become just a casual part of some people's experience.

That was what defined its elaborate ordinariness. What this place had become demonstrated what it had failed to be, daily mocked what Muldoon had seen it as being. Witherspoon had listed at one point numerous dignitaries who had visited Willowvale. They were mayors of here and MPs of there, businessmen and knights. The names were obviously intended to leave the reader awestruck.

Reading them, he had found it poignant that he had never heard of a single name. Their fame appeared to have lived as long as the local editions of the newspapers which had recorded it. Perhaps he was being unfair but, considering the sonorous emptiness of those names and the pomposity of Witherspoon, the only one of which he had any substantive evidence, he felt relieved that he hadn't been present at any of those august gatherings. He wondered if Muldoon had sat among his guests, puzzled that they could be as boring in the special setting he had made for them as they were anywhere else.

Nothing much seemed to have happened as a result of their well-fed and well-watered stays at Willowvale. No great theories for the betterment of society were recorded. Some charitable enterprises were referred to in the monograph but the implication was that these were no longer extant at the time of writing. For some years before Muldoon's death, Witherspoon's discretion hinted, Willowvale didn't resound with the chatter of many voices.

Standing at this window, he felt a kinship with Muldoon. Maybe what this place had been meant to be was a kind of humanist church, a place built to express a belief in big abstractions like progress and social conscience and the perfectibility of people. And just as real churches were being turned into discos and bars, it was natural that this place had become a hotel. Humanism as well as Christianity had fallen on hard times. What were supposed to be the monuments that housed the meaning of the future had become temporary accommodation for the pleasures of the present, nothing more. He had himself reduced Willowvale to that this weekend. He had defined the hollowness of his own pretensions here.

Through this window he saw his life as an elaborate pretence. Even his university career had been an exercise in self-delusion. He had always thought its purpose was to help people to grow into fully realised individuals. That involved academic rigour. Sometimes that rigour calcified into preciousness. He still remembered some lectures on Anglo-Saxon sound changes which he had attended as a student. He had found their irrelevance hilarious, like something out of Beachcomber (Dr Strabismus of Utrecht, whom God preserve). But at least that academic seriousness made demands on students. Now he felt universities were adjusting their degrees to fit the students, like bespoke tailoring.

It was right that universities should open up their formerly closed borders to the shifting attitudes and the dominant issues of the society in which they found themselves. But he would have thought the point of doing that was to submit our society's sense of itself to stringent examination, not simply to rubber-stamp its validity.

He remembered reading in the papers about Michael Jackson's visit to the Oxford Union. It made depressing reading, a performance of vapid sentimentality. There was nothing you could disagree with, unless you were a devout believer in cruelty to children. But then he didn't say much of any substance at all. He struck a series of compassionate poses and everybody took him at face value. In his case that was an interesting thing to do since, whatever his face was, it wasn't his own. And then, of course, he cried.

Yet all was mindless adulation. On television the faces of the students emerging from the hall glowed like candles at a Barry Manilow concert.

He knew Thatcherism had begun the process of obliging universities to sell themselves in the marketplace. But did that mean one of the oldest universities in the world should offer itself as a venue for unexamined cultural pap? Maybe, he thought, we can look forward to Bologna bidding for the Eurovision Song Contest and Salamanca hosting Miss World. Michael Jackson's tears? He would rather have Anglo-Saxon sound changes.

What had sustained him for so long was a fantasy. The realisation might come to him as a grief but the truth was that it expressed itself externally largely in terms of farce. Truth was always double-edged. It all depended on the angle from which you saw it. Even the tears that had dried on his face had led to nothing but snot. He closed the curtains and turned and felt for a handkerchief in his trousers, which were over one of the chairs, and blew his nose as delicately as he could, not to waken Vikki. Life undercut our dreams even as it encouraged them in us.

When she stayed with him on Friday night, they had simply slept together. Did this mean at that stage his infidelity had been less? The question was academic now. Maybe everything in his life had been academic. Tonight they had made love. At least that was what he hoped it had felt like to her. He had been surprised that his sexual urge remained alive. The experience had been awesome for him, like glimpsing the shore of a lost continent of feeling. But he wasn't exactly expert in judging how far the feeling might have been shared by Vikki. She had been very tender towards him afterwards. But he had already learned her kindness was such that her reaction could have been a conscious attempt to reassure him.

He gave up trying to understand. He gave up trying to understand anything. He put the handkerchief away, a small parcel of waste matter, which measured his sense of his own life at the moment. He suspected that what he had been confronting was not some sudden revelation but a truth which had been integral to his entire life. It was simply that some honest hours of contemplation in a hotel room, away from the affirming furniture of his life, had erased the dubious self-delusions with which he had overwritten that truth. He thought now, trying to give himself some bleak comfort, that such a bitter truth was what underlay all our lives, and our hopes were just a palimpsest that covered it temporarily and faded with our breath. Maybe each generation just wrote their own palimpsest of hallucinated hope, and that was living. If so, it was somebody else's turn. He was too tired not to face the truth.

His career, his education, his aspirations left him shivering in the cold. The feeling that took him back to bed was a sense of primal nakedness. He needed to borrow the heat of someone else's being to feel alive. He crawled into bed and put an arm round Vikki's warmth. She accepted him and automatically took his hand and cupped it round her left breast. He breathed deliberately quietly, not to interrupt her sleep. He did not know her eyes had opened and were staring into the darkness.

So what I am suggesting to you is that *Farewell, Miss Julie Logan* could be read as a kind of converse to *Dr Jekyll and Mr Hyde*. Dr Lawson talked yesterday about the almost total repression of Mr Utterson's nature. Well, J. M. Barrie's book could be seen as Utterson's story. It could be subtitled *Peter Pan: The Inside Story* or *Something Buried in the Kailyard*. It is like the autobiography of Barrie in code, a subversive account of his own career.

There wasn't much of David Cudlipp's lecture Marion wanted to make notes on, she had decided. It wasn't just that she didn't like the coldness of his voice. It was the feeling he gave her that everything was pre-decided. He wasn't inviting you to discover something for yourself. He was telling you that he had decided for you. Besides, she wanted to start on Harry Beck's talk about the Oedipus myth before they had to leave, and the subtle change of light in the room was telling her dawn was coming.

What is buried, of course, is the reality of the main protagonist's experience. The minister, Adam Yestreen, can come to no terms with his spontaneous, darker self but to wage war on it. His perpetual response to his animal nature is to deny it utterly. But he can't suppress it successfully. It remains as a fifth-column which constantly subverts his sense of himself. He gives the blacksmith his fiddle but its music remains seductive to him. He denies the existence of ghosts but creates his own. He falls in love with a woman no one else can see. And then he denies that he experienced her presence. He dies as a stranger to himself because he refuses to engage with the feelings in him he doesn't agree with. The man he is dies in a prison of who he thinks he should be without ever experiencing natural freedom. It is a story of empty and heroic folly. His life is a pathetically successful denial of his life. If Henry Jekyll can be seen as a terrifying warning against acknowledging the animal within us, Adam Yestreen can be seen as a perhaps more terrifying warning against denying it.

She was in the kitchen. It was her favourite room in the flat, large and comfortable. It was where she felt they could be most pleasantly together outside the bedroom. She was sitting at the long, rough wooden table. A cup of coffee had gone cold at her elbow as she read a book. Which one was it? She thought it might have been *Breathing Lessons*.

Outside the high window the evening was making a sunset. When they bought the place, the estate agent had recited the customary unconvincing list of the house's attractions. In it he had omitted what had become for her one of its quiet joys, a recurring pleasure. From time to time the kitchen window delivered spectacular sunsets to the room. David had joked with her that, when they came to sell, they should insist on including in the prospectus that Turner was commissioned to do the sky every so often. As she sat reading, the clouds had already turned into limitless embers.

David suddenly appeared in the kitchen, holding some sheets of paper in his hand. She thought he must have been pleased with something he had been writing in the small room he used as a study, for he was brandishing the sheets in a proprietary way and smiling at her. His hand hit the switch and the electric light banished the sun from the surfaces of the furniture.

'Read that,' he said.

He seemed so enthused, she decided to humour him. She was surprised to find that the typescript wasn't something of his own. It was a student essay written by someone called Veronica Hill. It was, she saw as she read, an attack on *Hôtel du Lac*, by Anita Brookner. She looked up at him. He was standing at the sink, watching her.

'I'd better explain,' he said. 'I decided to get away from the spoon-feeding. I took away the safety net. The remit I gave them was to choose any more or less contemporary novel. Read it and react utterly honestly. All they had to do more than that was to overtake their own reactions and justify them, as well as just having them. That's what Veronica wrote. Now read on.'

While she did, she was conscious of his movement around the room. He turned on a tap briefly for no reason she was aware of. He went into the fridge and took something out. The hissing noise suggested a can of beer being opened. She sensed him watching her from time to time. The feeling annoyed her, implying he was impatient for the affirmative reaction he was obviously waiting for. She didn't want to give him it. She felt the way she always felt when someone over-prepared her for something, a joke, for example. Statements like 'This is the funniest thing you've ever heard' always caused her laughter muscles to atrophy.

As she read on, she was glad that she didn't need his help not to give him the response he wanted. She didn't like the essay. One of the accusations it made against the book was snobbishness but she thought the terms in which the essay was conceived were themselves a form of snobbery. Expressions like 'bloodless' and 'emotional virgin' and 'boringness under a microscope' rankled with her. When she finally looked up from the pages, the sky was ash against the window.

'Well?' he said.

He was standing beside her now. He lifted her book from the table, turned it over to see the title and dropped it again, losing her place.

'Where's your Anne Tyler now?'

'I like *Hôtel du Lac*. I don't like this,' she said. 'She talks about a microscope. She might as well have read it through a telescope. She's missed all the subtlety of the detail.'

'What subtlety?'

'Have you read the book?'

'You know I have. And what you call subtlety I would call triviality.'

He lifted the sheets of paper.

'That's it then?' he said.

'That's what I feel.'

'Well,' he said. 'Not much point in preaching to the unconvertible. But that's a terrific essay.'

On the way out he took a slug from his can of beer.

It had seemed not much at the time, just another of those sudden meetings when people who are living together can find they've bumped into a stranger in the kitchen. Now, sitting alone in a hotel room that had been booked for both of them, she saw it differently. He had perhaps been more of a stranger all along than she had imagined. She had decided at the time that he was being proprietary about his ability as a teacher. But now it felt as if his reaction went deeper than that. Maybe he was being proprietary about the writer of the essay. Maybe he was playing two women off against each other and awarding marks accordingly. Maybe she had been failing some kind of test. The thought chilled her with anger.

As she took the bottle of pills and replaced it in her travelling-bag, something suddenly occurred to her. That woman who had come through the door of this room with him tonight. Was her name Veronica Hill?

Wasn't the dawn an incredibly reluctant thing? One lonely detectable glimmer of light and then nothing for ages, as if the day had been postponed. Please, no. It was like a workman determined not to clock on too early. Who put that ray of sun on? I told you to wait. You'd better leave it on now, but no more for the moment. Go and ask God what time he has. An aunt of his used to repeat, to the point of driving him crazy, 'A watched kettle never boils.' Maybe a watched dawn never happened. It had better. Trapped for ever in a hotel room with Jacqui Forsyth? Still, some people might not find that exactly a definition of hell. Without having to look, he was aware of her lying on the bed to his right. She was still wearing the black satin dress. It would be rumpled, showing her thighs and maybe more. It was a good thing he had turned the chair towards the window. No fraternising with the enemy. The last time he'd glanced over, she had been staring out of the window as well. She hadn't looked at him. She made a lot of noise. Turning and fluffing pillows and sighing. That was all right. As long as she didn't talk.

'What's your background?' she said suddenly.

'I don't have one,' he said. 'Only a foreground.'

That was neatly dealt with. He hoped she didn't ask him to explain it.

'What the hell's that supposed to mean?'

He felt too tired to say. He felt too tired to argue. But maybe talking would take his mind off the dawn so that it might actually happen. He thought about his own remark. Probably he had been telling a kind of truth.

'I suppose what that means,' he said, 'is I don't really think about that stuff a lot. I was born at an early age. My parents were my mother and father. I had two sisters, both girls. I grew up. And here I am. Sitting in a fucking hotel room. Waiting for dawn.'

He wondered if her silence meant she was digesting his words. He wondered what there was to digest.

'Had?' she said.

He looked across at her. Her left foot was resting flat on the bed and he could see the full expanse of her thigh. She was still looking out of the window. He returned to doing the same.

'Sorry?' he said.

'Had? Are your sisters dead?'

'No,' he said. 'Although maybe one of them might as well be. She's married to a man in Sheffield who is so boring that when he walks into a room . . .' He paused. 'He's like CS gas coming in. Everybody falls asleep. There's people falling off their chairs all over the place. But she accepts it. It's bizarre. It must be a death-wish or something. Suicide by husband. The other one. She was in Findhorn at the last census. Hugging trees or something. And probably hoping to meet the great god Pan in the woods. God knows where she is now. No. They're both alive. If that's living. It's just that we're all very much in the past tense to one another. Had.'

'What about your parents?'

'My mother's dead. My father has Alzheimer's. I was a very late arrival. I tried to visit him sometimes. But it was like having multiple identities. I never knew who I was supposed to be.' He paused. 'Maybe Sandra had it lucky. She was an orphan.'

He was checking the dawn. Still on hold.

'Were you abused?'

'For God's sake. Don't start with the DIY analysis. No. I was never abused. Unless tweeness and fear of life and living in the past are forms of abuse. Maybe that's why my sisters are screwed up. It's strange being born in a mausoleum. But I always felt my parents gave me one great gift. They made me want to get the hell out as fast as I could. And not look back. But definitely no deliberate abuse. Psychiatric session over?'

Strangely enough, he felt it had helped him to talk. It was like checking out the luggage he would be taking with him and deciding how little it would weigh. He would be travelling light. He had begun to think it was probably for the best that Sandra had found him out. The marriage wasn't working. Since she had given up her career and become a part-time librarian, her fixation with having children meant sex had become something they did in relation to the calendar. Getting a hard-on according to the phases of the moon. Every period sent her into mourning for the child that never was. And then the endless conversations about adoption. He could admit to himself now that he was relieved when the pregnant unmarried girl whose child they had been promised had changed her mind. It was better to get out before Sandra found another donor, then brought home a present it would take a lifetime to unwrap and work out exactly what it was you had been given. He didn't fancy the prospect of living with weird behaviour and always wondering where the hell it came from. Veronica would be simpler. He would see her tonight. He could arrange with Sandra tomorrow to get his stuff out of the house. It would take time but he was sure Sandra wouldn't cause too many problems. It wasn't in her nature. Without children, the financial arrangements shouldn't be too burdensome. First things first. Disentangle from Jacqui as cleanly as possible. He was almost there. Come the dawn, I'll be gone.

'So you're a self-made bastard,' she said.

She waited for a reaction. He continued to stare through the window as if she weren't really there. It irked her. This was like Kevin casually erasing her presence from his life. The difference was that now she was being obliterated by someone who was still in the room with her. It wouldn't do. If he was dismissing her, at least he would know she had been there. She would leave her mark on him.

'You sound about as substantial as a mayfly,' she said.

'Isn't that what we all are?' he said. 'With delusions of grandeur. At least I'm honest about it. I don't kid myself. Think about it. Any moment of any day. We come up against a bus, a virus, a slip on a staircase. Cheerio. I know a man who died choking on a chicken bone. Isn't that a pathetic epitaph? We can assassinate ourselves trying to change a lightbulb. Our heart's a time bomb. We're fragile fuckers.

132

Every day news comes in about how ludicrous our pretensions are. But we won't believe it. We live by denying our own reality. Well, not me. Life's a con. Take the piss out of it before it takes it out of you.'

She stood up from the bed.

'You are horrible,' she shouted.

He turned towards her.

'Why? Because I won't share your fantasies, you silly bastard?'

She was glaring at him.

'All this is just an excuse so you can treat people like shite. Even your wife. The unmentionable Sandra. You haven't even gone to talk to her. Why?'

'Because she's liable to start a riot.' (Or worse, accept a reconciliation.) 'You heard the way she went on. The whole hotel might be turned out. I don't need that.'

'You don't need anything. Or anybody.'

'I certainly don't need this. Fuck off.'

He was turning towards the window when his peripheral vision sent the message that she was on the move. Towards him, and coming fast. He stood up just in time to catch her wrist when she swung at him. He gripped her other arm as her body came against his. It wasn't unpleasant being assaulted by her breasts. What was supposed to be a wrestling match alchemised into a strange dance of lust. He developed an erection. Her arms went round him and they were kissing. They writhed each other towards the bed and fell there. In their haste to be naked, the top of her dress was torn slightly. It wasn't something she seemed bothered about. They undressed each other dementedly and he went inside her. As he ploughed desperately into her a thought came and went in her head like a scribbled note for later. This cancelled all the

133

distance there had been between them. As they climaxed together, his voice expressed his exultation.

'Oh, my God,' he wailed. 'Oh, my God, Veronica.'

In the first, faint dawn light the room froze around them like a glacier.

Dear Mr Beck

I understand from our bank that you have already cashed the cheque for twenty-five pounds which we paid you for the 'reading' you inflicted upon us some time ago. This proves that you are at least not a fool in financial matters, for it was our intention, after eventually meeting to discuss the matter, to stop payment of your fee. We felt that we had every right to do this since the discrepancy between what we understood was being offered and what actually took place on that unfortunate evening would render you liable to be sued under the Trades Descriptions Act.

The Committee of the Women's Guild has empowered me to write on their behalf, expressing our profound displeasure over many aspects of your 'performance'. First of all, let me explain the background to your appearance at our Guild. In this way you may receive some inkling of the responsibility you bear (something of which you are obviously not particularly aware) and of the damage you have done.

Ours is quite a small congregation but, I think I may say, an active and forward-looking one. Our minister is progressive without being trendy. While he may not play a guitar in the pulpit, he is open to happenings in the wider world. This tendency naturally spreads to congregational activities. We like to feel that we of the Women's Guild are particularly abreast of things. We are in the main a reasonably youthful group, mothers whose children have not long started school – that sort of thing. We have in our ranks two primary-school teachers, a lady who used to work in a bank before motherhood called her to another role and, I think I am correct in saying, at least one graduate. I myself am a writer of contemporary romances. There is, of course, a sprinkling of older ladies but we are anything but fuddy-duddy. We are an intelligent and interested group, successful women who are members of the Guild not out of the lack of something else to do but from thought-through Christian conviction.

It is because we are such aware people that we hit upon the idea of having a writer for an evening. I must admit that I do not feel wholly blameless in this matter. The other ladies have long known about my own career in writing and have frequently been agog with interest to find out what makes a writer tick. Here, I thought, was fertile soil for some lucky writer to cultivate. Here was an audience where a writer might sow his words with a certain relaxed confidence, secure in the knowledge that none of them would fall on stony ground.

How we arrived at yourself as the writer in question should perhaps also be explained. As you may or may not know, filling the annual syllabus for an organisation like the Women's Guild is no easy matter. Through lack of funds (I should point out that any funds we do acquire through such activities as bazaars and sales of work are given – to the last penny – to various charities, or to the fabric fund of the church), it is not our practice to pay a fee. Accordingly, the catchment area for our speakers is somewhat limited. We are dependent upon the freely given time of others. This can impose a burden on their generosity.

If I may illustrate this point. (If I seem to be labouring matters a little, that is purely because I would like to impress upon you the kind of people you have offended so deeply.) Mr Mayhew, the husband of one of our ladies, has every year, for three years running, given us a talk with slides on his visit to the Holy Land. This is a subject of perennial interest but we have not been unconscious of the fact that this is an unfair demand to keep making on Mr Mayhew. Nevertheless, he had again agreed to do it this year, in spite of being under considerable pressure at his work, and had been duly listed in the syllabus to that effect. Unfortunately, less than a fortnight before the date of his talk (i.e. the evening on which you joined us), his slides were stolen from his car. (Having given his talk to many other groups besides our own, Mr Mayhew frequently keeps the slides in his car for handiness.) We can only hope that once the thief (or thieves) discovered the nature of their swag, they were suitably chastened.

This left us with a gap to fill and not a lot of time in which to fill it. Since it is one of our boasts that we have never yet let our members down by failing to provide them with a stimulating and educational evening, an extraordinary meeting of the committee was quickly called. It was there that your name came up. I had myself expressed a willingness to step into the breach if no other solution could be found when your name was mentioned by Mrs Andrews. (She has subsequently offered her apologies to a full meeting of the Guild.)

She made the point, I seem to recall, that her husband – William Andrews – had been an acquaintance of yours at university and, while he had not seen you since, she felt that *perhaps this acquaintanceship might be enough to prevail upon your better nature (we were under the delusion at this stage that you had one) to help us in our time of crisis.*

The rest of the committee were immediately interested. As I have suggested, most of us have a natural interest in things literary. A few of us had seen you on television and one of us even hinted, quite jocularly, that at least we would have something decent to look at as well as listen to. I give this detail to let you see the goodwill that was waiting for you here when you arrived and which you have abused so unforgivably.

To come to the point, we were unanimous that you should be approached and post haste. I am sure you must be aware that this in itself was no easy matter. Mr Andrews informed us (his information seems to have come from a friend of his who seems to have bumped into you intermittently) that a letter was unlikely to elicit a response. Telephoning seemed to be the answer. I do not know if you are aware of how many times we phoned within the space of two days. Suffice to say, our financial expenditure was not inconsiderable. Eventually we learned that you would be willing, not to speak to us, but to give a 'reading'. The unexpected sting in the tail was that your fee would be twenty-five pounds.

This necessitated another extraordinary committee meeting, at no small inconvenience to the members. We had to meet in my house during the morning. I was, I am glad to say, against paying the fee. But some of the other ladies were, perhaps understandably, by this time keyed up at the prospect of meeting a 'celebrity'. One of them had borrowed Lodgings in Eden *from the library and had started to read it. In short, we acceded to your demands and there was even a tentative motion put forward that this be a regular fixture in* our syllabus – namely, that there be one evening each year when a literary figure should speak to us and that a small fee be put aside for this. We were to discuss the matter at our next committee meeting. Needless to say, the project has been abandoned. You have, perhaps irreparably, damaged the cause of literature in our small group.

Having reached the decision to employ you, we were then faced yet again with the problem of making contact. I shall forbear to detail the subsequent trials and tribulations that attended our attempts to get in touch for the second time, nor shall I itemise the expense involved. This left me, for one, with a certain lack of confidence that you would turn up. So nervous was I right up to the final moment that, when you appeared, I was checking through the notes I had taken the precaution of bringing with me (on what constitutes romance in the modern world) in case I should still have to fill the breach. It is perhaps a measure of my innocence that when you arrived I thought we were lucky.

All of the above, Mr Beck, may give you some small idea of the efforts we expended to have you with us, of the quality of audience that was waiting for you, of the opportunity for the advancement of literature that you have so wantonly thrown away. I cannot bring myself to list all of the ways in which you have let us down. It would be too painful. I shall content myself with some of the more salient features of your 'performance'.

You were, first of all, twenty minutes late. This may seem a trivial matter to someone of your 'stature'. I can assure you it is not trivial to our ladies. Many of us have to make special arrangements, baby-sitters and so on, and, being people who run houses as well as taking part in educational and cultural activities, we have to keep to a pretty tight schedule.

Consequently, punctuality is of the essence in our activities. It may interest you to know that Mrs Hughes, for example, had to pay her baby-sitter an extra five pounds for the 'privilege' of listening to you. I can promise you she doesn't think it was money well spent.

But the unkindest cut of all in the matter of your lack of punctuality was not merely that you were late but the reason for your lateness, which I assure you was patently clear to all of us. As soon as you came in, I had the distinct impression you might require a compass in order to find your way to the lectern. Your lateness was very obviously not due to rushing to keep your appointment but had been of a sedentary nature. Not to put too fine a point on it, you were drunk – a condition that became progressively clear (or should I say 'obscure'?) as you proceeded with your 'reading'. Mrs Jenkins, who is one of our more elderly ladies and is, as a result, a little hard of hearing, admitted to us later that for most of the time she was under the impression that you were reading poetry in a foreign language.

Any hope some of us may have entertained that you would 'talk yourself sober' was dispelled when we realised what was going on from time to time behind the lectern. Who would have thought something as innocent and naturally polite as providing a decanter of water and a glass in order to combat the 'dry mouth' so many speakers seem to suffer from could have been put to such a disgusting use? Whatever you added from the bottle in your pocket was no aid to sobriety. When you later added it to the tea we provided for you afterwards, I could not believe my eyes.

I have no desire to dwell on this débâcle any longer than is necessary. But the outrage felt by all of the Guild demands that I make one or two further points. At our meeting *following your 'reading', we worked out by pooling our impressions that in your poems you used two swear-words (three if you count 'hell' – though I am myself against including this one in this era of greater, if rather dubious, linguistic freedom). As I suggested to the rest of the committee at the time, I feel pretty sure that a reading of these poems in print would find these offensive words mysteriously disappear. In other words, I believe you put them in on the night for cheap effect or perhaps through simple lack of self-control. Shame on you.*

But I had thought your depravity was fully revealed on the night itself. I had not thought worse was to follow. Miss Anderson, who works part-time in a bookshop, had her suspicions aroused at one point in the evening. Next day she duly did some excellent detective work. As a result, I am now led to believe that you did not, in fact, write the extract from 'The Quaker Graveyard in Nantucket'. How you had the nerve not only to claim the poem as your own but to give a wholly fictitious account of how you came to write it, I shall never know. Mrs Barclay, one of our more compassionate members, confessed that she had been moved almost to tears by your account of travelling alone in New England and suddenly coming upon the stark bleakness of the place and finding what I believe you called 'a mirror for your mind, the skull beneath your own skin'. You are disgusting!

Rest well assured that you will never address our Women's Guild again.

Yours in contempt
Margaret Bauer (Mrs), Chairperson

Dear Mr Beck

Thank you for sending us the three poems, which I am afraid we cannot quite find space for at the moment. Although it is our editorial policy to offer comment to writers rather than the cold anonymity of a rejection slip, I find myself at a loss to define exactly the dissatisfaction I felt about these poems. Perhaps it is that they seem too raw, too confused, too involved in the naked pain of life to convey a clear message to the reader.

There is one in particular which seems to me very opaque. What is it about? I couldn't be sure whether it was about the alienation of being in a foreign country or the futility of art or the prostitution of talent or a hymn to misogyny. I found the quotations (echoes of The Wasteland?*) were too obviously tacked on, not effectively subsumed in the main body of the work. They are, I think, from Lowell? The incomprehensibility of the title didn't help either: 'Not Going to the Holy Land'.*

Please send us anything else in which you think we might be interested.

Yours sincerely
Geoffrey Marsten

The two letters, together with the one from the publisher, lay on the desk by the window. Sitting there, he glanced at them. Three rejection slips in one delivery. Maybe he could get into *The Guinness Book of Records*. Success out of failure.

He felt detached about it. It was as if they were dead letters, unable to reach the person they had been meant for. Not known at this address. The publisher's letter was rejecting a book Harry felt someone else had written. The editor of the poetry magazine was corresponding with a night of drunken mischief, which had seemed funny at the time. He shouldn't have gone to the pub before the reading, especially not on a night when so many drinks were to appear unasked before him, donated with good intentions by people who had decided they owed him one.

The letter from the guardian of the Women's Guild, prissy with outrage as it was, was definitely authentic evidence for the prosecution. But Margaret Bauer was talking to the prosecution's chief witness. She thought that was bad? He could bring evidence she couldn't imagine. She might get him fined for breach of the Women's Guild's peace. During a hangover, he had sometimes felt he knew enough about himself to justify bringing back the death penalty.

She was right on her own terms, though. (And hadn't she enjoyed herself, making an epic out of a complaint.) How could he have done that? A mangy literary lion among the ladies. It was pathetic. Next he could rampage through primary schools, reading Molly Bloom's soliloquy. At least he would pay them back the twenty-five pounds. He thought he might give them compensation and make it fifty. But he decided not to be abject about it. In fact, maybe he should deduct a five-pound penalty for the tweeness of the letter? No. Twenty-five pounds it was, a straight refund.

The answer to his dismay with his own past wasn't to put himself in hock to it but wave it goodbye and try to find a different future. He would like to have a try at social maturity before they buried him. But he knew he was going to miss some of those ludicrous times.

He wouldn't be having another night like the one with Big

Eddie. That had been a weird one. Like a holiday booked through Kafka Tours. You don't know where you're going till you get there, and even then you can't be sure where it is you have arrived.

He had gone into the pub he used at the time to have a quick drink before he caught the train to Edinburgh, where he was to do an evening reading in a bookshop. Big Eddie was just back from abroad where he had been working as a brickie. He had hands that made a pint dish look like a thimble. He was, he told Harry, absolutely loaded. He meant with money, but you could have taken it the other way without any loss of accuracy.

'Where you headed?' Eddie asked.

He told him.

'Mind if Ah come?'

'It's a reading, Eddie. I'm reading out a book. There's not going to be anybody pole-dancing or anything.'

'So? As long as Ah don't have to do the reading, what's the problem? Do they not have something like wine at these things?'

He took the point. He knew there could be risks. Eddie was a nice wild man but he was definitely a wild man. He had once jocularly introduced himself to a woman by asking her to take her clothes off. She slapped him so hard on the jaw, his head must have been reverberating like a struck gong for minutes. Eddie apologised sheepishly and went away. That was Eddie – he was so incompetent with women, he invited them to beat him up and get it over with.

He had seemed in calmer vein that night. He didn't look permanently sane but he did look as if he was having a lucid interval. The taxi to the station had to make a detour to Eddie's flat so that he could collect what he called 'some luggage'. Harry thought Eddie had a strange concept of a night out. He had wondered if it was Eddie's term for money. But Eddie came back out with a shirt in a Cellophane wrapper that said 'Made in Hong Kong'. Harry thought Eddie had a strange concept of luggage.

The reading in George Street had passed without serious incident. Apart from drinking enough plonk to make the young woman at the wine table panic about stocks and start to look nervously round the bookshop (perhaps she was wondering if there was a paramedic in the house or a bouncer), the most extreme thing Eddie did was to tell any attractive woman who came within earshot that he was the one who wrote the books and he just let Harry put his name to them.

When they hit the street again, they were both high – Eddie from the wine and Harry from the buzz of knowing that some people had actually read something he had written. Passing a casino, they decided they were high rollers. The man on the desk looked like a bull with a bow-tie. He explained politely to Harry that they had to be members to get in. It would cost five pounds each. Harry was taking out the money when the man said they would have to fill in a form and post it to the casino. The whole business might take a week or so.

Eddie was talking about offering the man a bribe when Harry noticed a woman leaving. He persuaded her to sign them in. She recognised him and, after signing them in, joined them at a table for a drink. Eddie left to play roulette and returned in ten minutes, saying he had lost seven hundred pounds. Their benefactor was called Marie. She had read *Lodgings in Eden* and she and Harry were discussing it when a small fat woman approached their table. She had a champagne glass in her hand.

'Excuse me,' she said to Harry. She pointed to another

table. A young man who looked as if he hadn't started shaving yet waved suavely, raising a champagne glass with his other hand. 'That's my husband over there. We got married today. We're having a party at our place to celebrate. And we'd love it if you would all join us there. Our treat.'

'My dear,' Eddie said, 'you're a charming woman.'

They lived in Pilton. When they all arrived in the living-room there was a skinny boy dressed only in jeans asleep on the sofa. He looked like something out of a Victorian print of destitution. He seemed to be about fourteen but the happy couple said he was eighteen and had been thrown out of his parents' house. He woke up and sat staring round at everybody during the subsequent party.

The party was a mug of tea each. As Harry began to sip it, the woman who had signed them in mouthed at him not to drink the tea. Check out the cups, her silent lips suggested. Her grimace implied they might be plague carriers. Come to her place, she secretly conveyed, and they could have a real party. They made their polite excuses.

At her place the party was tea in attractive cups. Harry was beginning to think that people in Pilton had a strange concept of a party. He fell asleep in his chair to be wakened by the woman telling him that he would have to leave. It was after four in the morning. It seemed Eddie had been through at her bedroom, trying her door.

Outside in the street in windy darkness Harry cursed Eddie elaborately.

'You know what?' Eddie said. 'She had a chair against the door-handle. Why would she do that?'

'You should know.'

'What? Naw, naw. She had the wrong idea. Ah was lookin' for the lavvy.'

Harry had a vision of dying of hypothermia in the street in the company of a man to whom coherence was a foreign country when they were saved. God sent a taxi to Pilton.

Dropped off in Princes Street, Harry said he must get some sleep. The door of the Mount Royal Hotel was open and they went in. Upstairs, no one answered the bell when Eddie hit it. Harry saw a key lying on the desk. The tab on it said '110'. He took the key and went along to the room, which, as if by arrangement, had two single beds. They stripped to their underwear and went to sleep.

Harry woke at half past nine in the morning to see Eddie finishing making his bed, tweaking the top coverlet meticulously. Harry made his own bed and suggested they have tea and biscuits before leaving.

'Let's not take liberties,' Eddie said.

There was no one on the desk when they came down and Harry left the key where he had found it. After the train, they took a taxi to the street where he used to live. When they parted, Eddie still had his shirt in the Cellophane wrapper. Harry wondered if perhaps Eddie liked to take a shirt with him in case he got arrested, so that he could look nice in court.

It wasn't that it had all meant anything. What he remembered was an escape from the necessity of meaning, a kind of social version of freefall which had its own exhilaration. He let other strange memories arrive with a kind of detachment. He simply touched them as they passed like emigrants boarding ship. They might revisit occasionally but their home would no longer be here. That time he had put his table napkin over the talkative woman's head, as if she were a budgie in a cage, passed by. He shouldn't have done that. He wasn't promising to cause no more trouble but he would try to make it more purposeful in future. He stood up and pulled the curtains. In the mass of grey that merged sea and sky, the dawn light was a lovely minute statement – like one sentence on a computer screen, he thought.

He wanted to make his own statement, however ineffectual. He wanted to reclaim his experience as his own. He might be as mad as Muldoon but he would make a small cairn of words. He had to do it now.

He opened the A4 notebook he had brought with him. He found a Biro pen. As he sat down at the desk, it seemed strange to be preparing to write a sustained piece of prose again with a pen. It felt good, though. Perhaps that was what he had been doing wrong for years: writing by computer. A pen seemed to connect the brain more directly to the page. Thought seemed to travel more carefully along the arm on to the paper. You earned the words more thoroughly, on your body. They didn't suddenly appear out of nowhere, as if random. You had to carve them out.

He started to write, while the dawn grew as if in personal response to his need for it.

So you thought Jekyll and Hyde and Adam Yestreen were bad news? (Harry Beck was talking.) You haven't heard the worst of it. Here comes their great progenitor. The daddy of them all. A man called Oedipus. Are you sitting comfortably? Well, don't. There's nothing here to make you feel relaxed about yourself. Here's the story: in ancient Thebes a child is born. When his father, King Laius, consults the Delphic oracle about the boy's future, the news could have been better. This boy, it is foretold, will murder his father and marry his mother, Jocasta. Cancel the cards of congratulation. In fact, Laius decides to cancel his son's life. It's the only way he can see to prevent such a horrendous prophecy from coming true. But this is his son after all. So he devises a way to kill him without getting too much blood on his own hands. He drives pins through his son's feet to cripple him and gives him to a servant to be abandoned on a hillside somewhere. Presumably to starve or freeze to death or to be eaten by animals. But the shepherd's only human. He feels compassion for the child. He gives the boy to a man who is travelling far away into Boeotia. What harm can the boy do there? Oedipus is adopted by the king and queen of Boeotia. Lucky fellow. He grows up knowing them as his parents. But in early manhood he overhears some man telling another about the prophecy that was made at the birth of Oedipus: he would kill his father and marry his mother. Oedipus is just as horrified as Laius had been and adopts his own strategy to outmanoeuvre the oracle. Thinking his adoptive parents are his real mother and father, he flees from Boeotia. How can he kill them when he will never be in their company again? Guess which direction he innocently heads in. On his travels he comes to a place where three roads meet. There he is ordered to get out of the way by a man being carried by his servants in a litter. Oedipus is nobody's pushover. He is a man of massive pride and quick to anger. There is a fight in which Oedipus kills the man and his retainers. The man is called Laius, although Oedipus doesn't know that. He presses on until he comes accidentally to Thebes. The city is being terrorised by a monster called the Sphinx, a kind of animal amalgam. Of every traveller it asks the same riddle. If you can't answer it, it eats you. Oedipus is the first to get it right and the Sphinx kills itself. Thebes is freed. As their liberator, Oedipus is made king of

Thebes and marries their queen. Her name is Jocasta. Many years later Thebes is caught in the grip of a terrible plague. Consultation with the oracle reveals that the city is harbouring someone unclean and, as king, Oedipus is determined to find the source of the pollution. With great difficulty he finally discovers that he is himself the problem, that the man he killed at the crossroads was his father and the woman he has married is his mother. Destroyed by the news, Jocasta hangs herself. Oedipus finds her and, taking an ornamental pin from her robe, he blinds himself. He's eventually banished from the city. He dies in exile. And there we are. When the ancient Greeks told stories, they told big ones. Just let all of that sink in for a moment. What can this avalanche of accidental horrors actually mean? For this wasn't some cynical Hollywood director cobbling together another blockbuster to make us spill our popcorn. The definitive version of Oedipus was written by Sophocles, a man with a profound understanding of human nature. He was giving us a message about ourselves in which he apparently believed. But what was the message? What is he saying about us?

'She's at it again,' he said as he came in.

'Who?' she asked.

'Mrs Fawcett.'

He leaned over to kiss her cheek but she turned her face up to his and their lips met full on. The magazine she had been reading slid off her knees. She pulled him down to her. He let his briefcase fall on the floor. They kissed for a long time. When their mouths parted, they were both breathing heavily.

'Come on,' he said.

'Maybe we should eat first,' she said. 'Dinner's on.'

'We can eat any time.'

She pushed out her bottom lip and tried to blow some ruffled strands of hair off her forehead.

'Is she really doing it again?' she asked.

Her face was flushed. He was warm too. He eased himself out of his jacket, removing first one arm from her and then the other, wriggling awkwardly out of the sleeves, so that he was always touching her. The jacket lay on the floor beside the briefcase.

'She is, she is,' he said.

'It's unbelievable.'

'Seems to be her mission in life.'

'That must be several times every day.'

They were looking into each other's eyes. He smiled slowly.

'Will you do that for me, I wonder,' he said.

'You'd have to fix the nameplate first,' she said.

They laughed. When he had tried to put up a nameplate, he had used the screw-holes that were already there. He had invited her out on to the landing to witness the ceremony. When he closed the door to get the full effect, the nameplate fell on to the doormat.

'I will,' he said. 'When I get hold of a bit.'

'Yes, but our nameplate's plastic.'

'We can change that. Incredible, though. How long's he dead?'

'Three years, she told me. Said they had been married fifty-eight years. Fifty-eight years. This is our anniversary, by the way. Three months today.'

'Is that a record?' he said. 'Let's celebrate.'

He stood up and pulled her out of her chair. They kissed

again and his hands were moving gently, rediscovering the strangeness of her body. She laid her head against his chest. She could see late sunlight illuminating the small room. It enriched the new furniture, seemed to deepen the colour of the wood.

'I like this place,' she said softly.

'It'll do for now,' he said. 'Until we get the mansion.'

'I don't know,' she said. 'Maybe this is as happy as we'll be.'

'It'll just get better.'

'I like this place,' she said softly.

'Let me show you the best room,' he said.

They moved awkwardly, rubbing against each other, towards the door. In the hallway, she took his hand.

'Wait,' she said. 'I want to see her.'

She led him along to the front door. She peered through the spy-hole. She saw Mrs Fawcett, distorted through the lens, rubbing furiously at the brass nameplate that said 'Alexander Fawcett'. Mrs Fawcett was, she knew, a small, frail seventy-nine-year-old woman whose wrinkled face suggested the unimaginable places she had been. But from here she seemed enlarged, a monument to endurance of feeling.

'Look, look,' she said.

He dutifully looked, one hand stroking her back. He turned back towards her and nodded.

'Uh-huh,' he said.

'It gives you faith, doesn't it?' she said.

'I've got that anyway,' he said.

'Come on,' he said. 'Come on.'

She took one last look.

'Come on, darlin',' he said.

'Aw,' she said. 'She's going back in.'

Mrs Fawcett closed the door. She went through to the kitchen and put the aerosol tin and the cloth in the cupboard under the sink, settling them in their familiar place that was easy for her to reach. She washed her hands slowly and thoroughly and dried them carefully. She smelled her fingers to make sure all trace of the polish was removed.

She took the crystal milk-jug from its cupboard. She filled it with water from the cold tap. She went through to her living-room and crossed to the potted plant where her husband's ashes were mixed with the soil. She watered the plant gently and lovingly. She went back through to the kitchen, dried the milk-jug, replaced it in the cupboard and put the carefully folded towel in its place on the lower edge of the spice rack.

She came through to the living-room and sat in the chair that had been her husband's. She glanced contentedly round the room from which all visible trace of her husband's presence had been removed. She smiled as she looked at the potted plant, which was a flower her husband had hated more than any other. She remembered again how she had read somewhere that, for the Egyptians, to remove a man's name from his funeral tablet was to kill his soul. She thought of the words 'Alexander Fawcett' dissolving in brass. She smiled to herself.

She lifted the evening paper which had been delivered, found her glasses and started to read.

After sitting holding them for a while, Kate put the three sheets of typescript down on the desk. She aligned them carefully, squaring the corners. She did it with care, for they seemed to her a part of the inside of Mickey's head and that was a place with which she thought she was falling in love. The body wasn't bad either.

She looked across at him. He was spreadeagled on the bed. Sleep had hit him like a car. The duvet was pushed down to his waist. With only torso, arms and head visible, he lay like a piece of broken sculpture. But the rest of him was there all right. She smiled slyly at the proof she had of that. The first light of morning coming through the closed curtains had the effect of the Vaseline she had heard could be put on a camera lens. The moment was soft focus. He would never look better than this, she was sure. Even the black eye merely increased his appearance of vulnerability. The hair would never be darker and the contours of his face would never be cleaner. The sense of time frozen was enhanced by the utter stillness outside. She felt she could hear for miles but there was nothing to listen to except her thoughts.

So this was love? It made her feel strange, as if she had just been introduced to herself. Pleased to meet me. This time would never come again and she would savour it. You could only feel this once. She felt double somehow. She felt her identity more intensely than she had ever done and she felt simultaneously distanced from it in a pleasant way. She was both inside her name and outside it. It was like being within the main character of a story, so that sometimes she occurred in the third person in sentences someone else seemed to be saying.

Kate Foster lost her virginity at Willowvale.

It had a good sound to her. She was glad it had happened here. It had the edge on having lost it up a tenement close in Glasgow. Willowvale. It made it more romantic. Willowvale. Wuthering Heights. Manderley. Not Busby. Dennistoun. Auchenshuggle. Even the exact circumstances in which it

153

had happened, although they might seem pretty tawdry to other people, were for her drenched in such a cascade of unfamiliar feelings, all she remembered was sensation. Place dematerialised.

The moment when the unimaginable suddenly loomed into possibility, she knew now, was when Mickey switched off the light. Their conversation had been the innocent approach to a place she had sometimes felt she might never reach. She was aware at the time of how unusual the way they were talking was. It would have needed an act of will to take their eyes off each other. They were like people who had met after a long separation and were happy to find each other again. She was telling him things she hardly remembered knowing about herself. Self-conscious mannerisms evaporated. She knew what she thought about lots of things she had assumed she wasn't sure of. He confirmed them and expanded on them and made them his own feelings. Ideas came out of them like fireworks.

Suddenly they paused. They could hear people talking in the darkened bar next door. She was offended, as if someone were spying on them, invading a space that belonged to them alone. Mickey put his hand on the back of her chair, leaned across her and switched off the single light that was burning beside them. Straightening up, he let his right hand come to rest on her shoulder and left it there. As she stared at him in the semi-darkness, he put his left forefinger to his lips and smiled. It seemed to her the most beautiful smile she had ever seen.

They sat staring at each other. Their eyes were a conspiracy of silence that lasted while they heard people come out of the bar and walk along the corridor and begin to go up the stairs. Mickey's right hand moved to the back of her head. It rested very gently there, touching her hair. Her breathing paused. He leaned off his chair on to his knees in front of her and his tilted head came slowly towards her and they kissed.

What followed, she imagined, was what going over Niagara two to a barrel might be like. The long gentleness of that first kiss exploded into furious, thrashing activity that took them along with it wherever it was going. They were on the carpet together, doing things she didn't know could be done, like the swift removal of knickers while sitting on the floor. She had no experience of unbuckling a man's belt but she learned instinctively. The hard heat of his body was shockingly exciting. When he went into her, the room did cartwheels. She found how enjoyable indignity could be, lying with her legs grappling his hips. Above her his head butted like a gentle beast.

She was left with warmth inside her. It hadn't taken long. It happened to her like newsflashes from another self. But, as some news can, it had changed things. That was what she mainly felt. The woman lying on the floor was never quite to be the same one who had been sitting on the chair minutes ago. She watched him as he leaned over her on one arm. She was surprised to see how diffident he looked.

'I'm sorry,' he said. 'I didn't know.'

He was staring at the floor.

She eased herself up past him and, in the glow from a porch light outside, saw what appeared to be blood on the carpet. It wasn't much. It was only then she remembered how slight the pain had been, breaking into pleasure almost immediately. Was that what all the fuss had been about? It seemed so little. She thought that perhaps her suspicions, during those times of physical exertion, that her hymen might have been damaged hadn't been unfounded. Maybe she had partly lost her cherry to the saddle of a bicycle or a tree. But this was better.

'I'd better clean it up,' she said.

His arm went round her and they sat there almost naked, holding each other. It was good to sit there, letting what had happened solidify from event into fact, and feel the sweat frost on her skin. The dark lounge seemed staid around them, its chairs and tables still rigidly in place throughout the room. It was good to have defied their rectitude.

'Just leave that,' he said, his face against hers as he nodded towards the blood. 'What can they think? That somebody cut their finger? They couldn't work out the truth of it in a year.' She burrowed into his neck and giggled. His left arm closed like a velvet clamp around her body. 'Anyway, I like it there. We'll always know it was there. And what it really means. It's our memorial. Kate and Mickey were here.'

She shivered pleasantly against him.

'Let's get you to bed,' he said quietly.

It was then she first thought that she might be in love. It was as if the sex hadn't been something separate from the rest of the time they had together. It was an expression of a continuity. It was still a kind of sex when he found her pants for her and watched her dress and had his arm round her coming up the stairs and let her into his room and they lay naked in the single bed together, talking for hours before she fell asleep. Wherever Donnie was, she was glad he wasn't here. Tonight in bed (last night in bed, she thought, aware of the growing light) they had made love again. *Kate Foster made love*. She thought she could get addicted to that. But it was to the presence of him she knew she could become most addicted. It enabled her to be more herself. She throve on it. She had never known how interesting she could be till she saw it in his face.

She looked at him still sleeping. She was in no hurry to

wake him up. She wanted to inventory the amazingness of this weekend. It was the fullest time she could remember experiencing. In two days she seemed to have amassed a library of new feelings. She wanted to browse among them. How could you be sure it had happened if you couldn't keep it? But they had talked about so much it wasn't easy.

Mickey Deans explained to Kate Foster about his black eye.

That was when he had left her before the Free-for-all began, saying he wouldn't be long. He was going to try to find Donnie Davidson. Donnie had brought his own pharmacy with him and Mickey was worried. He might try to swim the Atlantic in his underwear. Or decide the nearest pub was Tombstone and he was Wyatt Earp. He could go crazy on the stuff he took.

Mickey told her that he did find him in the nearest pub. Donnie had an unlit cigar. Mickey knew that wasn't a particularly good sign since Donnie didn't smoke. Nicotine, according to Donnie, was the only drug that was completely pointless. He was using the cigar like a prop, brandishing it extravagantly. Three young local men were standing round him.

'And then, of course,' Donnie was saying, 'the old man took to the drink. It was a catastrophic decline. We lost the entire estate. Twenty-five thousand acres. And so I stand before you, gentlemen. A cultured pauper.'

One of the three young men made a wide-eyed face at the other two.

'Is that right?' one of the other two said.

Mickey understood immediately what was going to happen if he didn't manage to stop it.

'It's funny,' Mickey told Kate, 'how something you've read ages ago can suddenly explain a situation you're in. It's like a flash of lightning or something. And you can see so clearly.'

What Mickey had read, he told her, was something about Edwin Booth. It was his brother, John Wilkes Booth, who had shot Abraham Lincoln. Anyway, Edwin Booth once played Richard the Third in front of a lot of miners in the backwoods somewhere. Edwin must have done it well. Because after the play a mob of miners were waiting outside to get him. They thought he *was* Richard the Third, an evil bastard. Edwin had to be spirited away before the miners got their hands on him.

What Mickey saw was that the three locals didn't know this was theatre. They didn't know that this was what Donnie did, go off on ridiculous verbal excursions and pretend to be somebody he wasn't. They didn't understand that he was taking the piss out of himself. They thought he was taking the piss out of *them*.

'Donnie,' Mickey said.

Donnie's head travelled in a gracious arc, his eyes tracing a line along the ceiling until they had landed on Mickey's face.

'Michael,' Donnie said. 'My friend. I've just been telling the chaps here about our family misfortune. They have seemed intrigued.'

'Come on, you,' Mickey said, taking Donnie's arm.

'You a mate of his?' one of the three locals said.

'Aye.'

'Where's *your* estate?' another said.

The three of them laughed very loudly.

'Right, Donnie,' Mickey said. 'Let's go.'

'What's your hurry?' one of them said.

'We're going,' Mickey said, pulling Donnie away from the bar.

'Take this with you.'

Mickey said he didn't know which one threw the punch. He didn't know if it was meant for him or for Donnie. All he knew was that he got in the way of it. The rest was noise. Fortunately, the barman came round from behind the bar at once and he was a very big man. The authority he instantly exercised among the locals suggested that he might have made use of his size a few times before.

When comparative stillness was restored, the barman was standing between Mickey and Donnie on the one side and the three locals on the other. Mickey's throbbing and watering eye seemed to demand revenge. But he still didn't know which one had hit him and the barman was in no mood for a rematch and the other locals in the bar were threatening to join in and it didn't take a genius to work out whose side they would come down on.

'You two,' the barman said. 'Out. And don't come back. I don't want trouble-makers in my bar.'

'I doubt if I will deign –'

Mickey managed to hustle Donnie out of the door before the people in the bar heard the rest of his statement, which he told to the night air outside, calmly and resonantly, as if it had been waiting like a crowd of reporters to hear it.

'– to visit your establishment again. The lower orders are revolting.'

Mickey said he walked Donnie as fast as he could, always checking for signs of pursuit. But nobody followed. No doubt they were all drinking to having driven off the aliens. Eventually, he let Donnie sit for a time at the side of the road. He asked Donnie what he thought he had been doing.

'I thought,' Donnie said, 'how sadly curtailed their little lives must be. So I brought them glamour. Where's my cigar?'

'Arsehole,' Mickey said. 'I wish it was you they'd punched. At least you deserved it.'

He managed to get Donnie almost as far as the entrance to

the drive at Willowvale when Donnie disappeared in the darkness into a small clump of trees. Mickey spent about twenty minutes looking for him but it was hopeless. It was then he had come back into the hotel to hear Harry Beck reading something he slowly recognised.

'Strange night,' Mickey said to Kate.

He remained worried about Donnie. A couple of times during the evening Mickey had gone out into the darkness of the grounds in Willowvale, vaguely hoping to come across him. He didn't want him to catch pneumonia or something. Kate liked that in him but, going out walking with him one of the times, she wondered why he bothered.

Donnie was all right, Mickey said. He just happened to be a chemical loony. Even then he wasn't nasty with it. He was just off-the-wall and funny. Before he got lost and ended up in the pub, he'd told Mickey he was dreading Sunday. He said he hated Sundays. He went into a whole riff about it, talking a lot more weirdly than he had been in the pub. It was a good thing the locals didn't hear him then. They would have thrown a net over him. Mickey wished he could remember it to tell Kate.

'He did it all in what I think was supposed to be a Yorkshire accent,' Mickey said.

'Why?' Kate said.

'How would I know? The stuff Donnie takes, I suppose he might as well be in Yorkshire. He probably can't tell Glasgow from Guatemala. But I wish you could have heard it.'

('It were a Soonday. I remember it as if it were yesterday. In fact, it were yesterday. Or were it? One thing I'm sure of. It were the day after the day before. I know this because our Bert were in the upstairs basement, trying to put wheels on the cat. I remember our dad calling up to him. Tha's mad tha is, he's shouting. If God meant cat to have wheels, where's the bloody axle then? Me mam were knitting a small loaf out of stale ends of bread. It were our Sal's turn for the book. We only had one and our dad would only let us read one page at a time in case some greedy bastard used up all the words before the others had a chance. Our George and I were playin' ping-pong wi' the budgie. Or were we throwin' darts at Granda? Or sucking one another's thumbs? Or did nowt like this 'appen at all? I don't know any more. One thing I do know, though. It were a Soonday.')

'I think,' Mickey said, 'maybe he can't bear to live outside his own head for too long. And maybe he's not alone in that.'

Kate Foster and Mickey Deans told each other about themselves.

She came from Graithnock. He came from Shawlands. She had had a maths teacher who taught solid geometry in mid-air, just by pointing and drawing imaginary lines with his fingers. It was tricky to follow. He had had a brief moment of triumph in primary school once. The teacher asked if anyone could tell her what BC meant. He was the only one who knew it meant 'Before Christ'. It was a brief moment because she then asked what AD meant. 'Ah, Mickey Deans to the rescue again,' she said. 'After the Death,' he had said brightly. It was only later he understood what a short life-span he was giving Jesus. She said Coldplay and he said the Strokes. She liked

Pacino and he liked De Niro. She said, 'Heathcliffe,' and he said, 'Mr Rochester – if they ever met in a pub, I know which one I'd bet on.' Her father had once been caught trying to put a pair of Y-fronts on Reba the dog because she was in heat and might get pregnant. Her mother had managed to stop him. 'Makes sense,' Mickey said. 'He was obviously trying to make the other dogs think she was male.' He had an uncle who knocked out his own brother when he came into the house in the early morning without putting the lights on. The brother was moving about in the dark so as not to disturb anybody. His uncle clocked him because he thought he was a burglar. He couldn't believe she thought Shirley Bassey could sing. 'Ferrari of a voice,' he said. 'Pity she can't drive. I read that somewhere, by the way.' She used to like going to Calella de Palafrugell with her family. That was on the Costa Brava. He had never been there. 'I've been to Saltcoats, though. Twice, as well.' She didn't go on holiday with her family any more. It didn't exactly offer a wild time. He thought maybe they could go together. Get student rail tickets and do the Continent. She fancied it. He thought Arnold Schwarzenegger had all the acting skill of a talking totem pole. He had read that somewhere, too. He'd had a maths teacher who gave a boy a terrible row for blowing his nose. Seemed to take it as a personal affront. Maybe there was something weird about maths teachers. No, he *had* been further than Saltcoats. Last year he went with two of his mates to Benidorm. But he thought he might like to go to Spain some time. Instead of just going on your holidays to an English pub with sunshine. She was a Catholic. He was an agnostic, or he thought he was. He couldn't be sure. Had she seen *American History* X? One of the best pictures in the world. Had he seen any of the *Lord of the Rings* ones? Just the first one. It was too long. He thought he might have rectal bleeding by the end of it. She liked them. She liked this place. Willowvale. It made her think of all the people who must have been here just after it was built. Maybe there were dances by candlelight, with beautiful ballgowns. The whole place lit up. Did he like this place? He really did. 'Especially now.' And he gave her the smile that excited her.

The memory of their being together so closely was all she would remember of this weekend, she thought. Everything else, the other people and the place, had just been a backdrop for them. They were the only show in town. She would have felt guilty about leaving Jacqui in their room except that she was too full of other things to feel. Anyway, if Jacqui had succeeded in what she was obviously trying to do when she came up to Mickey after his story was read, Kate was the one who would have been on her own. And she didn't imagine that Jacqui would have been alone for long.

The only thing that troubled her was that the feeling in her was too intense to last. Could Mickey possibly be feeling the same way she did? She took the lapels of his coat, which she had put on over her knickers, and pulled them together.

Kate Foster sat nude except for her lover's coat.

She didn't want the day to start. She rose and very gently pulled the curtains open. The dawn was up. The sky was ribbed with red. She sat back down and leaned her elbows on the desk and stared out of the window. She was suddenly wistful for a time she was still experiencing. She allowed herself to be absorbed into the stillness of the scene, the dark silhouettes of the trees, the grass growing slowly more green, the softly dissipating morning mist, as if they could hold her there.

His hands on her shoulders sent a shiver through her.

'Hullo, you.'

163

His voice was deep in its closeness. He lipped her ear. His hands crossed each other under the coat, each cupping a breast. They both stayed like that in silence a while.

'We'll never have this time again,' she said.

'We won't have to if we can stay inside it.'

She sighed.

'What if I become like the old woman?'

'What old woman's that?'

'The one in your story.'

He laughed. 'Come on.' He put on an old man's voice. 'That's just a story, hen. A wee story. Don't greet now. The bad monster has went to its bed. All better. And they all lived happily ever after.'

His lips moved softly against her face in a smile. She echoed it. But she wondered for a moment if the scene and the two of them being there in it weren't a mirage.

'I suppose I better put some clothes on and look for the mad Yorkshireman,' he said. 'That's two nights he hasn't slept here. Lucky for us, right enough.'

But she didn't move. She didn't want him to.

'I wonder where he is,' he said.

Donnie was sorry he had come. He didn't like this place. But he knew he couldn't go until the man let him out. The door was reinforced with steel on the inside. It was closed, with several large metal bolts pushed home. Making a run for it was not an option. He could hear people talking outside the door. Their conversation seemed deliciously ordinary. Somebody was talking about gardening. 'Perennials,' he was saying. 'Better with perennials.' Donnie wanted to be where they were but he knew there was no way he could do that. He hoped that one of the people would knock on the door so that the man would open the flap inset in the steel, check who it was and let them in. That way at least he wouldn't be alone with the man.

The man was frightening. Donnie admitted it to himself: he was afraid. He was very afraid. He was so afraid that he could barely follow what the man was saying. But he understood what his talk meant. It meant threat.

He seemed to hate everybody. Perhaps that was why the room was like a fortress. It was a very well-furnished fortress. There was a huge music centre from which such loud sound came that Donnie was more or less having to lip-read. There was a large ornate dresser. There were two chairs and a couch covered in what looked like purple velvet. In the corner of the room lay a black dog roughly the size of a Shetland pony. It stared constantly at Donnie. The man said it was his pet.

The man was almost bald except for his ponytail. He wore a denim shirt with several buttons undone and jeans. He had a lot of rings. He had a length of rope tied round his wrist. The other end of the rope was tied round the handle of a door, which was closed. The rope was very loose and dragged on the floor. Occasionally, as he talked, the man would make a face at Donnie and jerk his arm so that the rope rose off the floor and formed a straight line in mid-air between the man's wrist and the door.

'For those that misbehave,' the man said.

The man talked about hating the people he had to deal with, and Donnie was sure the hatred included himself. They were animals, the man said, and that was how he treated them. He held up a long knife. That was what he would give them, he said, if they caused him any trouble. They would get it in the guts. If that didn't sort them out, there was always the final answer. His arm tugged on the rope and the door juddered and the man grinned at Donnie.

'Right,' the man said, and produced a transparent packet of white powder and laid it on the table in front of Donnie. 'Your money.'

'How much?' Donnie said.

'One hundred pounds. Now.'

Donnie knew he had only coins in his pocket. The man was waiting. Donnie took out the coins and laid them on the table. The man stared at the money, then stared at Donnie.

'You bastard,' he said. 'Wasting my time. Your life's over.'

He jerked the rope at the end of his wrist and the door sprang open. A massive Rottweiler came snarling into the room, ran at Donnie and jumped for his throat.

Donnie woke up. The faint light lay on him like a benison, letting slowly materialise around him some harmless furniture among which he gradually found himself. It was the lounge of a place called Willowvale. He was lying on one of the double chairs, his feet protruding into the air. He lifted the jacket he had been using as a blanket. His torso was naked under it. He wasn't sure what had happened to his T-shirt. Sweat stood out on his chest like blisters. He wrapped the jacket back around him, wondering where Mickey was.

He drifted back into sleep, looking for a better dream.

The water soothed her, silk against her skin. She liked the way a bath seemed to cleanse the mind as well. She needed that. She lay letting vague thoughts pop like bubbles in her head. He was a nice man. The niceness went with him even into making love. It had been more slow waltz than tango. That had suited her. It gave her time to relearn the steps, even if she wasn't sure how often she would need them again, if ever. She suspected they had been relearning together. She wondered if, given his wife's long illness, it had been his first time for years too. She had heard that his wife was completely bed-ridden. She tried to rationalise her guilt by telling herself that the woman would never know what had happened. Perhaps what you didn't know had happened hadn't happened. (She remembered a lecturer saying someone called Bishop Berkeley had suggested something like that. Something about a tree in a quadrangle, she thought. If you didn't see it, it wasn't there.) But Andrew knew, of course, and so did she. She hoped the knowledge didn't hurt him too much. For herself, she tried to take some solace from the fact that his wife was not the only one who was ill. She pushed the thought away at once, because it seemed a mean thought and because she did not want to go there in her head for her own reasons. She had promised herself this weekend must be utterly self-contained. That was impossible. Thoughts didn't follow the instructions of your wishes. They arrived without invitation and you couldn't uninvite them. At least with their talk and the things they had done she had not allowed her fear too directly into her presence. Perhaps she had just been using him as an exorcist. But then hadn't he been exorcising something too? Perhaps the grief of his increasing loneliness.

She listened to the comfortable sounds he was making in the next room, preparations for departure. She liked hearing them. They were the sounds of ordinary life maintaining its preoccupied rhythm, regardless of what might be happening around it. She could luxuriate in banality a little longer. Her elopement from reality would soon be over but not quite yet. Let what was waiting for her wait. She would have her bath and get dressed and return to the room she was supposed to have shared with Marion. She was sorry about the distance she had created between herself and Marion but she had not wanted to compromise Andrew. Surely Marion would be understanding, knowing what lay ahead for her.

She began to wash herself slowly. As she soaped her breasts, she remembered Andrew's clumsily extravagant compliments. He didn't realise that his praise of them had been their epitaph.

Freud had his ideas about this as he had about so many other things. And new and arresting ideas they usually were. Enough to give Edwardians and Victorians the vapours. He could explain the hold the Oedipus story had on us, the meaning of the myth. Oedipus was a psychological archetype of the male unconscious. All men had, buried somewhere darkly in them, the impulse to supplant the father and claim the mother. It was shocking news, the Oedipus complex. Enough to make the dinner-table feel like a war zone, the bedroom turn into no man's land. It must have made family life seem suddenly to many like a masked ball, where you couldn't be quite sure who – or what – was behind the mask.

Marion paused the tape. She was thinking of her own family, the distortions of themselves they had created out of being together. Were her brothers, in what they had become within the family, anything like a just expression of themselves? Was her mother? Was she?

She supposed that was the legacy her father had given them. His own life had been suffocatingly narrow but that hadn't diminished his authority in judging the lives of others. She saw him as a kind of descendant of the Victorians, although in pygmy form, the runt of an exhausted lineage. He had their certainty with none of the vision that had sent them all over the world to fulfil that certainty.

Still holding the tape, she noticed that the curtains hadn't been opened. She crossed and pulled them and stood looking out. Contemplating the sweep of the grounds, she felt intimidated, not so much by the sheer scale of them as by the self-confidence behind them and the building she stood in. The Victorians could at least do this. They had built places she couldn't psychologically inhabit. She thought of a place she had lived in before she bought the flat. It had been part of a large Victorian house that had been subdivided into many bedsits. She and the other residents had come and gone like squatters in a grandeur that had never been their own. So temporary were their stays there, so vague their presences, so small the space their lives took up, they might as well have been living in tents pitched within the permanence of the building.

That same feeling of being inadequate to her surroundings, of being found wanting when measured against the size of other lives, had come back to haunt her here. Almost guiltily, she admired the Victorians. She had been taught them as being more or less defined by their hypocrisy but she suspected their hypocrisies might have come from the need to unfetter the energy of their idealism from some of the darker realities that would hobble it. Any critics of the Victorians she'd read always found themselves at least admitting their stature. She thought of Lytton Strachey writing about Florence Nightingale. He had peeled her image pretty well naked but even he had written a sentence which seemed like bowing reluctantly in print. She had written the sentence down so that she could keep it, like a definitive portrait of a woman who had always fascinated her. She tired to remember it now: 'She poured forth her unstinting usefulness . . . with a bitter smile upon her lips.' That small twisted woman had changed the future by sending her passion through the world like an antibiotic.

Florence Nightingale was an example of some kind to her. It wasn't that she wanted to be a nurse, just to do something of her own that made her not the almost invisible Mouse. The man they had been talking about this weekend, Stevenson, what was it he had said? 'Admire and do otherwise'? Or 'do other'? Anyway, it came to the same thing. Use your appreciation of other people's ability to have a larger life than is defined by the headstone. Find your own way to do the same. She thought of the computer in her box-room. She wanted in some way to memorialise the fact that she had been here.

The man who had built this place had certainly done that. Whatever his story had been, it seemed a big one to her. Like those Greek myths Harry Beck was so fond of. Oedipus. Watching a new day greening, she pressed the button on the machine, wondering what relevance to the brightening scene the words on the tape could have.

Yet, when you think of it, Freud gives what might be seen as a comfortingly chintzy interpretation of the myth. And he does this by twisting the terms of the story out of shape. The linch-pin of his interpretation is that it is *because* Jocasta is his mother that Oedipus marries her, and it is *because* Laius is his father that Oedipus kills him. But surely this is to take the more comfortable interpretation at the expense of the darker one. For the whole narrative line of the myth drives home the significance that Oedipus murders a man who *happens* to be his father and marries a woman who *happens* to be his mother. The point may be that, without the necessary, continuing and contrived set of social circumstances (which haven't been experienced by Oedipus), the most basic social relationship we have is meaningless. Its importance is not intrinsic to our animal selves. Our social selves have invented its importance. Now that is a truly frightening message. To tell a civilised man that he so wishes to possess his mother that he has, hidden in him, an urge to displace his father, that is surely upsetting enough for him. It means that the living-room is not perhaps all of his natural habitat. But it does still preserve the sacred importance of the basic unit of society – the family. His deeper motives are still a cipher, however obscene to some, contextual with his life within society. But to tell him that his mother has no particular relevance to his deeper nature at all, that if he takes her it is merely because she has the animal equipment complementary to his own and happens to be handy, that removes the keystone of society. It puts each of us in a separate wilderness, utterly alone to resolve the stresses and discords of our nature, and it tells us that society is never a resolution of these stresses, merely an imposition on them. I wonder too if, in Freud's interpretation of the myth, psychoanalysis didn't find its own 'place where three roads meet'. For there seems to me something in Freud's reading of the myth definitive of the use to which society has subsequently put psychiatry. The tendency with psychoanalysts has not been to liberate the divergent individual from the authoritarian pressure of his society so much as to liberate him from the conflict which that has created, to defuse the uniqueness of his identity, so that it can function without untoward danger (to himself, as well as to society, it has to be admitted) in a social context. In fact, to make his unique individual dilemma merely a part of the norm, to incorporate each psychic crisis into the static definition of what it means to be a social being. Instead of allowing it to fulfil the dynamism of the experiencer's drive towards his or her own individual freedom.

Marion clicked off the tape. She checked her own bed and Vikki's bed. Vikki hadn't said much when she came to collect her stuff from the room but she had seemed calm then, and at breakfast. Given the pressure she knew Vikki was under, Marion hadn't wanted to ply her with questions. Perhaps she might talk about it later. Marion made sure the bathroom was empty of all their things. She checked that her notes were safely stowed. She had heard the bus arriving and now she could hear the voices of the others gathering outside. Still holding the recorder, she took her key. She pressed the button.

I think Freud's interpretation only works by bypassing what is central to the myth – the meaning of the riddle of the Sphinx. When you focus on that, you begin to understand that the Oedipus myth is telling us not so much a psychological truth as an evolutionary one. Perhaps Freud's patriarchal preconceptions distorted his focus. The myth, it seems to me, is telling us not something narrow and gender-specific. It is telling us something species-specific. The high priest of its content isn't Freud but Darwin.

Darwin would have to wait. Marion silenced the tape-recorder and put it into her bag. She went round the room, checking that all the drawers were empty and that everything was in the place where she had found it. She lifted her bag, closed the door and locked it. As she came along the corridor, she noticed that the door of the strange woman's room – Sandra – was closed. She still couldn't imagine who could have tried the handle of her own door during the night. She paused and listened, but heard nothing. Having looked out earlier this morning when she had heard someone knocking at the woman's door, she had seen David Cudlipp. She assumed the woman must be his wife. If she were, something must be wrong there, for she wasn't letting him in. The problem between them must have been what the shouting that had frightened her last night was about. She wondered if the woman had left yet.

She checked her watch. Everyone else must have been gone for a couple of hours. The hotel sounded empty now. The two-day contingent had come and gone. The study weekend was over. All those voices, mainly young, had chattered into silence. Now there was only the occasional sound of some member of staff calling to another, the closing of a distant door.

She hadn't been able to bear the thought of leaving with the others. She didn't feel a part of anything any more. She had to work out who she was becoming. She had to know who it was who would be leaving. There was a place she had to get to before she could go on. She didn't know where that place was, except that it was inside her head. She just hoped that she would recognise it when she got there.

She must move soon, though. She had decided that. It was all she had decided so far. She would leave on the later ferry. It was the last ferry home, wherever home was. Gordon Mitchell had said she could stay as long as she wanted, whoever she was. He had been nice. Maybe David had told him something. Gordon had come to the room. They had spoken at the open door. He hadn't come in. He had asked no questions about what had happened but simply said she could stay until she felt like going and there would be no charge. He had suggested food but she didn't feel like it.

She looked at the open packet of sandwiches. One was half-eaten. She wondered when that had happened. She couldn't remember. It was as if a part of her had conspired against her bleakness, had secretly infiltrated her belief that she couldn't go on and subverted her denial of herself with supplies, however meagre. She rose, taking the glass, and went through to the bathroom, ran the cold tap till the water chilled her fingers and filled the tumbler. She came back through and sat down. She finished the stale remains of the sandwich, chewing methodically and helping the food down with water. The action was an admission made to herself, she knew, but she was also aware that it was a bitter admission. Perhaps that was why she ate the stale bread and not the fresher sandwich, which she threw, still in its package, at the waste-basket from where she was sitting, deciding that, if it went in, she would be all right. It did.

It was hopeless digging in the past of her marraige for meaning. She couldn't tell the significance of anything she unearthed there. Every certainty she tried to find crumbled on contact, atomised into such doubt that she couldn't tell his betrayal from her fantasy. She could get no purchase on the past. Shock had temporarily paralysed coherent reaction, like an emotional stroke which left her incapable of articulate response. She felt she would have to relearn the grammar of her nature painfully before she could understand her final reaction, let alone express it.

Her profound resentment somehow had to find a way to become the future. But it was the future she had carried in her to this place that he had most effectively destroyed. Him and someone else from the anonymous others. Veronica Hill? Those others, she thought, they had descended on the island like a flight of aimless arrows, one of which had hit her without her even being known as who she was. And it hadn't been noticed. Outside the window, she had heard them leaving at lunchtime, their self-satisfied voices babbling indifference at her. She felt the coldness of betrayal all about her. Permafrost would be cosy compared to this.

A memory appeared to her suddenly, like the ghost of who she might have been. She was in the garden at Langbank with Myra when Darren, who had been playing near them on the grass, came up to his mother and asked something very matter-of-factly: 'Mum. How do they make the sky?'

She would never be the answer to such sweetly impossible questions. That was most of all what she couldn't accept about what he had done. Cheating her of her past was painful. Cheating her of a future she had dreamed of for years was unbearable. It was how close he had let her come to the dream before casually erasing it that measured the depth of his contempt for her, shamed her before herself. His easy acceptance of her decision on Thursday evening not to come to Cannamore, which she had taken as a gesture of consideration for her at the time, meant something different now. Presumably he had already made his plans to be with that other woman. Each had had a secret the other couldn't know.

At least her secret had been benign, although that benignity had curdled into self-contempt in this room. If she didn't tell him that Angela had changed her mind again and had phoned to say they could adopt the baby after all, it was because she wanted everything to be definitely settled. She had wanted to surprise him with an incontrovertible fact: he was going to be a father. She had arranged to visit Angela on Saturday, which was the day she had said suited her, and finalise things between them, make certain there was no going back on the decision this time. There wasn't. Angela was utterly sure.

The euphoria of Saturday afternoon, every impulse of joy she had found expression for, came back to mock her now: the laughter mixed with sisterly tears she had shared with Angela; the insistence that she would call the baby Angela after her mother; the pleasure of holding something so minutely beautiful and feeling as if she were a perfect fit; the inability to wait until he came, to tell him of their incredible good luck; the adventure of travelling on the delayed ferry, crossing the darkened sea like the heroine of a romantic novel; the stranger who had driven her to the hotel, not knowing how casually important he was being; bringing the best of the Polaroid photographs she had taken so that David could see who had become the most important person in their lives.

She turned the photograph over. The small white face seemed effulgent to her, glowing out of the dubious half-light of her photographic incompetence. She couldn't bear to lose her now. But surely she wouldn't be allowed to adopt her into a broken marriage. That was how he had hurt her most. It was as if he had kicked her during a pregnancy and cost her the baby she was having. She couldn't accept that. But how could she avoid accepting it? That was what she had to come to terms with.

Three

The man was completely white. The costume that covered his entire body was white. The things that looked like cloth over-shoes were white. The gloves were white. What could have been a shower-cap was white. Even his face had been sprayed with the same metallic paint. His head jerked round in a series of broken movements, apparently scanning the small crowd around him. Then the head lowered itself in three distinct stages and his eyes became fixed in a stare. His right hand took a flower from the small bunch he had in his left. The hand with the single flower in it extended itself like a slide-rule until it was projecting straight out. With the arm held rigidly in front of him, he took a series of stiff and very slow robotic steps towards the crowd, his stare still fixed on whatever it was he had seen. Eventually he stopped in front of a small blonde girl, holding the flower out to her. Encouraged by her mother, she took the flower reluctantly, as if she wasn't sure what she was supposed to do with it. There was a smattering of faint applause.

'Uh-huh,' the small woman beside him said. She looked up at him. 'I don't know who's dafter. Him for goin' on like that. Or us for standin' here watchin' 'im. It's great whit ye see when ye've left yer gun in the hoose.'

She harrumphed and walked away. He laughed and threw a couple of coins into the cardboard box that lay not far from him. He wasn't rewarding the performance. He thought the small woman's review was fair enough. He didn't intend to stand here any longer, watching flowers being distributed slowly enough to give you softening of the brain.

The money was tribute paid to the city, its multitudinous crazy energy. It was good to be back. It was like plugging into a generator. The relentless thrust of living all around him pulled him into its careless force, let him feed off it so that he felt new possibilities.

The claustrophobic introversion of Willowvale seemed like an unhealthy self-indulgence, a sick-room he was glad to be out of. A Glasgow sky like a dustbin-lid banalised the problems he had imagined he had on Cannamore. Life was just something you got on with, whatever the weather. Jacqui Forsyth was only a worry if you were trapped in a room with her. He was glad he had managed to avoid her on the ferry and ignore the discreet opera of her tears on the bus back to Glasgow. If he had shown any concern, they might have had a full-blown Victorian melodrama: *The Rejected Woman*.

Also, he thought as he walked, maybe the money dropped into the cardboard box was payment for an idea the robot had given him. Flowers. He had been thinking about phoning Veronica before he turned up at her place. But it would be better just to appear, flowers in hand. And maybe chocolates. A suitor arrives. The initial surprise might prepare her for the bigger one to follow.

For Sandra's refusal to let him into the room this morning had clarified something in him with surprising speed. He didn't really want to talk to her about a reconciliation. He had stood in the corridor outside the locked door, wishing he hadn't left his key in the room when he went with Jacqui. He had felt foolish sending whispers through an imaginary megaphone ('Sandra, open the door, please.' 'Sandra, we have to talk!') until Marion Gibson looked out from a door along the corridor and he shrugged at her with elaborate playfulness and she went back in. What was that shrug supposed to have meant? 'Ah, there you are. This is just a little marital game we play. I know it's silly but we like it'?

He cringed at the memory. But at least the one response he had received ('No!') had reassured him that she was still quietly if bitterly present. And he was able to collect his toilet-bag from the corridor. If she hadn't caused too dramatic a scene during the night, she wasn't likely to do it when she had calmed down, was she? With the problem of scandal in Cannamore averted, he was spared the need to play conciliatory roles he didn't believe in. He could confront himself honestly and decide what he truly felt about the imminent break-up of his marriage.

The answer was: not much. Their relationship had been a travesty for some time now. The threatened adoption of a child had been the X-ray plate that showed him the incurable nature of their marriage. They looked at it and saw two different things. She saw it like a baby-scan, the promise of a future that stretched indefinitely ahead of them. He saw it like the shadow of a cancer. He dreaded what would grow remorselessly from it.

Yet he hadn't had the courage to tell her. When the adoption fell through, he had kept secret the massive relief he felt. But he knew it was just remission. The longevity scare was an early-warning signal, obliging him to face up to where he was. He was in a marriage he didn't believe in. For the first time he had obliged himself to see his infidelities for what they were. They weren't casual furloughs from the marriage, leaving it intact. They were sustained subversions of it, defying the possibility of its meaningful survival. The fact that it had taken him so long to admit such an obvious truth was proof of how unhealthily deceitful he had been, even to himself.

Whatever impulse had brought Sandra to Willowvale on Saturday, he couldn't regret it as some unlucky accident without which their marriage would have survived. It was an accident which had expressed the inevitable. Once over the initial shock, he had to admit that he welcomed it. At one stroke circumstances had brought him where it might have taken a lot of exhausting machinations to reach by himself. The relief he felt was not deniable.

It was as if a hair-shirt had been removed from him. It felt good again to be inside his own body. The day was alive with new beginnings. The world had dew on it.

In the flower shop he bought a dozen roses. The woman raised her eyebrows and said, 'Romance is in the air?' She didn't know the half of it. He wasn't just going to visit Veronica. He was going to snow her. She was unaware of it but they were going to set up house together. It was so much the obvious thing to do, he couldn't believe they hadn't done it already. Veronica had suggested it herself more than once. The time was now.

The choice of chocolates in the small grocer's shop wasn't lavish but he managed to get a box of After Eight. The charm of the Pakistani behind the counter was like an omen. All things were wishing him well. It was a little awkward carrying the flowers and the chocolates and his weekend bag. Still, it wasn't exactly a lot of luggage to carry into a new life with

184

him. A taxi might help, though. First establish his new base and then begin negotiations with Sandra.

'Clarkston Road,' he said.

The cab-driver kept eyeing him in the rear-view mirror in that way that warned him he was being sized up for a conversation. He didn't mind. Today his unexpected euphoria was something even strangers could share in.

'Have ye ever wondered,' the driver said, 'what would win in a fight between a crocodile and a shark?'

It was not an unarresting question. He had to admit to himself that in all his deep ponderings upon life's big issues, he had so far incomprehensibly ignored this one.

'No,' he said, a bit shamefaced. 'I can't say I have.'

The driver nodded, as if he'd known all along he had another unthinking automaton in his taxi. He let a few moments pass.

'Well,' he said. 'I bet you're thinking about it now.'

It seemed to him that the driver hadn't stopped watching him in the mirror since the cab moved off.

'I am, I am,' he said placatively. And wouldn't it be a good idea to give the road the occasional glance? Who knows, there might be another car there or something.

'And?'

'And?'

'So what do you think?'

He had to admit he was hooked. What would win in a fight between a crocodile and a shark? And, anyway, how would you ever know? Presumably, crocodiles and sharks weren't constantly bumping into one another. Had somebody arranged a special contest between them, like an Aquatic Championship of the World? The questioner obviously knew. Philosophers only like posing problems to

185

which they think they already have the answers. But what was the answer?

'I give up,' he said.

The driver had suddenly remembered that the road was something he should perhaps keep an eye on.

'Ah suppose it's obvious when you think of it,' he said, giving the stiff digit to a passing motorist. 'Certainly when Ah found out, Ah thought: Yes! Ya beauty! That had to be the answer.'

'Well?'

'Ye know how Ah found out? Ah'm sittin' in the hoose, readin' the paper one night. And Ah shouts tae the wife. "Jean," Ah says. "Know how Ah'm always wonderin' what would win between a crocodile an' a shark?" '

He had a sudden surrealistic vision of marital conversations between Jean and her husband. ('Nothing in the papers again today, Jean, about crocodiles and sharks.')

'Well, the answer's in the paper here.'

The road seemed to have become a matter of absorbing interest again.

'Well?'

'It seems there's a river in Australia. Got a big estuary, like. And the sharks swim there. Your Great Whites an' things. An' the crocodiles is waitin'. A square go between them is not unusual.'

'So what happens?'

'Same result every time.'

'Like what?'

'The crocodile, intit? Seems it takes one bite intae the shark. Holds on to the death. Ta ta, shark.'

He couldn't help smiling. Another nibble at the apple of infinite knowledge. He wasn't sure that he believed the driver, but so what? What sort of pedant would quibble about stepping into a Glasgow taxi to find himself swimming with the crocodiles and sharks? It was like Dorothy stepping from the black-and-white of a dull life into the technicolour of her search for Oz. This was his day all right.

'I'll get out here,' he said.

They were round the corner from Veronica's flat. He didn't want her to hear a taxi arriving outside her window. It would kill the surprise. He wanted to appear sudden and full-blown outside her door, bearing gifts and shocking her into acceptance of their new life.

He gave a good tip. To the alchemist his due. He walked round the corner and glanced up at Veronica's first-floor place. A sedate Sunday window. Soon the interior would contradict that.

It was one of only two tenements in Glasgow he knew of that had no secured door. He went into the entry, walked along the ground-floor level and climbed the stairs. Outside Veronica's door, he put down his weekend bag and took the flowers in his right hand, the chocolates in his left. He pressed the bell with his right elbow and waited. Nothing happened. He hoped she wasn't out. He rang again. The ringing dwindled into silence. He was about to curse silently when he heard movement within the flat. He prepared himself as he heard the bolts being drawn behind the door. He held his offerings behind his back.

The door opened. He couldn't have wished to see a sweeter image. She was wearing a white dressing-gown which didn't effectively conceal the voluptuousness of her breasts. Her long hair was dishevelled, as if she had been sleeping late. The face without makeup looked defencelessly sensuous. He was making the right choice. He had come home. He produced the chocolates and flowers with a flourish in front of her and held them up.

'Tah-dah!' he said.

'David?'

Didn't she recognise him?

'It's not a good time,' she mumbled.

'Veronica,' he said. 'It's always a good time. Come on. Let me in.'

But she seemed transfixed, staring at him. Her stillness spread to him. He stayed with his presents held in his hands. The feeling he suddenly had was of something bad about to happen. It was one of those long, frozen seconds when you realise that life has ambushed you once again but you still don't know where the attack is coming from.

Into the stillness in which they stared helplessly at each other came a padding sound, as of something very heavy approaching. Behind her appeared what might as well have been the Creature from the Black Lagoon, so exotic was its impact. It put a large paw round her shoulders. It spoke. Even the voice was on steroids.

'Is there a problem, Nica?'

I hope not, he thought, looking at the size of the man. The flowers and chocolates are for you. You can decide which ones you want to eat first. The man must have been about six feet four and he had the kind of body you used to see only in comic strips. He was wearing only jockey shorts, which looked as if he had stuffed a piece of the furniture into them, perhaps as a secret weapon.

The familiarity of the 'Nica' was interesting. It distracted him irrelevantly, like a condemned man noticing a fly alighting on the barrel of the rifle that is pointed at him. It suggested a certain length of acquaintanceship which he didn't feel like questioning at the moment. He just remembered that Veronica had begun going to a gym. It looked as if she had started bringing one of the exercise machines home with her.

What is the Sphinx? For the Greeks it has the body of an animal, the wings of a bird. Out of that body grow the torso and face of a human. It is, as I've suggested, a kind of composite of the animal world, a composite of which we are an integral part. We are harmoniously combined in it with the other animals. But notice that the part by which we are represented includes the head, where the mind is. The part which enables us to unravel the riddle.

Marion turned off the tape to make some coffee. As she moved about the kitchen, she suddenly felt the strangeness of what she was doing. Combining Harry Beck's news from what he thought was the darkest place with having a coffee. I suppose we *are* a strange species, she thought.

'There is surely intelligence among the young,' Democritus was saying, 'and lack of intelligence among the old. For it is not time that teaches good sense but timely upbringing and nature.' And 'The desire for more destroys what is present.'

189

'Poverty and wealth are names for lack and satiety; so one who lacks is not wealthy and one who does not lack is not poor.' 'A life without feasts is a long road without inns.' 'A man of sound judgment is not grieved by what he does not possess but rejoices in what he does possess.' 'Learn to feel shame before yourself rather than before others.'

He replaced the book on the shelf, where it merged with the lines of others, another brick in the walls of words around him. He had instinctively come here, to his office in the university, rather than go directly home. He felt guilty about extending Mhairi's time for looking after Catriona but he had felt the need to locate a sense of himself again, to work out who it was who would be entering his own house.

The words hadn't helped. It wasn't that he didn't feel their relevance. He still experienced that quiet thrill he had often felt when reading an old text. Here was a man writing two and a half thousand years ago and telling him about himself. The weekend had been for him an unexpected inn on a long road. He was certainly learning to feel shame before himself rather than before others.

But, instead of confirming him to himself as they had so often done, the books in this small room seemed to call him in question now. What had been his psychological bunker for so many years, the place where he had stored the essential purpose of his life, was breached by an alien presence. The alien presence was himself, the man he had been with Vikki. The sense of new potential he had discovered with her, of unexplored space in himself, made the place where he had felt most securely at home feel suddenly and pointlessly narrow. He understood as he looked round the room how safety could be dangerous. It could stultify. A refuge could just be a fancy name for a prison. Like Dr Manette, so conditioned to confinement that he couldn't bring himself to pass through the open door of his cell in the Bastille, he was afraid of the possibilities that seemed to be before him. To pursue them would be a negation of what his life had meant for so long. But their very existence was a contradiction, in any case, of who he thought he had been.

'The desire for more destroys what is present.'

That had already happened. He couldn't return to his life with Catriona as the man who had left it two days ago. He had subverted the meaning of their time together. He came back to their relationship as someone who had already undermined it. The treachery seemed all the greater because he couldn't meaningfully confess it to her.

The sense of a self-deluding life extended to this room. He looked around it. The motes drifting in two shafts of grey sunlight gave it a sombre, tomb-like atmosphere – and around him the serried experience of the past, bearing names. It was as if they had thought the meanings they had found were of permanent significance. So had he. But were they?

In the quiet gloom he noticed the screen of the computer he had never learned to use effectively. It glinted at him like a malevolent eye, as if it knew his time was up and its time was only beginning.

He thought about having visited a school last year to talk to some sixth-form pupils about coming to university. He had met with them in the school library and had been aware, as they talked, of the computers there were around them in the room, like an electronic assault party in the citadel of Gutenberg. The computers might be few in number but their presence seemed to him to dominate the room, silent spies who already had so much authority here that they constrained the students' responses to him. He was listened to politely but he learned sadly that only one girl acknowledged reading as a habitual activity. The rest admitted that it was something they hardly had any time for.

The sadness he felt wasn't mitigated by his understanding of some of the reasons for it. It had occurred to him that the virtual monopoly the book used to enjoy as a pastime to engage the mind had broken up into several alternatives. The nineteenth-century appetite for novels the size of a small outhouse was there because they were mainly what the imagination had to eat. The culture now was a smorgasbord of passive options. The book had to take its chances.

He also knew, from being aware of his own pattern of recent behaviour, that most of us tend to spend our leisure on the softer options. Television, for example, was something he could often watch without having to engage the brain. Late at night he could sit in its warm glow as if it were a sauna. Sometimes he might object to its pointlessness but he was liable to go on watching in spite of himself, muttering things like 'How did this tripe get to be on the box in the first place?' and 'I don't believe this,' as if the remote control weren't resting on the arm of the chair. The tendency could be compounded by the fact that ease itself is habit-forming, so that we may not only settle for the easier medium but progressively for the less taxing forms of that medium, as if suffering from a mild degenerative condition.

The book makes heavier demands on us, he thought, looking round. A scene in its pages doesn't appear ready-made before our eyes, so that all we have to do is lazily record it. We have to construct it in our imaginations. It is a much more participatory medium, more our own creation. It's a DIY experience, he thought. The practice of it empowers us with a sense of ourselves by demanding our own individual interpretation be earned in decodifying it.

Luddism was pointless. He stared across at the computer he didn't like and saw it as a sign of an irreversible change in the way we conceive our lives. But he couldn't simply put his faith in it. He thought of the politely baffled confrontation he had experienced in that school library, a kind of cultural Mexican stand-off. There was more than age dividing him from those students. He suspected they saw him as if he had stepped out of a time-machine, apparelled in quaint attitudes. He knew that he saw them as dangerously self-assured, dismissive of the very medium which had not only been central to the evolution of their society but which could have deepened their awareness of who they were in it.

Yet he had to admit that they were far more in tune with the times than he was. There was surely intelligence among the young, even if it seemed to him to be intelligence in the sense of information rather than creative thought. It was a kind of intelligence that made them travel much lighter than he had ever done. Taboos for them seemed to relate to things like wearing the wrong style of clothes and enjoying the wrong kind of pop music. Sex was demystified. He sometimes wondered if the id had gone public. These days it was often photographed and liked to appear on television.

It came to him that the pupils in the library and his own younger students at Willowvale would have found it bizarre to be agonising over a weekend with a strange woman. The pleasure he had found with Vikki made him wonder if they might be right. Maybe what you thought were the deepest feelings of your heart were no more than adopting the fashion of the times. Had all his well-known moral objections to what he regarded as the shallowness of the present been no more than the jealousy of a generation that missed the party?

But he still had to honour those objections, even when they related to himself. Especially when they related to himself. He would take his guilt home with him and try to make the only kind of expiation he could, in caring for Catriona. It was all he could do.

He lifted the phone and dialled his own number. When the connection was made, he heard only silence.

'Mhairi?' he said.

'Andrew? Oh, Andrew. Catriona. Catriona has—'

The suddenness of her tears drenched him in knowing. The feeling in his gut, like being disembowelled, knew how to complete the sentence she hadn't been able to speak. The feeling also knew that, for his unexpiable guilt, it was a sentence for life.

'These piles are killing me,' Dan Galbraith said, shifting in his chair.

'You still bothered with them?'

'Bothered? On a bad day I've got an arse like a baboon.'

'Thanks for sharing that with us,' Sylvia said, bringing in three glasses and laying them on the table that had a map of the world under its glass top.

'Sorry, Syl. That wasn't meant for your ears, obviously. Just a bit of locker-room badinage.'

Dan was wrestling with the cork of a bottle which was misted with chill.

'But there's an operation for it, isn't there?'

'Harry,' Sylvia said. 'Puh-lease. Do not mention the operation. Peter. Dan's brother. Had the "operation". I've heard about it so much, I sometimes think it was me that had it. He talks about it the way some people used to talk about the war. Only the operation was worse, it seems.'

Dan popped the cork and poured the wine. Sylvia lifted two glasses, gave one to Harry and sat down with the other.

'Anyway, to matters less mundane,' she said. 'How—'

'Mundane?' Dan said. 'Having purgatory in your underpants? That's mundane?'

'The weekend. How was it for you?'

'I'm still not sure,' Harry said.

'Oh, here,' Dan said. 'I've got another wee word-test for you.'

Harry smiled, knowing the sort of thing that was coming. Perhaps because he worked as a sub-editor on the newspaper, Dan almost made a hobby of trying to find examples that illustrated the importance of nuance in language.

'I like this one,' Dan said. 'What happened was that I was watching an old black-and-white film. I can't even remember the name of it now. But that actor was in it. Is it Mary McCarthy's brother? Kevin? The one who was in *Invasion of the Bodysnatchers*. Anyway, there's a scene where a mother is annoyed with her son and she makes a threat. A couple of minutes later I was trying to remember what she said. And there was one word I couldn't get. And it struck me how dialogue can convey almost subliminal information. And I worked out this wee scenario.'

'I hope it's not *Gone with the Wind*,' Sylvia said.

'Right. A film relating to the forties is being shot. A woman is supposed to be threatening to chastise her eight-year-old son. He's given to telling lies. She's fed up with his fantasies. She says, "If this doesn't stop, I'm going to have to take the hairbrush to you." The writer interrupts, ruining the scene. He tells her she's got the line wrong. When he explains what the line should be, the crew are annoyed. They think he's wasted their time for no good reason and he's costing the production money. The writer won't budge. He says the line she said has quite different implications from the one he wrote. He makes them do it again with the mother saying, "If this doesn't stop, I'm going to have to take a hairbrush to you." Was the writer justified? If so, why? If not, why not?'

'Leave it with us,' Sylvia said. 'The weekend. What do you mean you're not sure, Harry?'

'Just that. It was a kind of strange weekend. I don't know.'

'Mystery,' Sylvia said. 'I love it. So?'

Pausing before he spoke, he thought at first that he resented Sylvia's inquisitiveness but then he realised that this was why he had come here, to give his feelings to his friends for clarification. He had known that Sylvia would be brusquely direct with him. He had come here on impulse after getting off the bus in Glasgow. This was why, he now understood.

'That woman at the party on Thursday,' he said. 'You know her well?'

'What woman?' Dan said.

Sylvia looked at Dan.

'What's your problem?' she said. 'Senile decay? Are you sure that was just your fiftieth we were celebrating? They went out as if they were surgically joined. The woman who came with Alec. What's her name?'

'Mary Sue,' he said.

Sylvia nodded.

'That's right. She's American.'

'Poor old Alec,' Dan said. 'He couldn't bite his nails by the time he left. He needed instructions to get through the door.'

'They're not seriously connected, are they?'

'Harry.' Sylvia was shaking her head. 'I think Alec is only making occasional connection with himself these days. Drinks like a fish? He should have gills by now.'

'Yes,' Dan said. 'Alec's lost it by now, I'm afraid. I think when Frances packed it in, that was him. Took a header into the bottle.'

'No wonder Frances left.'

'So how does Mary Sue come into it?' he said.

'Alec asked her to come with him, I suppose,' Dan said. 'He seemed quite pleased with himself. God bless him. As if it meant he could still pull. I suppose she was his beard for the night. I don't mean he's gay. His hormones would still need to be alive for that. But maybe she let him act as if he's still a player in the game.'

'Maybe she works for the Samaritans,' Sylvia said sadly.

'Oh, well,' he said. 'That scene. I suppose the difference is. If the mother says "the" hairbrush, it means cruelty to children. Because it would imply that it's a regular event. Something the boy is familiar with. Whereas "a" hairbrush would suggest something with which he isn't familiar, not something he recognises. And probably an empty threat. I'm with the writer on the importance of the difference.'

Dan made a face and raised his wine-glass. He reciprocated the gesture. But they were toasting different things.

What the Sphinx asks Oedipus is this: what walks on four legs in the morning, two legs at noon and three legs in the evening? Oedipus works out that a child crawls on all fours, that we walk upright on two legs and that we may use a stick in old age. He says the answer is man, human beings. The Sphinx kills itself. What Oedipus thinks he is doing is answering a question. What he doesn't understand he is doing is volunteering for a destiny, and an unfulfillable destiny at that. The death of the Sphinx is the authority of the animal world, of nature, apparently abdicating in favour of the supremacy of our species. But the Sphinx had given us a riddle that has a much darker meaning than the one Oedipus attached to it. To prevent the Sphinx from ingesting us, we are effectively obliged to ingest the Sphinx, to take its darkness into ourselves. If we refuse merely to be another part of the darkness of the animal world, that darkness will remain a part of us, endlessly compromising who we think we can be. The riddle is not just a question. It is also a prophecy. Whoever has the ingenuity to answer the riddle is condemned to live the prophecy. Step forward us. What walks on four legs is an animal, what walks on two legs is most definitively a human, what walks on three legs is a mutant. Tell me. What animal has three legs?

Marion still couldn't think of one. Someone had suggested afterwards in the dining-room that a flea might have three legs but this was disputed by several voices, although fortunately no one had the physical evidence on them at the time.

The painting suited his mood. It was called *Crucifixion*. It showed an empty spangled Elvis Presley one-piece suit against a nondescript pale background, suspended in space with the arms extended. What could have been blood ran in two rough lines downwards from the empty armholes. It was like a pastiche of a religious artefact. The painting seemed to him to fit the man who wasn't in it. It seemed to celebrate and mock at the same time.

He had liked Elvis. He thought he had embodied the social rebellion that was rock 'n' roll more effortlessly than anyone else. In his early films, almost uniformly dire as they were, what was always unmistakable was the coolly subversive threat he gave off. He had the amused, self-confident eyes of a man who knew he had an awful lot of testosterone in the bank and would spend it exactly how he chose. He looked like a breaker of the rules. He looked dangerous. But long before the end, the threatening stud had turned into a confused and conformist fat man, eating junk food and popping pills and dying in the lavatory. The adulation was empty. It was always empty. Think of the self-serving hysteria that had erupted round the death in New York of John Lennon, a talented musician who for most of his adult life didn't know his ass from his ashram.

He stood in front of the painting for a while, letting it remind him of the emptiness of things. He didn't know if the meaning he took from it was what had been intended by it. Maybe the artist was just another worshipper at the posthumously established Presleyan Chapel. He certainly seemed to be inviting us to compare Elvis with Jesus. Maybe there was no intended irony. He didn't care. He saw in it the folly of investing banality with a depth of feeling it couldn't carry, like putting a midget on stilts and then being impressed by his height.

He let the thought chasten him. Hadn't he been doing the same? He cringed at the memory. That big bastard. He obviously wore the jockey shorts to advertise. Showcasing his only talent. Dennis, she had called him? Denis? No, Dennis. The greater width suited him.

'It's all right, Dennis.'

The cow. He should have told her that to her face, except that he didn't particularly fancy being knocked down a flight of stairs. Instead he had stood there, with the flowers and the chocolates advertising his silliness. The gifts denied him any means to make a dignified retreat. They made him feel as if he had wandered into the wrong play. He had no part here. He might as well have been someone in flannels and holding a racquet who appears suddenly in a kitchen-sink drama, saying, 'Tennis, anyone?'

Fucking tennis? Only if you're the ball, my man. He might have been standing there yet, staring into his own stupidity, if the Incredible Hulk hadn't given him his exit line.

'You better leave, pal.'

'Hm,' he said, and turned to go.

'Your bag, David,' she said.

Trying to put all of his contempt into one last stare, he picked up his bag and came downstairs. A stare was safe enough. He imagined he could have been in another country by the time Dennis worked out what it meant.

Anyway, he supposed the contempt was really for himself. It was a long time since he had done anything as naïve as that. It would be a longer time before he did anything as naïve as that again. Hopefully never. The flowers he had placed neatly and ceremoniously in the trash can in the street had seemed symbolic, a bouquet laid at the grave of his sentimentality. It wasn't just the flowers he was putting in the trash can. Belief in the trustworthiness of anybody else went with them. RIP. Even Sandra had turned out to be devious. Why had she turned up at Willowvale after saying she couldn't possibly come there?

He wandered away from the painting. He had always enjoyed coming here to the Gallery of Modern Art. It was like a kind of anti-church for him, a place for mortifying your delusions, for reaffirming the absence of any lasting significance. He liked the gimcrack nature of some modern art, how it often made itself out of any oddments of life that came to hand. It seemed to him an iconoclastic assault on the pretentiousness of the past. Like Rachel Whiteread's subversive plinth. Asked to devise a statue for an empty plinth in Trafalgar Square, she put an upended, pale and ghostly plinth on top of the stone one. She stood reverence on its head. She seemed to be commemorating the emptiness of what we are trying to commemorate. Think of the crumbling significance of a statue of Field Marshal Haig. She seemed to be commemorating the insubstantialness of our ability to commemorate. Think of some grand mausoleum in a deserted graveyard. All we can really commemorate, her plinth seemed to be saying, is our desire to commemorate.

He came upstairs to brood over a piece that he liked. It was called *Inner City*. He stood studying it again. It was like the model of a set for a film, an abandoned back lot in a studio that had been adapting a seedy story by someone like Raymond Chandler. It was hauntingly detailed, a shadowy staircase and office windows and blind apartment blocks that drew you into their dark ambience, making you wonder about what kind of lives would be lived there. It was eerily empty but he thought he could imagine the sort of people who belonged in such a place.

They would be the kind of people Duane Hanson had created – those fibreglass figures, painstakingly constructed from body-moulds, nearly all of them dressed in working clothes or the leisurewear of their time, every one of them rendered in a meticulous detail that records each sagging jowl, each fold of fat, the shadow of minute hairs on the forearm. Painted into what could pass for living flesh, they stand or sit, staring bleakly past any attempt to engage them in eye-contact.

He could imagine them here, blue-collar America trans-ported into this environment: a weary waitress bored into being a submissive automaton, housepainters having a break they don't seem to know what to do with, a fat man wondering why he is mowing a lawn, tourists who stare vacantly upwards, baffled by what it is they are supposed to be admiring. 'We have worked the work,' the expressions on the faces of Hanson's people always seemed to be saying, 'we have bought the tickets, and we have reached a place which is nothing like the way we were told it would be. Is this all there is?' They were the morning-after supplement to Norman Rockwell's *Saturday Evening Post*. The shining-eyed inclu-siveness of Rockwell's Americans became in Hanson the dislocated stare of the dispossessed. They were fixed in their eternal bewilderment, resonant anti-icons, individuals who represented nothing more than their own intractable indivi-duality, the loneliness of the unique bodies in which they were trapped. Harry Beck had mentioned Auden. 'In headaches and in worry vaguely life leaks away,' Auden said. Hanson's people were staring into the truth of it. They were the labourers in the vineyard of the American dream who never got to taste the wine.

He wouldn't be making the same mistake. There was no

dream, American or otherwise. There was only the way things are and what you can do with them. He studied *Inner City* dispassionately, as if it was a map of where he was, and turned away. Here endeth today's lesson.

By the time he came out into the street, he knew what he would do. He would find a hotel and it would be a good one. Don't mourn rejection, celebrate release. The freed man ate a hearty dinner. He would do that. He needed a little more time and a comfortable place to clarify his immediate future. Veronica Hill hadn't narrowed his options, she had expanded them.

'Are you all right?'

'Hm. Why?'

'You look as if you've been crying.'

'Just lack of sleep, I suppose.'

'It was that kind of weekend, was it?'

'Well, you tend to sit up late. Discussing lectures and stuff.'

'And stuff?'

'That's everything, I think.'

She stood watching her mother separate coloureds from whites to be added to her parents' washing. It occurred to her how convenient it was that the thong her mother was holding, before placing it in the appropriate pile, was so skimpy. There wasn't enough of it to retain much dust from the time it had spent on the floor of her room, not to mention being kicked away by David Cudlipp. In the difference between what the thong meant for her and what it meant for her mother she saw an expression of the distance between them. It was a good thing she had been careful not to take the torn dress out of her bag when she removed the other used clothes from it.

'It's been fixed for June,' her mother said.

'What has?'

'The wedding.'

'Wedding?'

'Jennifer's wedding. It's in June.'

'That's nice.'

'Well, I hope so. I just hope she isn't showing too much.'

'She's pregnant?'

'I told you that. Honestly, I think nothing registers with you if it isn't in a book. Or comes by email.'

Email, she thought, and her mother's voice receded from her and the sound of her father mowing the front lawn before the rain came seemed as distant as her childhood.

So, we're nature's freaks. Very impressive freaks, but freaks. We can't just live. We have to dream our lives as well. In taking over the animal world, we interrupted nature with unanswerable questions. No other creature does that. In one of his poems Auden points out that fish are seamlessly a part of nature, in contrast to us. Fish don't begin the day by wondering, Should I swim left today or should I swim right? They just swim. They inhabit their element totally. We stand on our three legs both inside and outside our element. Edmund Blunden has a poem where he talks about going for a walk to get relief from something he's working on: the question of who wrote Shakespeare. All around him he sees a world fulfilled in simply being, a world from which he feels excluded. He notices a flower and thinks how lucky it is. It has no worries like him. He says he 'beheaded it for blooming insolence'. We can't just be in nature. We have to argue with it. We contradict it. We introduce God to it. Even death we haven't accepted as final. People talk of the worm in the apple. We're the apple in the worm. We can't just be. We distort the nature of being with our dreams. And the dreams, we have demonstrated over millennia, are unfulfillable. Open any newspaper any day of the week to see the incursion of the naked animal into society. Think of the horror of the bru-tishness that is happening daily all over the world. We haven't grown out of our animal origins. We have perfected, refined, technologised them. Some of you will have been reading *Heart of Darkness* this term. Human history has located that place precisely. The heart of darkness is the darkness of the heart. Our dreams don't work. But we can't stop having them. We can't just inhabit the present. We try to foresee the future. Even the past can't just be the past. We have to keep ransacking it for meaning to find out if who we were can tell us who we are.

On the bed she looked as if she was lying in state. The light coming through the gauzy curtains from the street-lamp outside softened the furnishings around her, making them look as mysterious as the artefacts in an Egyptian tomb. The dimness also gentled the suffering which had been etched for so long on her face, completed the cosmetic ministrations of the undertakers. The dress was the one she had worn on her last evening out before her living space finally contracted to a wheelchair. Although this stillness had grown upon her by inches, its totality was shocking. She had become sheer fact, immutable.

He stood at the bottom of the bed, staring. His thoughts buzzed aimlessly around her body like flies, still trying to take sustenance from the dead. He was glad he had told the undertakers to leave her here tonight. He had to find a way to take his first farewell. He imagined he would be taking other farewells for the rest of his life. He was glad this was the dress he had chosen. She had loved it, and it was as if he had released her into who she had been before her illness.

If he had had a mobile phone, he would have known earlier. He had phoned regularly from Willowvale, checking on how Catriona was, but Mhairi had given no forewarning that anything was different. But how could she tell? Catriona had spent so long precariously poised between living and dying that she was always liable to leave discreetly and without warning. Between a whisper and silence is no great distance. As far as he could tell from Mhairi's tearfully fragmented account, Catriona had probably died while he was on the ferry. It struck him that he still didn't know the precise cause of death. The doctor had used some technical term which he assumed related to breathing but he had been too disorientated to ask for clarification. He remembered the word 'airways'. He would have to speak to the doctor again. He didn't know what difference the knowledge would make but it was important to him to have it. It seemed disrespectful to let her die without knowing exactly why. He should have had a mobile. He felt as if his aversion to modern technology had caused her to die without him. But then he felt that this thought was just a screen for the one he didn't want to face: he had already abandoned her by being with Vikki Kane.

He stood before her like a penitent for whom there could be no absolution. Her ignorance could never forgive him. She was a shrine to emptiness at the end of a pilgrimage he had rendered meaningless. He hadn't paid Mhairi for the weekend. She hadn't asked for the money and probably never would now but he should see to that. No. It shouldn't have happened like this. Not like this. This wasn't the way it should have ended.

He remembered how it had started, as a casual little accident in a kitchen. 'It's a good thing we don't know what's in front of us,' his mother used to say. She had meant what's in the future. But that moment in the kitchen had literally been right in front of him and he hadn't imagined what it meant. But life is deceitful. It fills our time with countless, successive minutiae and suddenly one of them develops elephantiasis, overwhelms everything else and comes to dominate our entire existence. A careless step into the road that leaves us crippled. The pallor of a child that becomes meningitis. The minute lump that is cancer's calling-card.

He remembered that day clearly now, the brightness of the sunshine flooding the kitchen, the laughter they were sharing, the bottle of wine that was rubied with light. Thanks to the wisdom of retrospect, it was all imprinted on his mind like the memory of an ordinary Eden from which they had been expelled. Did he truly remember those things or had regret constructed them? It didn't matter. Either way, the loss was just as sore.

He had been chopping vegetables on the breadboard, which he had placed on the worktop, when he heard the noise. He turned and saw her face vaguely bemused, as if she had no idea how what had happened could have happened. The broken cup was lying on the floor. The brown ingredient for the sauce she was preparing to mix had spread on the tiles like the map of an unknown country. And that was it. Catriona had dropped a cup and their lives were smashed. The casual remorselessness of it gave him hurt still, for both of them.

The incident was erased with laughter at the time. He kidded her about the side-effects of menstruation. But, like the other early responses they were to try, kidding proved to be inadequate. Being deliberately more careful didn't cure her growing clumsiness. Diet didn't help her lethargy. Being tested for spectacles offered no way round her deteriorating eyesight. There was no diversion they could take to avoid the road they were travelling. Catriona had multiple sclerosis.

The term had closed round them like a shared strait-jacket, inhibiting the movement that their lives could have. Once he knew, there was, of course, only one reaction he could have. He was devastated for Catriona, for the dimming that would come to the brightness in her eyes, for the slow congealing of the vivacity of her nature, for her outgoingness relentlessly turned inwards. He felt both rage for her and determination to help her to defy the disease as far as possible.

But he had also learned, against his will, how the only thing to do can be a terrible thing to do, how contracting your life to one natural response can painfully, over the years, blunt and suppress so many other natural responses that you lose touch with who you might have been, even with who you are. He could never regret devoting so much of his life to Catriona's illness. He couldn't not regret the effects of the devotion on himself. You had misgivings either way. Maybe that was why his life had become a guilt-machine, manufacturing doubts like small obstacles to everything he did.

There were no obstacles now. He could do anything he wanted. But there was nothing he could think of that he would ever want to do. Why couldn't he feel what he should feel? She lay there like a final demand for all his love and he had nothing to offer. He stood there, a stranger contemplating a stranger. Nothing was happening. Something more than this had to happen. He walked round the bed, leaned over her and kissed her forehead. It wasn't a final meeting, it wasn't a final parting, it wasn't anything. Stone was kissing stone.

He came out of the bedroom and came slowly down the stairs. He went into the living-room and sat down in the darkness. He had phoned Aileen. She had arrived at the house and looked at Catriona and cried for her sister. He and she had embraced across a void that had only ever been bridged by Catriona. She would tell her mother, who had dementia and was in a home. That would be a strange meeting.

He had to do something. He would phone somebody. Catriona had been so isolated for so long that he wondered who might find her death remotely meaningful. As far as most people were concerned, she had probably been dead to them for a long time. He thought of how much she had enjoyed the presence of Harry Beck. He got up and put on the light and looked for the list of those who had gone to Willowvale.

As he was dialling, he stopped, as if the phone had given him an electric shock. He had begun to dial the number of Vikki Kane, which was on the same sheet of paper. He stared at his hand the way he might have looked at a friend who had betrayed him. He very deliberately dialled Harry's number. The connection was made at the second ring.

'Hello?'

'Harry? It's Andrew.'

'Andrew. How are you?'

'I hope I'm not disturbing you.'

'No, no. I've been trying to do some scribbling. Listen.

Thanks for having me on the weekend. It was . . . an experience.'

'Harry.'

Andrew instantly felt the finality of what he was going to say, as if the silence were stone on which his words would be carved.

'Catriona's dead.'

He was waiting for Harry's reaction like confirmation of something he didn't quite believe.

'My God. Andrew. I'm sorry. I'm sorry. I'm sorry.' There was a pause. 'When?'

'It happened when we were on the way home. I suppose it's been imminent for a while.'

'That doesn't make it any easier when it does happen. Ah, that's hellish news, Andrew. I only met her a few times. But she was such a nice woman.'

'A lot nicer woman than I've ever been a man, I'm afraid.'

'No, Andrew. I can't go there with you. I'm sure Catriona couldn't either. Would you like me to come round?'

'Thanks. But no. I'm all right.'

'Are you sure? I can get a taxi and be there in twenty minutes. Not a good time to be on your own. Maybe you need somebody with you just now.'

'That's kind. But I think I have to be alone tonight.'

'Do you want to talk a bit?'

'No. I just wanted to tell somebody she liked. And liked her.'

'At least I qualify for that. I thought she did terrific with what she got. And so did you. You're two of my heroes, Andrew. I'll be thinking about you both.'

'Thanks.'

'I'm sorry, Andrew.'

'Thanks.'

He had to put the phone down quickly. He was crying. The warmth of Harry's voice had thawed him into feeling. He had touched the reality of what had happened by proxy and it had come home to him. He didn't know whether he was crying for her or for him or for everything.

He took another After Eight, placed it carefully on his tongue, sipped his whisky and let the two tastes argue pleasantly in his mouth, before kneading them into unity, and swallowing. He did it again. He liked the economy of it, recycling waste into consumption, turning his folly into sustenance. That's what he would have to do. There must be ways.

The obstacle is the path. He had read that, somewhere he couldn't remember. He hoped it wasn't in a self-help book. Sandra had bought a couple of those recently and he had glanced through them. More full of shit than a blocked toilet. He hoped he hadn't picked up any germs of hand-clapping optimism from them. The obstacle is the path. He thought it might be from Eastern thought. He supposed it meant that being required to solve a problem resulted in creating new possibilities, that an enforced diversion could open up another direction. At least he had his career.

He adjusted his position on the big comfortable bed. He felt relaxed in just trousers and a woollen sweater. He studied his bare feet. He took another thoughtful sip of whisky, wayfarer at the crossroads. Fair enough. This was a good hotel. He liked hotels. They asked no questions, except those to which the answer was a credit card. The meal had been good and now the mini-bar attended, a barman who never said a word, just silently dispensed maintainers of your mood.

This was all right for a night, but provision had to be made for tomorrow and after. He had to think about that. Veronica Hill was dead to him. He drank to her interment in the past. He had successfully extricated himself from Jacqui Forsyth. Calling out Veronica's name had been more effective than hours of argument. One word had amputated them from each other. He was free. He liked the feeling. Now there were other possibilities. He wondered about Alison Miller. She had been interesting. But he needed a temporary safe-house, a vantage-point from which to plan ahead in comfort. The flat was the only available option. It might not prove easy but it would have to be done. He couldn't afford to stay too long in this place, and he would need time to transfer as much money out of the joint account as he wanted.

He would have to phone. He would use the mobile. Every time you used a hotel phone, they seemed to link you up via America. He reached across and took his mobile from the bedside table. He lay jiggling it in one hand while he held his whisky in the other. He was preparing himself for the call. But he didn't want to overprepare. Flexibility was the key, pre-paredness to manipulate whatever responses you received. He touched out the numbers carefully, as if they were the combination to a safe.

He came upon instant profit. The vulnerability of her voice on answering made it seem easy to persuade her not to put the phone down. He kept talking quietly but steadily, explaining that they had to meet and the sooner they did the better it would be for both of them. She answered monosyllabically in a dead monotone. She agreed that he could come to the house tomorrow and they would talk. Killing the connection with his thumb, he dropped the phone on the bed and punched the air. He took another After Eight. As well as the chocolates, maybe he should have kept the flowers as a peace offering. Crossing to get another miniature of whisky, he caught himself in the wardrobe mirror. Staring at his reflection, he put a clenched hand inside his sweater at the shoulder, so that it looked like a hump. He made a demonic face at himself.

'I'll have her,' he said. 'But I will not keep her long.'

When she had put the phone down, she crossed to the fridge and took out one of the bottles of champagne. Uncorking it with difficulty over the sink, she filled a glass and sipped. What she was celebrating, she decided, was the departure of naïvety. If she could maintain for long enough the appearance of a successful marriage, surely she would still be able to adopt Angela. As far as she was concerned, they were already divorced. Their past was a mockery of what she had thought it was. But she would play him any way she could until she had the only thing she wanted from the emptiness between them, the child they had never had. She sipped again, noticing the similarity between an effulgent sunset and a dawn.

The pub was quiet except for a small man who seemed to be arguing half-heartedly with the barman. There weren't many other people in the place besides themselves. Three older men were talking quietly at the bar. She and Mickey were sitting at a table. At the only other occupied table two old men were staring ahead in unison, like matching ornaments. It wasn't the kind of place she could remember having been in before but she felt safe being here with Mickey.

'You all right about coming back?' he said.

'Of course,' she said.

'It's not exactly a penthouse.'

'I suppose it's got a bed,' she said, surprising herself.

'Two, actually. And it's not as bad as it was before Donnie moved out. I've made a few kind of gestures towards house-work. You'll be fine if you keep your eyes shut. You feel all right about not going back to your own place tonight?'

'Maybe I feel all right about never going back. Jacqui was weird today. She didn't want me to sit beside her on the bus. And all that crying. I hope Alison can cope with her. Anyway, I'm fed up sleeping on the fold-down bed. What about Donnie?'

'He's still alive. That amounts to a triumph for him. You know why he slept in the lounge? Couldn't remember the room number. Got fed up trying doors. Good thing for us, eh?'

He stood up.

'Need to hit that hole-in-the-wall,' he said. 'Finance our amazing lifestyle. You okay? Won't be long.'

'I'm fine,' she said, and smiled.

But when he went out she had an immediate sense of risk, the vulnerability of being alone in a strange place. She felt herself as an unprotected presence. Maybe that was one thing losing your virginity meant. Brute reality had found a way in. She was aware of its proximity now, the harsh truth of its nearness in this garishly lit room. Perhaps fantasy had its uses. She thought of a time in the flat.

Jacqui and Alison had been talking about sexual experiences

and the conversation came round to the first time you had done it. When they had finished laughing and turned towards her, she waited for a moment and then told them about Davy.

He was a boy who was at school with her, who had since become a professional football player. She described the place where they went one night – under a bridge in Inverness during a school trip. They did it standing up. She said she felt he was assaulting her with some kind of object.

'Well, that's what sex is,' Alison had said. 'Benign assault with a blunt instrument. And sometimes not so benign.'

There was water dripping all around them, she said. She described it as like doing it in a cave. Then she was dripping, too. He was very concerned about the blood. She still looked occasionally for his name in the papers, under the results, where they put the goal-scorers but she didn't know which team he played for.

'He certainly scored that night,' Jacqui had said and they had all laughed.

She was surprised at how easily the confession had come out, especially since none of it had happened. There had been a Davy at school but the most physical thing he had ever done to her was wave to her once in the street. She was glad they hadn't asked for his second name. It was bad enough inventing a liaison with somebody without passing on his surname as well.

After that, she created a couple of other assignations with phantom lovers. Once in a dingy flat. Once in the bedroom of someone with wealthy parents. That was an exciting episode in her life. The furnishings had been amazingly plush. One wall of the room was lined with the mirrored doors of a fitted wardrobe, in which they could see themselves making love. It got her so interested she almost believed it.

Perhaps the exposure she was feeling now was just the result of being out of the swaddling clothes of make-believe.

A young man came through the door of the bar suddenly. He was gasping and red-faced. He seemed to come too quickly into the middle of the room. You could tell he had been running. His stride was slightly out of control, as if the message from his brain that he could stop running now hadn't yet reached his legs. The blind look in his eyes was something Kate used to associate with the eyes of her friends coming out of a cinema matinée. It wasn't only a matter of adjusting to the light. The recent past had seemed more present than where they were. They were having to wait until the vivid images of where they had been receded before they could see clearly.

The man focused. His awareness seemed to arrive to join his body. He crossed to the bar. The barman came along to stand in front of him.

'Could you get me a half-pint of lager and a taxi?' the man said.

'A taxi?' the barman said. 'What kinda drink's that?'

'No, I mean a real taxi.'

'One with a driver in it?'

'That would help. I've had a bit of bother. I know it's a liberty to come in and ask you like this. But I don't fancy going back out on the street.'

'That's all right. I thought you meant something like a Sidecar or that. The names of these drinks is changing every week these days. I'll get the drink first. You look as if you need it.'

When he had served the man, the barman phoned.

'That'll be about ten minutes,' he said. 'So what was the problem?'

News of the taxi was like an instant readjustment to the

man's thermostat. He shook his head. He took a small sip of the lager and replaced the glass on the bar. When he started talking, everybody was listening except the small man, who seemed to be continuing the argument with the barman in his head.

He was going home alone when someone shouted at him from across the street. He was lost in his thoughts and it took him a moment to locate the sound. Opposite were several teenagers – he thought there were five of them – and they were moving their arms backwards and forwards in time with one another to point at him, like a football crowd, he said.

'Five of them?' one of the men at the bar said. 'They must support ma team. That's the kinda crowds we get.'

The teenagers were jeering and they started to chant. 'Say goodnight, wanker. Say goodnight.' They started to run towards him and he ran away. He was lucky some passing cars delayed them long enough to give him a good start. They chased him for a couple of streets until he heard one of them shout, 'To hell with it. Let's get that old bastard over there.'

She was starting to worry about Mickey when he came back in. She repeated the story to him as the taxi-driver arrived and the young man went out with him. As Mickey and she chatted she was aware of the men at the bar talking about how things had changed in their lifetime, like a descant to their own voices she couldn't quite shut out.

'It's great we found each other.'

'Think of thirty years ago.'

'I know.'

'You've paid your dues. If you can't see any difference between then and now, ask for your money back. You've missed the show.'

'We're going to be good together.'

'No rules to violence now. About as macho as pulling the wings off a fly.'

'As long as you learn to like Tolkien.'

'Don't know. Sometimes love can ask too much.'

'Private terrorism. The weaker the victim the better they like it.'

'I'll listen to Coldplay.'

'I think I'll emigrate.'

'Where to?'

'Same everywhere. Nowhere to hide.'

Mickey took her hand and smiled. She was remembering that Mickey's only reaction to the story of the incident in the street had been to raise his eyebrows. It was the first time she had felt it might be possible to be alone in his company.

She thought of Willowvale. She had supposed it had been what an idyll is. But perhaps idylls were only recognised in retrospect and you couldn't travel deliberately towards them. Certainly, as Mickey released her hand, winked, stood and lifted their bags, she couldn't imagine how to get to a place that wouldn't have the kind of hurt in it that must have happened to the old man the teenagers had decided to settle for. She just wanted to try.

Mastectomy. Chemotherapy.

The words waited for her like instruments of torture under which she wasn't sure she could hold her nerve. She had heard them often enough before, words that went in and out of conversations, evoking a sympathetic shiver, like news of a mugging that had happened to someone else. Now they had come to live with her, frightening presences that stared at her when she woke up in the darkness, looked over her shoulder at every book she read, made an irony of Jason's casual treatment of her, accompanied her to the supermarket, biding their time. Their time was now.

She had looked them up in the dictionary several times, as if to confirm that they really existed, as if to verify the address of a place she was moving to. The dictionary didn't tell her much about what it would be like to be there: 'the surgical removal of a breast'; 'treatment of disease, esp. cancer, by means of chemical agents'. She liked the casualness of the *esp*. She had thought of trying to find out more but she had decided not to. She suspected that to know too much about a dread, to pace out its dimensions too precisely, made it overwhelm you more effectively. It was enough to know that the words had climbed out of the dictionary to find her. To meet them she needed the irrational defiance of a certain amount of ignorance.

She had managed to sustain that until now. She had wept a lot at first but the tears had begun to space themselves out, just punctuation for the resolution she was trying to make herself express. She would try not to let them happen tonight. She touched her left breast, as if reassuring herself that it was still hers.

Her breasts. She remembered a summer day before she and Alan were engaged. She would be twenty. She was to meet him at his office in Bath Street to go for lunch.

The day stood like a crossroads in her memory, a time when she took a turning from which she was still trying to find her way back. She sometimes felt it had led her insidiously, step by step, to where she was now.

It had been a day of fierce sunshine, or so it seemed to her now. It had certainly been bright and she remembered it as very warm with the kind of heat that makes you aware of your skin, conscious of the fact that, no matter what you are wearing, you are really clothed in your own flesh. That day she didn't simply know what nubile meant. She lived it. Her breasts were like antennae sussing out summer. She had by then come to accept the effect they had on men. She should do. She had had plenty of time.

They had arrived early when she was a girl, as if nature had mixed up the dates and had her down as sixteen in its records. She was twelve when her breasts became alarmingly obvious. She couldn't have been more embarrassed if she had been a boy who had started to go bald at twelve. She was miserable.

She started to find excuses for not taking gym. She tried to learn to sleep lying on her chest. She pleaded with her mother to buy her blouses in a bigger size. She slouched around, furtively aware of being someone with a sad deformity, the Hunch Chest of Notre Dame. Some of the girls began to treat her as if her sudden development were the result of a personal choice, the flamboyance of a show-off. Their eyes followed her like gossip. She often worried about what the gossip was. Some of the boys took to sniggering as she passed. She didn't want to know what they might be saying, although some of the remarks, fired at her from the safety of the group, gave her more idea than she wanted to have.

She knew now what that painful phase of her life had been about – three or four years in which a girl was obliged to walk around in the body of a young woman. Her body had been delivered to her like a DIY kit without instructions included. She had all the parts but she couldn't put them together, so she was obliged for a long time to provoke reactions to which she could find no imaginable response.

But something happened. Slowly the feelings came to fit the

body she had been given and she began to feel good inside it. It was then that the misery she had experienced turned to something positive. The standoffishness of other girls revealed itself as jealousy. The threats of the boys became immaturity. She wasn't an ugly duckling. She was a swan.

Having been a woman for years before she knew she was one, she seemed to have a kind of accrued, retrospective maturity to draw on. She started going out with older men. But she handled herself carefully and by the time she met Alan, who was five years older, she was still a virgin. Three weeks after she met him she wasn't.

It had seemed so right at the time. She was glad she had waited. She was enjoying exploring sex. He made her laugh a lot. They knew they were going to get married. Any problems that arose were just part of making the necessary adjustments to becoming a couple, like that day in summer.

She had been very clothes-conscious then. She chose to wear a tight pair of black jeans. The memory made her conscious of what she was wearing now. She stood up and looked at herself again in the mirror. She turned and looked over her shoulder. She seemed as trim now as she had been then. But what surprised her was that they might have been the same jeans. She had bought them on impulse, unaware that she had been replicating a moment from eighteen years ago. Was she trying to erase the intervening time and begin again?

The thought depressed her, not just because she knew it wasn't possible. You could move beyond the past but you couldn't deny it. You could transform its meaning but you couldn't wipe it out. What really depressed her was that perhaps the attempt to contradict Alan's influence so determinedly, if that was what she had unconsciously been doing, might merely be a way of acknowledging it.

She looked at the Lycra top. At least that was different. But not very much different, she had to admit. For a start, it was white. That day she had worn a white cotton bustier. How different was that? Not exactly the transformation of Vikki Kane. She drained her glass and went through to the kitchen to get the wine-bottle from the fridge.

That summer day the bustier had accentuated her breasts nicely. She hadn't minded that by then. She had grown used to the way men appeared to be fixated by them. She had suffered enough in coming to terms with them; she could enjoy them now. She had earned her tits, she had decided, the way they said knights used to earn their spurs.

So when she resolved to walk to the lawyers' office where Alan had recently begun to work, carrying the woven black bag over her shoulder, she felt good in herself. The glances and the whistles didn't bother her. She could afford innocently and accidentally to flirt with the world because there was only one man she was interested in and she was going to meet him. He was the armour that made any incidental advances harmless.

In Bath Street scaffolding had been erected in front of a building maybe fifty yards from Alan's office. As she manoeuvred herself round it, she heard the chorus of workmen from above her. Hullo, hullo there. Does yer mother know ye're out? Room for one more up here. Jesus Christ, look at those.

She thought they must have an interesting view from above and she would have become seriously flustered if she hadn't seen Alan emerging on the steps outside his office. He was watching her as he came down on to the pavement. She kept her eyes fixed on him, smiling as she came. He was her protection against this and she came into the haven of his presence gratefully. She didn't realise the haven was an ambush.

'What the fuck are you doing?' he said, as she leaned towards him.

What should have been a kiss felt like a slap. She stared at him. She thought she had been walking along the street. She felt immediately vulnerable and isolated, standing between the workmen and Alan, caught between two simultaneous expressions of the one aggression.

'Jesus Christ,' he said. 'Look at you. You might as well be carrying your tits on a silver salver.'

He glanced up at his office window and started to walk quickly away in the opposite direction from the workmen, obliging her to teeter after him. She could barely keep up. She felt towed in the wake of an anger the force of which was wildly in excess of any reason she could give it. She was aware of how dusty the street was and she felt suddenly cold, as if the weather had changed.

'It didn't occur to you to put clothes on?' he said.

'I thought I had,' she said.

'Did you?'

'I'm wearing jeans, for God's sake.'

'No, the jeans are wearing you.'

She had no idea what that was supposed to mean. She wasn't sure Alan did either. His mouth seemed to be working of its own accord, making gasping noises and hisses and contorting itself strangely.

'And that,' he said. 'What the hell is that?'

'It's called a bustier.'

'No wonder it's called that. That's what it does, all right. They should call it a massive-tittier. You never heard of decency?'

'Listen, in my book this is decent.'

'What's your book? The *Kama* fucking *Sutra*?'

It was a dire day. They raged at each other as they walked. There was no way he was going to lunch with someone dressed like that. There was no way she was going to lunch with someone whose mind was so narrow he could have worn a thimble for a hat. They parted simply by taking two different directions at a corner without saying goodbye.

She was furious and, when someone whistled as she passed, she became more furious at the gawky stranger and went into Marks & Spencer and bought a fine black cardigan, which she wore on the way home. What she had convinced herself at the time was an attitude of defiance to the attitudes of all men had come to seem to her now a gesture of submission to the attitudes of one man.

Sitting with a fresh glass of wine, she saw that black cardigan as her beginning to conceal the reality of who she was. She might as well have bought a mask.

It had been a trivial thing to do but perhaps it had become definitive. It seemed to her that, since then, readjusting her sense of herself to come closer to his demands had become a habit. It hadn't happened dramatically but by an accumulation of tiny deaths of instinct and impulse that grew together like a coral island, on which she was stranded. For the truth was that all her small submissions hadn't brought them any nearer. The further she had gone from the spontaneity of herself, the further she had gone from the possibility of maintaining any dynamic connection with him.

It seemed so obvious now. But she reflected that the minutiae of our behaviour are often too small to decipher until they cohere with time into one massive statement which we can sometimes only read when it is too late to make significant alterations. When Alan phoned her in the evening of that summer day, for example, she had still been very angry. But he was apologetic and he explained that the intensity of his love for her made him sometimes irrationally jealous. Wasn't jealousy one measure of love? And then they both had to laugh at the outrageousness of their reactions. *Kama* fucking *Sutra* became code between them for saying that one or the other was becoming stupidly jealous.

It had appeared funny at the time but maybe they had been laughing all the way to the divorce courts. Meanwhile, behind the laughter, she supposed that the more she was adapting herself to fit his image of her, the more he was becoming bored with her. And the more, perhaps, she was becoming bored with herself. Perhaps that was why she had changed the spelling of her name from Vicky to Vikki after Alan left her. In spite of what Andrew had said, it was a sympathetic magic which didn't seem to have worked, she had to admit.

Not much had worked, she thought. Not the attempt to change her mind as well as her name by going to university at thirty-seven. Not her commitment to Jason. She had managed to talk to him tonight. He had sounded so happy that it depressed her. She felt completely unnecessary. She thought she had got everything wrong.

She remembered Harry Beck mentioning *Heart of Darkness*. One of the passages she had underlined in the book was apposite to the way she felt, she suspected. She went to retrieve the book now and found what she was looking for, marked by an asterisk in the margin. She was hesitant to read it again.

'Droll thing life is – that mysterious arrangement of merciless logic for a futile purpose. The most you can hope from it is some knowledge of yourself – that comes too late – a crop of unextinguishable regrets.'

She had plenty of those. She sat feeling locked inside the quotation like a condemned cell. But she couldn't resist wishing that some message might still arrive there, a reprieve, no matter how tenuous or improbable. Or temporary.

Like a ringing phone? With Andrew at the other end?

In the sunlit office where I booked my ticket on a different day and in another town, they had given me the traditional choice between sun and shade – sol y sombra. I had opted for the more expensive sombra. This evening in Girona I see I needn't have bothered. Sombra is your lot. The sky is like a lead casting. It will leak spasmodic rain throughout. This is just another working day in the bull-ring.

The crowd is sparse and we seem to be mainly tourists. Like people who may visit a solemn cathedral just to say they've been there and to loot its imposing stillness with their cameras, some of us might be said to be cheapening the meaning of the place with the shallowness of our motives. But that won't matter too much here. Unlike so many modern events, where hype replaces judgement with hysteria and glamorises mediocrities into superstars, the bullfight contains at its heart something so purely dark that it defies super-ficiality of response. Superficiality may be all you bring to it, right enough, but then all you are cheapening is yourself.

The parade they call the paseo is over. The matadors, the banderilleros, the picadors, the drivers with their small har-nessed horses which will drag out the body of the bull – all have paid their respects to the president's box. The old men with their flat wooden rakes have made smooth again the surface of the sand. One of them had a long cigarette dangling from his mouth. It was startlingly white in the dully lucid air.

There is a stillness, a brief congealing of time. The ring is empty. I am aware how remorselessly the space is defined by the red-painted barriers of wood between the ring and the barrera, behind which a man who is in trouble or who has abandoned his nerve can find concealment from the bull. These are the burladeros. Behind them wait the matador and his banderilleros, each with no more protection than his tight-fitting suit of lights and a cape.

The entrance of the bull will always be one of the most physically electrifying things I have ever seen, like a surge of primal memory in the blood. Suddenly, in the carefully contrived structure of the ring, there appears the essence of the animal, as if summoned by necromancy out of a darker past we used to share with it. It is like watching a Lascaux cave painting come to life. The span of the horns is shocking. The beautiful power of the bull is overwhelming.

You realise what a frail species we are. In the gasp of the crowd I sense admiration and envy and fear. We are lucky to be sitting in our man-made safety, out of distance of its questing rage. We were not always. It is trotting relentlessly around the ring, its head on a high and threatening swivel, looking for anything that will challenge it. How, you imagine, could such majestic and fearless power ever be subdued? But then that is the story of the bullfight. It is the story of ourselves.

For see what happens. Throughout the six encounters with six bulls the same ritual forms will be repeated in the same exact sequence. First, the matador and his banderilleros will show themselves slightly beyond the edges of their shelters and shout to the bull: 'Hoy, hoy, hoy. Toro.' Having encouraged it to make maybe half a dozen long and powerful charges, they will have withdrawn again just in time behind their burladeros to let the bull horn the wood. Then they will play it gingerly and briefly with their capes. Then the picadors will enter on their horses, which are heavily protected with metal and padding. With their wooden lances tipped with steel, they will stick it. If they are good enough, they will wound it only in the morrillo, the hump of muscled flesh that rises at the base of its neck when it is angry. This same place will be the target for the banderilleros who follow. Holding a banderilla in each hand, they must time their lateral run across the horns of the charging bull and place both of the harpoon-tipped dowels wrapped in coloured paper in the morrillo.

Finally, the matador will have his dance of death alone with the bull. He must give it its chances with his cape, invite it near but past his body, work close to the horns, make a graceful ballet of the danger he is in. At moments of arrogant confidence in his mastery, he will turn his back in the immediate vicinity of the standing bull's head and strut slowly towards the facing crowd, inviting plaudits. When the bull's head hangs low enough, he will sight along his sword and, as the bull advances, sink the sword to the hilt, if he is good, in the one small space on the shoulders that isn't blocked by bone. The bull sinks slowly. The death of the bull is elemental and it is infinitely sad. Its vast strength thaws into death before your eyes, like a mountain melting.

Six times it happens here tonight, with differing degrees of skill from the matadors and the banderilleros and the picadors. But one thing is constant. It is the awesome power the ritual holds in itself. The more you watch honestly, the more it unfolds its dark meaning.

It begins with a gang against the bull, for no single man

could take on the beast in its primal state. Man had to hunt in packs. It proceeds by using the tamed part of the animal world against the untameable part. The broken-in horse will be man's servant in the killing of what is wild. Only after the horses have carried the picadors will two men take on the bull in flight, with weapons. And only then will the matador alone elaborately demonstrate his authority over the bull to the point of death.

We have been watching the enactment of a tragic myth – the story of man's mastery of the animal world. All the bull has is the power of his blood and we drain him of it before we can face him one on one. The bull has one trick – fearless strength. We have many. The bullfight symbolises these.

It has always been a shaky myth, one we are not entirely sure of – which is why the bull must die or the myth won't hold. It has always been a cruel story, which is why it must be told with such great style. The dignified grammar of the bullfight is how we make an art of our cruel mastery, to justify it. At least we have grace. It is not so much an evolution myth as a civilisation myth. It is how we came to be where we are.

Now that we are here, many would no doubt wish to ban the bullfight. But I don't see how we can, at least not ban what it stands for from our natures. It would be like putting lace doilies over ineradicable bloodstains. They may not be visible that way but they're still there. They still mean what they meant.

Bring your attitudes of refined outrage to the bullfight if you wish. I will not share them.

Later, in the centre of Girona, I eat a long slow meal alone. It is a soft evening. I am remembering a small blond boy in front of me who cried through much of the bullfight. Those were wise tears. I am watching people eating and talking and walking in the colonnaded square. I am feeling how sweetly fragile life is. I am thinking how thin the membrane of civilisation is on which our lives walk delicately, liable to fall through at any moment into darker places.

Rereading the sentences, he wondered where the compulsion had come from to write them. Those bullfights had happened a long time ago. He had watched them and come away and finally taken a taxi to the airport. In the time between then and now he hadn't realised how vividly the capes were still swirling and bulls still subsiding into stillness on the sand somewhere in his memory.

It was strange that he should have resurrected that day for himself now. It occurred to him that perhaps the theme of the weekend had brought it to the surface and his mind had been working quietly away, like a clerk collating further evidence for a lawyer's case. But the words he had written felt more personal to him than that. When he had sat down in the dawn light at Willowvale he hadn't been looking for evidence to support an argument, he suspected. He had been looking for evidence of himself.

What had taken him back to Girona was the intensity of what he had felt then. It was the need to reclaim a moment where he had thought he might find an utter authenticity of feeling, unalloyed with self-delusion. The man at the bullfight then was nearer to himself than he was now. In revisiting him he had been trying to meet with a sense of who he was that went beyond the improvisational performance he knew had become his daily life. It was a performance that didn't quite convince even himself.

He thought he knew why he had felt the need to discover that earlier sense of himself. Something had been quietly haunting him all weekend, and it wasn't the ghost of Willowvale. It was something he had felt the morning before he left, when he was in his flat with Mary Sue. It was an emanation of himself which suddenly confronted him like a doppelgänger, the ghost of who he might have been.

It was almost as if Mary Sue were talking past him to where she knew he really was. She accepted the levity he had refined into an unguent to let intimacy pass painlessly into departure. She had maintained the levity, proving better at it than he was, but she had done it abstractedly, as if waiting for who he might really be to show up. He wished he *had* shown up because, in turning himself into an identikit of the casual lover, he hadn't allowed her the space to do more than be the same. He had sustained it to the end. Even inside the cab, before he dropped her off, he had defied closeness by sustaining a three-way conversation involving the driver.

He felt in a way that he had missed the chance of meeting her because there hadn't been enough of him present to make up a couple. That doppelgänger was the missing part of him that should have been there. At least he had found him sitting alone in a sparse crowd on a dull night in Girona.

He would want him along if he met Mary Sue again. He looked at the phone on the desk beside him. He picked up the piece of paper on which he had written on Friday morning and checked the number, although he already knew it by heart. But he wondered how you recovered something when you weren't sure what it was you had lost. He dropped the piece of paper back on the desk.

He looked again at what he had written about the bull-fights, skimming it. He couldn't imagine any use to which he could put it. But that was how he had started to write years ago, reclaiming his experience for himself, earning a sense of himself from what happened to him rather than letting it just happen. It was what he told his students: even if they never published anything, there was a value in what they were doing. It would at least make them better readers. More importantly, the most inalienable right anybody had was the right to try to arrive on their own terms at an honest under-standing of their own experience. To wrestle it into words wasn't the worst way to go about that. Wasn't that what he had been trying to do? To travel back through words for a purpose no more rewarding than an arrival at an attempted understanding of his own experience. It certainly put his latest rejection in a perspective that modified its significance. In the process he had also been doing something for the sake of trying to get it right. That was it.

How long was it since he had been as honest as that to himself? He sat at his desk as if he were in the dock, letting people he barely recognised file in and testify against him. Were they really talking about him? Were they telling the truth?

The woman from the writers' conference. He couldn't be clear where or when the conference had taken place. She was a very attractive woman and in the bar afterwards they had talked so suggestively that he vaguely assumed they had made an assignation, though perhaps his reception-system had been several drinks beyond precision. Later he heard her give her room number to another writer and retire. The chosen man loitered casually in the bar for a long time, holding forth to a small group of devotees. Having listened to enough of the writer's self-advertisement, he went upstairs to the woman's room, quietly opened the unlocked door, stripped and climbed into bed with her in the darkness.

'You took your time, darling,' she said huskily.

She embraced him fervently and suddenly drew back. She stared at him in the dimness while he waited for the police to be summoned. She smiled.

'Oh, it's you,' she said. 'What a pleasant surprise.'

After they had had sex and had fallen asleep, he was wakened suddenly by a loud scuffling noise at the bottom of the bed. A shadowy ogre stood there in the dark. It was the other writer. Naked under the duvet, he lay watching the man with a certain nervous fascination, unaware of any book of etiquette that told you what to say in situations like this. But the writer seemed to have read one.

'I,' he said, 'could write you under the table any time,' and swept from the room, leaving the door open.

He thought he had better close it. As he came back to bed, the woman spoke.

'Don't worry,' she said. 'I don't really know him.'

That's all right, then.

Thinking back, he couldn't believe that he had once done that. He couldn't have been the person who risked being arrested to climb into bed with a stranger. Who was that masked man?

He couldn't stand having any more witnesses recalled. It was enough. He pleaded guilty to whatever the offence was. Trivialising human relationships? Undervaluing his own life and, by implication, those of others? Any women like that had been innocent. All they had done was unselfconsciously express the individuality of their own sexuality. He respected them. What he couldn't respect was his own part in those experiences. He had reduced sex to a game of solitaire for two. The other person was just the deck you were playing with. If you spent your life body-surfing, you couldn't expect to come ashore at some significant place. You had to accept that you would run aground in the same old anonymous sand. He was guilty all right. What troubled him now was what the sentence might be. Turning into Sunbed the Sailor? Perhaps he was already serving it.

He thought of that night in the Ubiquitous Chip, when the three women he called the Post Romantics had casually disembowelled Sunbed with a few oblique sentences. He had been condescending enough at the time to feel sorry for Sunbed. But might they not just as well have been referring to him?

He had sat briefly with Mary, Fran and Christina that night and was about to move when Sunbed came in and went to the bar to order, an act that in itself might mean he would be in for a while. It might be better to stay seated in case you had to talk to him. The nickname had emerged mysteriously from the vox populi and gained currency. You could see why. His face wouldn't have looked out of place hanging from an orange tree. And often when he had ordered the regular Cockburn's, he would hold it up and look at it and say, for the benefit of anyone within earshot, 'I see a girl in every port.'

'Oh, no,' Mary said. 'Look who it is. If he comes over tonight, he gets it. All right? As we rehearsed it.'

Fran and Christina nodded. Those were ominous nods. If their heads had had thumbs, they would have been vertically down. Sunbed had decided that he fancied Mary and had once told him in confidence that reciprocation of the feeling was eventually 'inevitable'. Perhaps the word Sunbed had been looking for was 'impossible'. He was dealing with three divorcees who hadn't liked the settlements.

'Take your cue from me,' Mary said.

Wearing his Clint Eastwood coat as if it could protect him from words, Sunbed came smilingly over with his glass of port and sat down.

'How are you, ladies?' he said. 'Your evening is now complete.'

Nobody said anything. Mary nodded.

'Anyway,' she said. 'As I was saying. Maybe when we get past the male member as fetish, we'll be getting somewhere.'

'I know what you mean,' Christina said. 'And the conditioning starts young. Though I'm hoping my two girls have managed to escape it. I remember changing Ewan's nappy once. The girls are watching. Anna would be three. Sophie six. "What's that?" Anna says, pointing at his penis. Sophie's recently seen a friend's son just after he's come out the hospital, with the umbilical cord still projecting. "Oh, that," Sophie says. "It's all right. It falls off in ten days or something."'

'At which point, no doubt,' Mary said, 'Ewan refilled his nappy and said his first word: "No-o-o!"'

'But maybe Ewan hasn't escaped the dreaded male conditioning,' Christina said. 'Another time. He would be about four. He wanders into the bathroom when his dad's having a bath. And I hear him saying, "You've got a really big one, Daddy." I hear Vince laughing and he shouts, "Say that again, son. I don't think your mum heard you." "I did," I shouts back. "And that boy gets his eyes tested tomorrow."'

'I think it's called forty–forty vision,' Mary said.

'Maybe Vince was playing with the loofah again,' Fran said.

Or words to that effect. And so on. Sunbed didn't try to proposition Mary that evening, seeming to need another drink

235

very quickly. Maybe he should have joined him. He did so now, in a way, by getting up, pouring a whisky, watering it and coming back to his desk.

But he didn't want to belong in that foetid locker-room where Sunbed seemed to feel at home. He suddenly remembered that Mary Sue had referred to having a child. Or was it children? Yes. A daughter and a son. She said they had been staying with friends the night of Dan's party. The name 'Mark' emerged from somewhere, hovering around him in a menacing way. They could be problems.

He absently fingered the piece of paper with Mary Sue's number on it.

I suppose what I'm suggesting is that the oracle consulted by the father of Oedipus is articulating our animal identity, the way we are born. And that the life lived in attempted defiance of the oracle is our social identity, the way we try to be. And that the conflict between them is never quite resolvable. What we have conceived of as humanity is a state we aspire to constantly rather than one we live in. For us, to live is to be endlessly conflicted. Think of the beginnings of this story. Even the initial act of the father is fatally compromised. He doesn't just kill his son, like a wolf devouring its young. He cripples him and gives him to someone else to leave on a hillside. It is neither the animal act of conscienceless slaughter nor what we would think of as the fully human act of sparing a life. It's a crossbreed, not fully of one species or the other. The maiming of the feet. Oedipus becomes the duality of our nature. His father abandoned him, which in itself would simply have restored him to his animal nature. But the father also has the human ingenuity to pierce his feet, which cripples his animal nature. The whole play is the tragedy of compromise, the compromise that is our nature.

He closed Witherspoon's pamphlet and let it rest on his lap, wondering why he had taken the trouble to search for it in the first place. Perhaps, being alone with the body of Catriona in a house now uselessly adapted to her survival, he felt a kinship with Muldoon in Willowvale at the end: both had ended up living in a house the purpose of which had become meaningless.

That must have been a strange time for Muldoon. He could imagine the visionary wandering the empty chambers of his vision. It was then he added a few haphazard features to the building. It was as if he already knew that Willowvale would never be anything but the tomb of his ambitions and he would make it express what his life had taught him.

One of these features, like a bitter afterthought, was the series of six gargoyles on the eastern corner of the structure, facing the mainland. Five of these were traditional grotesques, as if copied from some medieval handbook of frightening faces. The sixth looked strangely modern, might have belonged to Muldoon's time. It showed the face of a young woman, a face which might have been beautiful except for the distortion of its expression. The mouth was distended horribly, wide open in what seemed to be a scream no one would ever hear. Whatever the eyes were staring at, you hoped you never saw it. The frozen hair streamed upwards as if the wind had caught it. Her agony was perpetual.

He suspected he recognised her. There had been an incident in Muldoon's life that Witherspoon referred to briefly as being indicative of his subject's compassion. It could have been equally expressive of his guilt. A young woman in one of his mills had had her hair caught in a loom, was pulled into the machinery and partly ingested by it. The burial of what was left of her was paid for by Muldoon. He also made what was for the time a generous settlement on her family.

His conviction that the event must have been a constant companion of Muldoon seemed to him supported by the presence of that face placed startlingly on his house towards the end of his life. Perhaps that death was to him what the Homestead Strike was to Carnegie – a parallel between the two which Witherspoon carefully didn't draw.

Carnegie was always evasive about the brutality with which Homestead was crushed, an attitude made easier because he had been abroad when it happened. Perhaps he had needed to do that to believe in the purity of his philanthropy. Blood-stained idealism foretells the impossibility of its own realisation. Muldoon as well may have understood in the failure of his own idealism the pollution of its source in things like the death of the young woman. His good intentions were corrupted by what was supposed to enable them.

The gargoyle woman was perhaps the key to the story of Willowvale. More than the unnecessarily large foyer that suggested it would never quite be merely a hotel, more than the impractically grand staircase that renovations had so far failed to make conform to common sense, she defied the present's mundane definition of the place. She silently declared the truth of Willowvale.

It was a stone dream. But part of the dream was nightmare.

Of course. Perhaps that was why he had wanted to read about Willowvale again: it was a massive monument to the kind of futility his own life had been tritely expressing, and some part of him had always known it. It gave him understanding. Or perhaps it was just that he had needed to connect the tawdriness of what he felt his life to be to something big, an imparting of grandeur to his small failure, the way religious people say farewell to brief anonymous lives in hymns that resonate stubbornly with eternity.

He, too, wanted more than this for Catriona. She shouldn't die as unnoticed and quiet as a leaf. She would have no hymns, having always wanted a humanist funeral. She would have no monument, wishing her ashes to be scattered in Loch Lomond. But the rest of his life would be her commemoration. It wouldn't be lasting, but how many things were?

He would live in memory of her. That meant there could be no repeat of his earlier compulsion to phone Vikki Kane. He sat thinking deliberately about Vikki. He contemplated her long and carefully, naming her parts honestly but emotionlessly to himself, as if performing an exorcism. Her eyes confirmed you just by looking at you. Her mouth imparted its hunger to your own. Her smile could induce a sweet derangement in you. Her breasts were awesomely exciting. All right. But all that was over for him now.

It was then he became aware that he had an erection.

It seems to me that every aspect of Sophocles' play feeds into the same central meaning. The prophetic blindness of Teiresias, for example. Teiresias is a blind seer who was claimed to have had the experience of being a woman as well as a man. Oedipus summons him to find out what is polluting the city. Very reluctantly, Teiresias eventually leads Oedipus to the truth – the pollution is himself. Teiresias in his double sexuality is like the incarnation of one of the polarities of our nature. He is the social being in complete ascendancy. He is all knowledge that is lost in the natural world, that leaves the animal side of him a helpless hulk that has to be led around like a dog on a leash. He is power paralysed, unable to fulfil itself in action. He is mind that is almost omnipotently present everywhere and is crippled in its immediate context. Oedipus is his counterpart. He is all action, which has taken him beyond any deeper knowledge of himself. He is virtually omnipotent in his immediate context but power-less to understand that context in its wider implications. The one knows more or less everything about himself but can do nothing about it. He can only know. The other can do just about anything he wants but doesn't know himself. He can only be. Where they meet is in the last stage of the riddle. Each fulfils the last stage of the Sphinx's prophecy. Each incarnates the mean-ing of the riddle, tapping his way forward with a stick. They are the three-legged animal, nature crippled by the ability to conceptualise. The Sphinx's revenge. The Sphinx wins.

She called, 'Mark?'

It was often the first word she said when she came into the house. The question always followed the name like a plea to the Fates. If he answered, it meant that he wasn't lying somewhere hopped out of his head or in hospital or dead by his own hand. The teenage world he lived in seemed to her full of shadows she dreaded would some day materialise into a disaster, the grief from which would then set up house with her for the rest of her life.

Tonight as she shut the storm doors she decided it was all right. The television was blaring from the living-room. That couldn't be Samantha. She lived inside her own routine as if it were a separate apartment. She would be in bed by now.

After locking up, she pushed open the door of the living-room.

'Mark.'

No one was there except a dark man shooting someone on a lonely street, with no witnesses besides herself as far as her house was concerned. She turned off the television and pulled out the plug. As she went upstairs, feeling the initial flutterings of panic begin to happen in her, she was already regretting that Mark was now too old to be obliged to accept a baby-sitter. If he was still out . . .

She opened his bedroom door. The room was in darkness and the bed was empty. She was about to go and waken Samantha when she made him out against the faint, cloud-filtered moonlight. The curtains hadn't been closed. He was standing there, staring up at the sky, like Dracula with earphones. Perhaps he was preparing to fly off into the night. She could hear the muted, persistent thud of the beat from the doorway. God, he was tall. Having his hair gelled up into careful disarray made him look even taller.

She didn't want to go up and touch his shoulder in case he jumped out of the window. He was a tightly wound boy. If she made him start, he would resent it. It would spoil his image. And he certainly couldn't hear her if she spoke.

She switched on the light. He spun round, wide-eyed, then

put on his nonchalance immediately. The light had instantly
created his habitat around him: old socks, discarded sweat-
shirts, scattered CDs, what she called the 'handles' for his
PlayStation, a plate with a fork on it and three empty glasses
on the floor, sticky with residue. He looked like a derelict on
wasteland. Before he could turn away, she signalled him to
take off the earphones. He pulled them down round his neck.

'Hi,' he said.

'Everything okay?'

He nodded vaguely, as if his ears still hadn't cleared
themselves of the music.

'When are you going to tidy this room?'

'Yes.'

She sometimes wished she had an interpreter with them
when they talked.

'When?'

'I'll do it.'

'And it's time you got to bed.'

He nodded.

'Soon. Goodnight, Mark.'

'Goodnight.'

It was nice to have a family chat. As she went out of the
door, he spoke again:

'You have a good night, Mum?'

'Fine, thanks.'

'That's good.'

He put the earphones back on as she was closing the door.
Always that delayed connection, like light arriving through
space long after it was sent. The night had been 'fine'? Only if
your idea of a good time was listening to Janice enumerate the
problems of her marriage.

She went back downstairs to make sure that all the lights

were off and all the plugs pulled out and that everything was generally all right. She felt too tired to be bothered with this but, with someone as careless as Mark in the house, she had turned going to bed into a ritual as compulsive as evening prayers must be for some people. Habit, keep us safe this night.

In the kitchen she noticed again the huge pot of peeled potatoes Alice had left on Friday. She sighed. When Janice had recommended that Alice could come to her for a half-day every week, she didn't explain that it would be like having a poltergeist in the house. Things changed position inexplicably and sometimes disappeared altogether, to turn up months later in strange places. Alice was a good worker and pleasant enough company any time their lives crossed if she came home from work early. But Alice could not be given advice, let alone instructions. She followed her own compulsions.

Potatoes were one. They seemed to exert some kind of mystical influence on Alice. If there were potatoes in the kitchen, she peeled every one. Sometimes coming home, you could find two large pots filled to the brim with potatoes in water. No notes left could stop her, no phone-calls from work expressing a profound longing not to have potatoes tonight. The only way to save their skins would have been to take them with you. Alice had her own special relationship with potatoes. If she looked at one, it peeled.

She also seemed to have selective kleptomania for cleaning fluids. To use them was to take them with her. Discreet questions as to their subsequent whereabouts merely evoked a sharing of your puzzlement. Perhaps a more authoritative sternness was called for but, if things went too far and Alice quit, the untidiness of the house might become such that the three of them lost sight of one another among the clutter.

As she looked at the kitchen now, the possibility seemed very real. Some of Mark's discarded clothes lay on the floor. They were close enough to the laundry basket to suggest that he had at least made a half-hearted effort to throw them into it. There were used plates and cutlery and a box of cereal and a packet of salt and an opened sachet of pâté, all sitting where he had absentmindedly left them while he was transfixed by whatever was on his mind – the meaning of some abstruse pop-song or a topless woman he had seen in one of the magazines he kept under his bed. As she stacked the plates and put things away, she came upon a screwdriver. She wondered what he could have been doing with that. It came from a cupboard with no food in it and, therefore, one that he never looked into. Replacing the screwdriver, she noticed a newspaper pushed to the back of the cupboard.

That was another thing. What was Alice's problem with the printed word? Anything with words on it was hidden away wherever she found handy. Pulling the paper out and closing the cupboard door, she went towards the bin. It was then she noticed that the paper was open at Harry Beck's article on dogs.

He hadn't phoned. Maybe he was just another crossing on Cunard. He didn't deserve to have the article read again but she took it upstairs anyway.

She checked on Samantha, who was sleeping. It was difficult to believe she didn't think she was good-looking.

With the bedside light on, she settled herself to read.

. . . I once visited a man – once was enough – who lived with a Doberman that was a terrible bully. The man was nice enough but he seemed to think that his dog was the house-holder. So did the dog. I'll call it Snarl to protect the guilty . . .

She felt sleepy. It had been a long day. She was finding it hard to keep the thread.

. . . wondering why the man didn't just buy Snarl a twinset and pearls and marry it . . . a progressive tendency in our society: treating animals as people . . . beaches for dogs . . . umbrellas, showers and meals in restaurants . . . Now Bruce . . . this was Wittgenstein with a tail . . .

The paper slipped from her hands and she sank back in sleep. It was a sleep so sweet that when the phone rang she wanted to ignore it. But her hand reached out automatically and took the receiver.

'Hm?' she said.

'Hullo, you,' a dark voice said.

She almost surfaced into suspicion.

'Who is this?'

'Harry. It's Harry Beck, Mary Sue.'

'Oh, the late Mr Beck.'

'Well, I've been away. As you know. But listen. There's some things I want to tell you. I've been thinking about you all weekend.'

'That's nice,' she murmured.

But she wasn't sure if she meant that it was the sentiment which was nice or the voice that expressed it. The voice was deep and gently undulating and very soothing. It was easy to weave it into her sleep. She felt as if she were dreaming. And soon she was . . .

'. . . and I hope you understand what all this means. I don't know when I last felt like this, if I ever did. I'm sorry to have gone on about it for so long. But I had to tell you. I had to tell you before I lost my nerve. I hope I haven't put you off, Mary Sue . . . Mary Sue. Hullo? Mary Sue. Hullo . . . Hu-fucking-llo!'

He switched off and slammed the phone down. How about that? He poured himself another whisky. Maybe he shouldn't take any more. Maybe it was the drink that had ambushed him into trying to write love-poems with his mouth. But he needed pain-killer. He went to the sink and put water in it. Jesus. He walked up and down the kitchen, taking his drink with him like a medical drip. Could you believe that? An elaborate declaration of love that acted as a sedative? It was a new experience. Not one you could enjoy. Jesus. Maybe he should patent himself. He could make a business out of it. What happens is people who can't sleep give him a call and he talks to them. A couple of minutes or so and they're in a deep sleep. He replaces the receiver. Quite a few advantages to the system. You only pay according to the length of time it takes you to fall asleep. Judging by her, it shouldn't be long. Cheap oblivion. You go to sleep with the phone still in your hand. Nobody can disturb you for the rest of the night. Next morning, no woozy chemical side-effects. You've just had a deep and naturally induced sleep. Serious possibilities there. Dial-a-Coma, he could call it. Bugger it.

What was the point? You build yourself up to be able to say something you really mean and it vanishes into the air. He could never find the words to say it as well again. He sat down at the kitchen table, sipping his whisky and stoking his anger. When the phone rang, he stared at it for a moment. He thought of leaving it but it might be Andrew. He took it up. Her voice was muffled.

'Did you call me there? What were you saying?'

'Oh, piss off!' he said, and cut the connection.

But even in his anger he couldn't be sure that he meant it.

So this is why I am writing to you.

She stood up from the computer and walked around. She wasn't sure she should write the letter. She couldn't believe that Alison wasn't here. She had known exactly when they were coming back. And Kate? It was true that she had told Kate she wanted to be alone on the bus but she didn't have to sit so far away. It was as if she couldn't bear to leave Mickey Deans. Love's young wet dream. Very wet.

My life as a leper. She began to wander round the flat convincing herself that she was just saying hullo again to the place, as if she had been on a tour of the Far East. But she knew she was really casing out her own incredulity and making sure Alison hadn't fallen asleep in a cupboard or something. The place was as empty as the way she felt. As empty as the wardrobe Kevin had left her with.

It was as if the world was a conspiracy against her. Were they trying to tell her something? Well, maybe she was getting the message. 'Oh, Jacqui. I won't be back tonight. I'll see you tomorrow. All right?' That was all Kate had said when they got off the bus. And winked. Winked? All right? Kate knew she had been crying on the bus.

And where was Alison? She had thought they were all so close. They shared just about everything, she had thought. So where were they now? It didn't used to be like this. Not since the night that Kevin had dumped her and she phoned them and they came round to help her through it and she told them what had happened.

She had been sitting in the flat she and Kevin shared, with the table laid for a romantic supper. Two red roses in a thin vase. A candle just waiting to be lit. Two places set. The coq au vin was cooking nicely. A bottle of red was opened, becoming what Kevin had told her was *chambré*.

'The pretentious bastard,' she said to them.

It was the anniversary of the night they had met in the Halt. She didn't mind that he hadn't remembered. She had. She wasn't wearing any underwear, just the sheer blue mini-dress. It showed off her thighs, which she thought one of her best features. She was so excited waiting for him, her nipples were like obelisks.

'What an idiot I was,' she said. 'The only thing that got laid was the table.'

She was doing that nervous double- and triple-check thing you do in your head when you really want everything to be just right. Roses, wine, the tie from Liberty in its folded cardboard thingamajig. It would look good in his office. She checked that the coq au vin was simmering nicely, not turning into leather. Then she suddenly wanted to put on the necklace he had given her.

'The only bloody present he ever did give me,' she told them.

She went through to the bedroom to find it when she noticed the door of his wardrobe slightly ajar. When she pushed it, it clicked shut immediately. As she turned away

248

towards the dresser where she kept the few bits of jewellery she had, she suddenly stopped. Something wasn't right. Something didn't fit her habitual sense of things. She worked out what it was. His wardrobe door had never shut so easily before. She had always needed to press some clothes in carefully and release them just at the moment the door was closing or it wouldn't click. She crossed back to the wardrobe and opened the door.

'It was a weird feeling,' she told them. 'As if I was looking at how my heart suddenly felt.'

The wardrobe was empty. She checked for his shirts and pullovers. Nothing. For his shoes. They had walked. Even his Dinky Porsche (promise to himself of all the money he would make some day) had driven off into the sunset.

She was so dumb she sat on the bed, writing Gothic novels in her head about what had happened to him. He had been murdered by burglars and they had disposed of the body and his clothes, so that nobody could ever prove he had been there. He had been abducted by aliens and they had atomised his entire wardrobe. He had amnesia and had packed and was travelling aimlessly round the country, trying to find out who he was.

Then it slowly came to her. If he didn't know who he was, she did. He was a bastard. He had sloped off without even leaving a note. He hadn't even had the courtesy to sit talking soulfully into the early hours of the morning, telling her all that crap about needing his space and mouthing that it's really for her sake because he can't give her the total kind of love she deserves and she'll be better off without him and maybe later it will be different and he'll always think of her with love.

It might just be sleazeball-speak for 'I'm screwing somebody else', but at least it was nicer than vanishing so fast you caused a draught that hung around for months. Your average arsehole would at least do that. But not him. He was gone, leaving her like loose change that had fallen through a hole in his life.

Then, drifting around the place like the ghost of illusions past, she found his key in the kitchen. Mad? She thought the top of her head would come off. She remembered wishing she could even grow back instantly the hair she had shaved off her legs earlier that evening. When Alison and Kate came round in answer to her phone-calls, they brought more wine and a large supply of fresh perspectives on the departed Kevin, like secret photographs they had been hoarding but had hesitated to show her until now. They formed a drunken coven of witches, each throwing her own ingredients into the pot while they drank, casting spells that made a physical grotesque out of what had previously been a reasonably presentable man.

It was then, in the early hours of a drunken morning, that they remembered how horrible the black hairs sprouting out of his shirt collar had been. His fingernails looked as if Godzilla had been chewing them, didn't they? And what about the hair? He was still nurturing the thinning remains, but he would have to own up soon. It was lucky for him baldness was a fashion statement these days. Why is it that baldy men need to have such hairy bodies? And what use could he have had for those 32DD tits? He must have made her feel like Mia Farrow.

And it went on. At one point, peering through two bottles of wine, she had felt panic suddenly and wanted them to stop. She explained that she had had a thought. What if he had taken all his clothes to the dry-cleaner's and would come in any minute now lugging them with him, to find them sitting here among his dismembered remains? There was a brief waiting silence until the three of them collapsed into raucous laughter.

'He's had his coq au vin, then, hasn't he?' Alison said. 'He can lick the plates.'

They all looked at the debris of the meal they had eaten, still lying on the table, and somehow the sight of the empty stew-pot and the greasy plates seemed to them amazingly hilarious and they collapsed again in hysterics. Then Alison came back from a trip to the lavatory, holding up a plain piece of plastic in one hand.

'Exhibit A,' she said.

'That's his,' she said, nodding. 'He's forgotten his shower-cap.'

'Maybe he left it towards the rent,' Kate said. 'Maybe he wasn't all bad.'

And that seemed funny as well.

'Maybe he was afraid the force of the shower would be enough to remove what was left of his hair,' she said. 'Like electrolysis.'

'Shower-cap?' Alison said. 'Oh, that's a pity. I thought maybe I'd found one of his Durex.'

They laughed until she had started to cry and said through her tears that he wasn't that bad in bed, though. They comforted her and agreed that they would all sleep together tonight.

That was the night their friendship became a mutual protection society and they decided to share a flat. Their solidarity was the wagons in a circle and the rest of the world were the Indians.

Now it was just her against the Indians, it seemed. She wandered about the flat, absorbing its emptiness like a lesson that had to be learned by someone who was slow of study. It was on her third visit to Alison's room that she saw the ashtray.

It was made of transparent blue glass, a small curved bowl with one indentation on its rim where a cigarette could sit. Since none of them smoked, they kept it in the kitchen for the use of any visitors with a death-wish who might decide to make a pit-stop here on their way to the grave. It was sitting under Alison's bed. Its blueness shone faintly in the gloom as she stood at the door.

She switched on the light and crossed the room. Going down on her knees, she pulled the ashtray out from under the bed. She held the bowl in her cupped hands, staring at it like an archaeologist who has made a significant find. Knelt there, she thought she could interpret it. Here was time burnt to an ash that held a litter of cigarette stubs. She counted them. There were eleven. Alison's weekend reconstructed in her mind. History essays didn't seem to have been an important part of it. Two people had spent a long time in this bed. She put the ashtray back where it had been. Do not disturb the scene of the crime.

She stayed kneeling in a kind of anti-prayer. There was nothing she could think of that she believed in, not even her friends now. Alison's praise of Willowvale had been a device to keep her out of the flat. Kate was with Mickey Deans. And David Cudlipp. How much did you have to take before you gave it back? In spades, as Kevin used to say. And he should know.

Why had she expended those useless tears on the bus today? She hadn't been able to explain herself to any of the people who had tried to console her. For all they knew, she could have been crying for anything. Rape, for example. No, not rape. That would involve an elaborate court case, the need for incontrovertible proof. But then she could make it clear that she had no wish to pursue the matter in a court of law. She merely felt obliged, for the sake of others, to register the distress her experience had caused her. It was a distress a bus-load of people could vouch for. The university wouldn't be able to ignore it. Her tears would have a purpose after all.

She straightened up, remembering something else. She stood up. She switched off the light and went to find her partially unpacked bag. She opened it and took out the black satin dress. She examined the tear in it and found it suitably ragged. She laid it over a chair. Exhibit A, right enough. She would finish the letter.

Sitting at the computer, she thought for a moment before resuming typing. It was true that his wife had seen them cuddling as they came into her room. But then sex had only happened after that, hadn't it? Perhaps it was knowing that his marriage was damaged anyway that had made him take advantage of her. If he was paying the price, why not demand the goods? She began to type.

While Dr Cudlipp was in my room, he forced himself on me. The sex was not consensual. The force used was such that he tore my dress.

Ladies and gentlemen, we've been sphinxed but don't let it spoil your weekend.

She paused the tape and started to spool forward. She was looking for a moment during the question time that followed Harry Beck's lecture. Mickey Deans had asked a question in a tone of such aggression it had stirred the room from somnolence into tension. Eventually she found it.

'You mentioned in class once that you still regard yourself as a socialist. How is that possible when you have such a jaundiced view of humanity?'

She thought she could almost hear Harry Beck's sad smile.

'First thing is, I don't think it's jaundiced. I think any kind of hope begins in honestly trying to confront what you see as the truth. That's all I've been trying to do. It's the darkness of that truth as I see it that makes me a socialist. After all, the dark is where the dawn comes from. I don't believe in Utopia. You won't find it on any map we can ever make. And if it did exist, we couldn't breathe the air there. It would be too pure for us. But I believe in our ability to drift endlessly towards dystopia. We seem to be programmed for it. As if we were saying to ourselves: if we can't beat the dark, let's celebrate it. I'm against that. I'm a dystopian socialist. Socialism is an attempt to share as justly as we can with one another the terms of human experience. Don't do the dark's work for it. If it's only void out there, let's write our own defiant meaning on it. And make it a shared meaning. I think believing in good is the good. Against all the odds. Even if I'm part of the odds against us. I think it's what makes us what we are.'

She switched the machine off. She had finished her research, as she liked to call it. Tomorrow would be a good day to start. But she remembered reading somewhere about a writer who said in an interview that the moment he had finished one book he wrote the first sentence of the next. John Masters, she thought his name was. The fact that he had started a new project, however briefly, seemed to guarantee that he would at least continue with it. She liked that idea and her first sentence had already shaped itself in her mind. She would fix it in its place tonight.

But she sat on a little longer, slowly arranging the papers in front of her into categories for convenient reference. She was tired. She had managed a little sleep on the bus to the ferry but the fuss that was being made of Jacqui Forsyth meant that any sleep she had was only fitful. She had noticed that one person who had seemed conspicuously uninvolved in whatever crisis Jacqui was going through was David Cudlipp. He had read the passing scenery like a whodunit. She had managed to get more sleep on the ferry and on the bus back to Glasgow. The woman in the room hadn't travelled with them. She wondered why. That was interesting.

Sitting back, she looked at her ordered notes. The work would be difficult and she felt no certainty that she would succeed. But her loneliness had developed a determination and ferocious persistence in learning all sorts of different skills, physically and mentally. There had been no one else to rely on but herself. Stubbornness was her main gift. Even her father would have given her that.

It was all he would have given her, she thought, but perhaps it was enough to let her work her way out of the meagre sense of self in which he had for years tried to entrap her.

She had seen that entrapment close inescapably round her

mother and her two brothers after her father died. She understood it with her mother. She had been a mill-girl who married a bank teller after meeting him at the dancing and becoming pregnant by him. He condescended to marry her. She became a mixture of awe and guilt, which he could play on for the rest of their life together.

Her mother had been so innocent of the nature of all things academic that she had come to ascribe a formidable intellectuality to someone who had managed to get a job in a bank and then become the manager of a small branch. Her mother's tragedy was that her husband agreed with her assessment. Instead of freeing her kindly from her preposterous overestimation of his abilities, he had locked her inside it, became the jailer of her innocence. Slowly her potential to grow on her own terms had withered.

That tyrannical authoritarianism became a domestic necessity for him, one which extended to his children. He hadn't achieved his authority by shouting or bullying. He had achieved it by small subversions of the spirit. He shook his head at their opinions. His mouth curled in distaste at their turns of phrase. He explained in a long-suffering way to their mother what she really meant. 'Give me strength,' he said into his soup. He wondered how Michael and Thomas would ever make a living. He couldn't understand where Marion had acquired her stodginess of body. At least her mother was slim. Most effectively of all, when he was displeased with any of his children, which was every day, he would stare at their mother in a way Marion had learned to interpret. She took it to mean irreparable sadness at how the purity of his bloodline had been polluted.

It was as if no thought that happened in his house could be taken seriously that did not have his approval stamped on it.

He had literally, she thought, staring at the viscous surface of her coffee, intimidated all of them out of their minds. In her case, she thought sadly, he had intimidated her out of her body as well.

Her mother had learned to live in the corners of herself his arrogance allowed her. She wondered if her mother had managed to nurture any hidden dreams for herself she kept out of his reach, like pets she fed in secret and took out to stroke when he was asleep. She couldn't imagine so, since after his death her mother had become the keeper of his spurious reputation. 'Your father would have said . . .' she said. 'That's one thing about him . . .' she said. The one thing was usually an enormity gilded by time and offered as a virtue. 'He never looked at another woman,' her mother said. In case the truth about himself looked back, Marion thought. What other woman would have given his ego such unfettered freedom to act as it wished?

Her brothers and she hadn't helped. Perhaps he had got to them too early, dismantled the means of effective rebellion before they even knew they would have need of them. Denied belief in their academic abilities, Michael and Thomas had recourse to expressing themselves physically. They became enthusiastic rugby players at school, as if they could only succeed in an area which was alien to their father. Sport was a foreign country to him, full of a primitivism he found distasteful. But his contempt was less potent there since sport spoke a frivolous language he obviously couldn't understand.

She herself had only one method of resistance against him. It was sullenly and defiantly to become what he thought of her, she had decided on looking back. That must have been why she left school at sixteen and went to work in a shop. If he saw her as one of life's menials, she would act like one. She

257

let the banality of her life close round her like a fortress. Since she made no attempt to disprove what he thought of her, she became invulnerable to his contempt. More than that, she was able to retaliate by giving him back his sense of her, which was so obviously painful to him.

It was how she had survived the daily attrition of her self-confidence. None of the rest of her family had. Once their brief and none too successful prime as amateur rugby players was over, Michael and Thomas seemed to return their spirits to his keeping, drip-fed daily on his disappointment. Michael was an alcoholic in his early thirties. Thomas became a security guard in a shopping precinct, an occupation which was seen as a deliberate and pointed insult. Their father declined swiftly in retirement. He died having cast himself in the role of some biblical patriarch, looking on in wise and helpless sorrow at the ruin of his tribe.

What annoyed her most was how death had sanctified the cruelty of his life not only with her mother but with his sons. His shallowness of mind became unspoken wisdom. The emptiness of his heart turned into the sternness of the just. Her mother and her brothers made a conspiracy of three against the brutal truth of what their family life had been. Perhaps that way they didn't have to admit to the guilt of their weak acquiescence in the stunting of their own lives.

She wouldn't join them. She knew the one bravery she must have was the courage not to deny the disastrous consequences of her own cowardice. Having endured the darkness of his life, she wouldn't light candles to it in his death. She would let in the sun at last.

It was that which split them. Her difference was a constant accusation to them. She embarrassed them. For her the house was a phoney church where what they seemed to take for incense was the stench of his dead presence.

She stayed until her mother died. It didn't take long. Perhaps the world was too big for his widow with his overwhelming dominance out of it. The last thing he gave her mother was a kind of terminal flu of the spirit from his absence. Her breath fluttered out apologetically in the bedroom they had shared, where Marion had often wondered whatever happened that was warm.

Her brothers bought out her share of the house with some of the money their mother had divided equally among them. She was glad to let them do it. She felt sorry for them. They would never find more space than he had allowed them. They would die in the prison he had made for them.

Her own escape had come too late to be more than partial, she knew. It was already unlikely that she would fulfil her physicality. But she could perhaps live it by proxy, in her mind. She would people her loneliness.

She went through to the box-room, switched on the light and sat down. She activated the computer and waited. The people on this weekend might not know who she was but she thought she knew who they were. She should do. She had studied them closely enough. They might not have formed any attachment to her but she had formed her own secret attachment to them.

She smiled to herself at the way some of them had kidded her on the bus about her performance at the Free-for-all, calling her 'dark horse'. Now she suspected she knew why she had done something so unusual. If she had the nerve to do that, she had the nerve to do this.

As she found her way into the file she had prepared for the purpose, she smiled again. A smile as inscrutable as the

Sphinx's ever was, she felt. The Mouse's revenge. She made a space and started to type the first sentence but she stopped after the first few words, staring at them. They fascinated her as they appeared suddenly out of nowhere. They were a doorway into cyberspace. They were leading to a place where these people would always be with her, their essences floating helplessly there as if in formaldehyde.

It was that time when

Acknowledgements

Thanks to Patricia Lombardi (not forgetting Dom); Alan and Elaine Gillespie; Colin Beattie and the staff of the Tiree Lodge Hotel (not forgetting Doodan); Frank and Ruby Donnelly; Wendy and Gary Anderson; the two Bettys (Trodden and McCluskey); Bob Cooper; *The Herald* and *Scotland on Sunday*; the woman who bumped into me on a Glasgow street, grabbed my arms and told me that I was 'a great wee writer' and that she sent my books all over the world, and then vanished into the throng; Hazel Orme and, assuredly not least, Carole Welch – midwives all but not to be blamed for the baby.

Sphinx

It was an animal committee,
Same question for each candidate.
Failure to get the question right
Involved you in providing lunch.

Oedipus was a vagrant who
Just happened to take the interview.

'What walks on four legs in the morning
Two legs in the afternoon
Three legs in the evening?'

He commuted the times to a life-span,
Thought of babies and sticks and answered, 'Man.'

The committee demitted its lofty shelf
And, as it were, dissolved itself.

The job was his, and with him mine
And yours in perpetuity.
But before we pass the cigars around
Consider the question once again.

He didn't get it right at all.
It was a trick. Yes, babies crawl
But what *walks* is an animal.

Man walks on two legs, let's agree
But only a mutant walks on three.

The animals knew that pushy man
Was bucking for boss of the whole shebang.
So what did they do? They said, okay.
He wants the job, we'll fix the pay.
He may become lord of creation
But the pension is his malformation.
He's not content to be animal?
We'll make him nothing much at all,
Neither insect, fish, nor beast, nor fowl,
Content with nothing, health or wealth,
Lord of everything but himself.

When evening comes, he'll blow the job,
The world, the lot, three-legged slob.

It's been evening now for quite a while.
No wonder that bloody sphinx could smile.

– Harry Beck

WILLIAM McILVANNEY
The Kiln

Alone in a rented flat in Edinburgh in the 1990s, Tom Docherty calls up the past like a necromancer, reliving the summer of 1955 in search of the key to his present state. As he recalls the intellectual and sexual awakenings of his youth and the paths he took as an adult, he discovers that only by understanding where he comes from can he make sense of his life.

'A pitch-perfect blend of warm lyricism, limpid observation and excrutiatingly funny comedy. It is a beguilingly brilliant portrait of the artist as an adolescent'
Sunday Times

'Delightfully funny. McIlvanney can whistle up a joke from anywhere – and his wit keeps us laughing, reading, and finally feeling for his troubled narrator. He is a compassionate writer and leaves an impression both of high seriousness and great charm'
Sunday Telegraph

'A tour de force, a wry and witty novel, shot through with deep reflection on how, in a materialistic world, we come to terms with ourselves, with society, and with those we love and hurt . . . Finely judged and beautifully written'
The Times

'The best novel yet from the finest Scottish writer of our time'
Allan Massie, *Daily Telegraph* Books of the Year

'On almost every page it offers matter for reflection and the sudden stab of emotion that comes from reading something that is truly evoked or created . . . It is rare and it is wonderful'
Scotsman

'McIlvanney plumbs, in language of luminous precision, the tortured psyche of the Scottish character. It's Greek tragedy, hilarious to boot'
Mail on Sunday

SCEPTRE